Penguin Books
The Scarlet Sword

Born in 1905, H. E. Bates was educated at Kettering
Grammar School and worked as a journalist before
publishing his first book, *The Two Sisters*, when he
was twenty. In the next fifteen years he won a
distinguished reputation for his stories about English
country life. In 1941, as 'Flying Officer X', he wrote
his two famous books of short stories – *The Greatest
People in the World* and *How Sleep the Brave* –
which were followed in 1944 by *Fair Stood the Wind
for France*. These, and his subsequent novels of
Burma, *The Purple Plain* and *The Jacaranda Tree*,
and of India, *The Scarlet Sword*, stemmed directly or
indirectly from his war experience in the East, won
him a new reputation and, apart from their success in
Britain and America, have been translated into
sixteen foreign languages. His writing took a new
direction with the appearance in 1958 of *The Darling
Buds of May*, the first of the popular Larkin family
novels, which was followed by *A Breath of French
Air*, *When the Green Woods Laugh*, and *Oh! To Be
in England* (1963). *The World in Ripeness* (1972) was
his last book. H. E. Bates died in 1974.

H. E. Bates

The Scarlet Sword

Penguin Books
in association with Michael Joseph

Penguin Books Ltd, Harmondsworth,
Middlesex, England
Penguin Books, 625 Madison Avenue,
New York, New York 10022, U.S.A.
Penguin Books Australia Ltd, Ringwood,
Victoria, Australia
Penguin Books Canada Ltd, 2801 John Street,
Markham, Ontario, Canada L3R 1B4
Penguin Books (N.Z.) Ltd, 182–190 Wairau Road,
Auckland 10, New Zealand

First published in Great Britain 1950
First published in the United States
by Atlantic–Little, Brown Books, Boston, 1951
Published in Penguin Books 1958
Reprinted 1974 (twice), 1977, 1980

Made and printed in Great Britain by
Hazell Watson & Viney Ltd, Aylesbury, Bucks
Set in Linotype Times

1

Father Anstey shuffled into the hospital garden, on the third of five terraces below the Mission, through the archway of crimson peach-boughs, beyond the vines, just in time to see the sun strike the great spur of rock that projected across the gorge of the river below. It hung there like a glittering brown extended claw.

His eyes as he lifted them to the mountains glowed with the crinkled softness of a pair of blue walnuts; they had the troubled dryness of a man who had not slept well. Down below him a single bullock-cart raised smoky yellow dust from the river bank, beating it finely up above avenues of leopard-patterned trunks into the dying leaves of plane trees. Along two lines of long white house-boats, moored side by side like long gigantic water-leaves, there was no sign of movement: partly because it was too early, mostly because of all their European owners only Miss Jordan and Miss Shanks now remained to live there. He remembered that Miss Jordan and Miss Shanks were coming to tea; they would eat grape-jam and scones in the garden by the prunus tree; but the thought left him without comfort and he looked once again at the brown and savage claw of rock reaching out above the narrow gorge of water. Beyond it lay, in gigantic fold after fold, a million other rocks, rising from the great snows of Nanga Parbat in the nearer distance to Kangchenjunga and all the greater snows at the invisible end of the range: yet the nearer single claw of rock was something that never failed to awe him into the oddest feelings of calamity. He could never see it without remembering that once, more than a thousand years before, the whole of the mountain beyond it had fallen, obliterating the valley below. He did not know why that event, so far away as to be almost legendary and happening in any case to a mountainside that had otherwise nothing more spectacular to it than the hills of his native Yorkshire, should always disturb him so much. A mountain that had fallen once, he realized, could not fall again; so chance a catastrophe could hardly recur; yet he was always disturbed by the notion of its recurrence as he was still, at seventy, sometimes frightened by the recurrence of a childhood dream.

This old habit of perplexity was like an ache in the bone; too old and too deep for cure. It was as hopeless as trying to cure in his colleague Father Simpson the mystic irrationalities that, in ungenerous moments, he called pure laziness. It was like trying to cure the ache of India by placing a sword across it and slashing it into two bloody portions like a lump of beef. There could be no such simple partition of fear from flesh; and now also to all his old habitual fears were added others.

As he waddled down the path, hands still folded in his sleeves, looking for Father Simpson, he kept his face uplifted to the sun. The air from the north-eastern ranges of Kashmir was quite cold, with a dry crispness of snow, although in the morning haze, half mist, half smoke from nomadic hill-fires, no snow could be seen. Nanga Parbat, always a difficult mountain to see, always rare in revelation, was not visible today. Sometimes he thought Nanga Parbat was like God; immense and splendid and omnipotent, yet so often hidden and so rarely revealed.

As he walked, screwing up his eyes against the sun, so that they looked more than ever like a pair of old blue walnuts, centrally and exquisitely lighted by a touch of fire, he was worried not simply by the incurable ache of old calamities or by the incurable dreams of Father Simpson. He was worried by rumours that drifted in, every day now, from Srinagar. He did not like Srinagar. It was filthy and it spewed rumours and it was very hot. It was constantly being burned or flooded or devastated by afflictions never quite vast enough to settle it completely. Yet he could not ignore any longer the rumours that came in from Srinagar for the simple reason that they came in from everywhere else too. Even up here, behind the

6

insulated walls of the Mission, cut off as they were from almost any sort of outside manifestation, political or racial or ideological, absorbed in their small life of service, the apple-crop, and the potatoes: even up here you were bound sooner or later to hear an explosion if it were loud enough. You were bound to be touched, even if it were ever so little, by the slashing sword that was parting India in two. Far more terrible than that, he thought, was that the sword might slash Kashmir in two. Kashmir was very beautiful; almost too beautiful; it was truly the country of God. They said that Indian troops had been flown into Srinagar – that, if it were true, was because the Maharaja wanted to save his skin and had acceded to India. Very simple, he thought, but what if Pakistan replied in kind? He could not get the picture clear. He did not read the papers; he supposed that really no one had got it clear. There had been ghastly massacres. He had never liked the religious intolerance of the ruling families in Kashmir; the wealthy Brahmins were notoriously tyrannical and selfish; most Kashmiris were timid liars; but now there were rumours that down in the plain Sikhs and Hindus were simply butchering Moslems everywhere to make a Hindu holiday.

But what if the Pathans came down from the frontiers, as rumour kept saying they were coming down, and began butchering Sikhs and Hindus to make a Moslem holiday? The Pathans were Moslems: fanatics, terrific and ruthless fellows, a warrior people. Supposing they came down and began making holiday among Sikhs' beards and Brahmin or Hindu boasters? There had been all sorts of expeditions against the Pathans up there on the frontier for about a hundred years – you had to keep these people in check – but they had never really suppressed them. Pathans were not like the people of Bengal: to be crushed by famine and over-breeding and the wretchedest filth and poverty; they were a mountain warrior people, proud, loving blood, thriving on war. India was a violent place; you felt violence in the air; all the East had become violent; but the North West Frontier, with its Pathans, was most violent of all. God help Kashmir, he thought, if they ever come here – he had got the picture clear in his mind at last, as clear as the rock about to fall and the sword about to descend – God help us all.

By now he was out of the fruit garden and could see below him, on the second of five garden terraces, Father Simpson. He was digging, in his shirt-sleeves, among the potatoes.

There was no accounting, he thought, for the way Father Simpson dug potatoes. It was rather as if you had put a spade into the front feet of a cow. Father Simpson at intervals held the spade aggressively poised and then rushed forward, driving the spade among the yellow haulms. An explosion of dry earth flung white potatoes about him like a nest of scattered eggs. Father Simpson then held back the spade, rushed forward again and threw into the air a second explosion of dust which completely buried the potatoes unearthed by the first. Father Simpson then fell on his knees in something of the attitude of a praying cow. His fat body, cut off at the knees, had a beautiful cow-like gentleness as one by one potatoes were rediscovered by his dreamy podgy hands and laid reverently in the basket of bamboo.

Father Anstey stopped for some moments and gazed down across the terraces. His hands and feet were really quite cold. He was glad to let the sun fall on his face; it was softly warm already on the closed lids of his eyes. When he opened them again he turned completely round from looking at Father Simpson to a contemplation of all that lay behind him: the church with its little pepper-pot tower and the central rect-angular mass of mission buildings, including the small hospital, in white-cream stone, crowning the garden terraces. They were surrounded, farther up, by walls of sun-bleached plaster that were frames for the hills that lay behind. These hills were never the same colour on two successive mornings in that rare high air, and already this morning they were red. They seemed still to be smouldering, as they so often did, with abandoned creep-ing tribal fires, the soft smoke of which had fallen in the night, in bags of opalescent mist, to cover the thicker woodland below.

He was never tired of saying that he liked this view, terraced from the potato-patches to the hill-tops in a series of immense steps, better than anything else in the world. There was a view from the Pennine Range, in Yorkshire, about Ingleborough, that he liked almost as much, but it was harsher and darker and he knew that it was really distance and nostalgia, some-times secretly excruciating, that gave it enchantment. It had in it no touch of unearthliness, as you had here in the gardens when the peaches flowered, when the whole hillside seemed to be tied to a crowd of pink distended parachutes, pulling in the wind, so that it seemed about to fly away.

In a distant corner of the highest terrace Father Simpson kept a collection of tame white rabbits, housed in depressing wooden hutches. It was a little difficult to breathe when the wind blew that way in the heat of summer but when the rabbits were feeding on the orchard grass it was if they were a flock of white pigeons and they were very beautiful. But that was like all India, everywhere. It was a country of enchanting distances always resolving into ugly realities. From the hospital windows you looked down on the curve of brown river, clustered about with pleasant house-boats and white poplars, with marshy tributaries covered with pink lotus-flower, and a village that rose, in a series of terraced huts, to deep folds of trees. It had such splendour and magnificence from the hospital side of the gorge that when you went down there it was shocking to find nothing but an interminable human rat-run boring between foetid hovels of corrugated iron and bamboo filled with the stench of warmed-up sewers.

For a moment longer Father Anstey stood watching the hills turn from red to a burnt brick colour before he realized that that colour was really the colour of the first maples turning to autumn. And he remembered also in that moment what he had really come to speak to Father Simpson about.

It was really very urgent and he thought, 'I'm getting as daft as he is. Dreaming here.'

'Father Simpson!' he called. 'Father Simpson!'

Half-waddling, half-running down the path, he saw once again the fat, cow-like figure on its knees among the potatoes. It seemed to him more than ever like a flabby, baggy creature waiting to be milked. It aroused in him waves of Yorkshire impatience, flowering to mischief, so that the crinkled walnuts of his eyes were lost behind dark slits of fun.

'Father Simpson! Father Simpson! You didn't lock the rabbit hutches and the rabbits are everywhere!'

'Oh! no, Father, no –!'

Father Simpson raised his fat startled face; his podgy cream fingers hung in the air like the distended teats of a cow.

'They're all among the vines. They're everywhere. They're like the little foxes –'

'It can't be, Father, it can't be –'

Father Simpson began to scramble across the potato-patch, shuffling small clouds of dust.

'Father Simpson!'

'Yes, Father!'

He turned and stood in the potato-patch, shaking.

'Did you remember to lock the hutches?'

'I remembered. I know I remembered.'

'Are you sure?'

'Absolutely, absolutely. The rats will get them. They always do.'

He turned, scrambling up the slope again.

'Did you remember something else?'

'What, Father, what? What should I remember?'

'Do you remember what day it is?'

'Saturday, Saturday. Isn't it Saturday? I think it's Saturday.'

'It is, it is. And what happens on Saturday?'

'Does something happen?'

'Don't you remember who comes today? Don't you remember who you had to meet from the boat?'

'No, Father – no – oh! Father, yes –' He raised podgy horrified hands to his face. 'Oh! Father –'

'You'd better hurry because the boat will be in and if you are not there –'

'Yes, Father.' He scrambled away, halted and turned again and came back, sweating, in distress. 'What was his name – I don't remember –'

'Mr Crane.'

'Oh! Crane, yes, Crane –'

'Your memory's going to pieces.'

'No, it isn't my memory. It isn't. I was thinking of something.

10

I was thinking of something awful Colonel Mathieson was telling me yesterday. Oh! my dear Lord, the rabbits – what about them?'

'It was a fib,' Father Anstey said.

'A fib? You were telling me untrue things –'

'Simply to wake you! You know the boat will be in.'

Father Simpson began once again to scramble up the slope, raising clouds of reddish dust, talking as he went.

'I was awake. It was simply this ghastly rumour of Colonel Mathieson's.'

'You are getting to be a regular Kashmiri, listening to rumours.'

'Yes, but this was an appalling thing – appalling –'

He ran. Father Anstey stood watching the cow-like figure hurrying away, pressing squabbily against the incline of the terraces, and then he remembered Colonel Mathieson. The Colonel was a youngish experienced man of unexcitable temperament not given to rumour. That made it more than odd. And suddenly the mischief went out of him, leaving him unexpectedly cold. His eyes became once again dry and leathery and he called:

'What rumour? Father, what rumour was that?'

Father Simpson had reached the fourth of the terraces, and he turned for the last time before disappearing between the bush peach-trees and the vines. He seemed about to call.

Father Anstey saw his mouth open and close again as if in one of those infuriating fits of forgetfulness.

And when he spoke it was almost in a little shriek, to make himself heard:

'It really wasn't Colonel Mathieson. It was Mrs Mathieson. I remembered. It was she after all!'

'Yes, but what was it?'

'It's too long! I'll tell you when I get back!'

His voice, strained to shout so that it rose above tenor into broken falsetto, went above the garden and across the gorge of water to make its echo against the hills beyond. And instinctively, following it and waiting for the thinner mocking return, Father Anstey looked at the spur of rock, sword-like and brilliant in full sunlight now, overhanging the valley across which, in half an hour, Father Simpson would be bringing Mr Crane.

It seemed more than ever about to fall.

2

What Father Anstey had called a boat was nothing but a raft
of planks lashed to empty oil-drums and Crane, as he sat on it,
did not notice upstream the spur of rock that had troubled and
fascinated the priest so much and would not have given it
another thought if he had. He was very tired; he too felt as if
he had an ache in the bone. He had travelled from Bombay as
far as Lahore by plane and from there had taken the night train
north, as far as he could go, coming by truck the rest of the
way. The sweating gritty hours in train and truck had twisted
him like a rag. He was not interested in spurs of rock that
would or would not fall; or in Kashmir; or any longer in India
itself. Kashmir was simply another place on the map: dirtier,
smellier, if that were possible, than the rest. India, that text
books always warned you was a sub-continent, as if that fact
diluted its horrors or eased its complexities or sweetened its
smells, was a problem that through sheer surfeit and thinning
of blood he had given up. He was a tall brown-haired young
man of thirty but now he felt twenty years older and there had
been no one to play chess with on the train. He carried his
miniature set of ivory chess-men in his hands, too night-dazed
and tired to put it in his pocket, and it was some time before he
noticed that he was the only passenger, besides a Hindu girl in
a yellow and orange sari sitting on a cheap fibreboard attaché
case, smoking sullenly, who was sitting down. All the rest, including Father Simpson, stood watching the four sweating and
crying Kashmiris poling the raft: not out of pure interest, but
rather like a collection of scrawny and nervous hens who could
not swim. Only the Hindu girl and himself did not seem to care.

'That is the Mission,' Father Simpson said and pointed upward and across the river with a wave of podgy fingers.

Out of politeness Crane looked up. The mass of cream-white buildings, pleasantly framed by trees, had something of the appearance, exposed from below, of giant cubes of sugar.

'A very nice target for somebody,' he said and did not realize, until he saw the fussy horror on Father Simpson's face, that he had not meant to speak aloud.

'Nobody makes targets of missions, I hope,' Father Simpson said.

'Nowadays they make targets of anything.'

'It's unthinkable.'

'The more unthinkable it is the more they think of it.'

Crane for a moment had an impulse to tell Father Simpson of unthinkable things: of war in Burma, war in England, even of war that was beginning in India now. Perhaps, he thought, the Reverend Father would not care for these things. It would be rather like speaking to a child and he wondered how long the Reverend Father had lived up here, in this high insulated world, unshaken and unbruised by things outside it. How did the Reverend Father manage his conscience? A Hail Mary or two when things were tough, he thought, a Pater, an Ave, or a Gloria here and there? He longed to see the reaction on the unworldly, unbruised face as he said these things; but he did not speak. He was tired of playing war correspondent; satiated with rushing about continents looking for a war about which to correspond. He was tired of India and tired of himself. He was tired most of all of cables from London that sent him on infuriating and fruitless assignments in impossible places. His journey to Kashmir was one of them. The only war he wanted to find, he thought, was one between himself and a forty-pound mahseer in a snow-fed stream.

He looked up to find Father Simpson gazing with melancholy unrest at the Hindu girl. Her scarlet elliptical mouth was blowing smoke against the sun; her yellow and orange sari was cheap and tawdry and too bright. Her head was so thrown back that her big turquoise earrings were like painted blue slides holding up the fringes of her black hair and her fingers were so covered with rings that they were like slender silver barrels tipped with scarlet thimbles.

14

He remembered suddenly seeing just such girls, with just such resentful sullen eyes, down the dock roads of Bombay.

'She doesn't belong here,' he said.

'She is a bad girl.' Father Simpson stared away from her, at the opposite bank of the river, pleasantly thick with white poplar and willow and plane trees, with its line of painted house-boats beyond the landing stage. His cheeks were a little flushed; he seemed guilty and embarrassed at being caught in the act of looking at her.

'She came up on the truck.'

'I know. I saw her.'

'She's just a prostitute. She has to live –'

'Don't use that word. Don't talk of her.' Father Simpson took sudden jumpy steps, seizing Crane's suitcase. 'We are here. We are getting off.'

He pressed forward among the Indians, aloof and miserable and affronted, his corpulence aggravated, his brown habit winged about by fluttering dhotis. In the few moments before the raft hit the jetty piles his mind pranced wildly about, seeking less inflammable things for discussion.

'We may have to walk. Do you mind? You are lucky to get a rickshaw that will go up the hill.'

'Anything you say.'

'We are very glad to have you here and it was very nice of Dr Mackenzie to tell you about us.'

'Oh! God,' Crane said, 'I forgot. Mackenzie sent all the very best to you.'

Mackenzie was a tough and melancholy West coast Scot whom thirty-five years of medical trial in India had not succeeded in defeating. Year by year he had seen India repeat her eternal cycle: fecundity, birth, fecundity, death: filth, stupidity, bigotry, blindness. Revulsion had grown to a sort of hypnotized attachment and attachment to a kind of defensive and blasphemous love until gradually he became resigned to the fact that he had no home, and wanted no home, except the one he had made for himself exactly where he had landed on India's eastern sea-board thirty-five years before. Mackenzie, untravelled, attached by a Presbyterian conscience to the hospital

15

grindstone with a grousing fervour that gave himself only one reluctant leave in two years, seemed to manage at the same time to know everyone there was to know. Crane had merely to mention his assignment to Kashmir for Mackenzie to say: 'Go and see Anstey. He's a priest and a damn good one. I'll telegraph him you're coming. He'll put you up. You can stay there,' and simply because he had greater faith in Mackenzie than in anything he had found in India Crane had ignored his hatred of Catholics, his mistrust of missions and an intolerant love of living by himself and had let the telegram go.

That had been four or five days ago. Tired, sucked bloodless by a long summer of ruthless heat, he had struggled up country by train and truck through an atmosphere of tense and growing jitteriness. Stupid cow-like crowds and an explosive vapour of the air had revived all his impatience with priests and the peculiar uselessness of all priesthood at a time when it seemed likely that one half of India was about to butcher the other: until now, faced with the nervous ineptitude, the jellified adolescence of Father Simpson, he felt himself caught in an excruciating and ridiculous trap. He had come up to find the truth about Kashmir and had simply got himself entangled with an example of priesthood that had as much relation to war as a skein of knitting wool. He bitterly regretted coming; there would be no telegraphic facilities, no contacts, no means of sifting truth from rumour, nothing. He saw himself spending his days trying not to offend the priests, the Catholic susceptibilities; trying not to look at the nuns as if they were human under their anonymous façade of starched cardboard. He had been tricked into a backwater of peculiarly irritating stagnation and was more angry with himself than with the priest who puffed and sweated at his side. Already he could smell that curious dry holy odour of the complete dead-end. It would have been better to go to Srinagar.

The priest too was worried. He shuffled forward, silenced and nervous. Here is a man who looks at prostitutes, he thought, and swears by God. Frantically his mind searched, once again, for changes of subject. He talks of prostitutes; he swears by God: how on earth are we going to get on with each

16

other? A cloud of dhotis began to slide from the raft. The pressure of weight against the jetty flung passengers forward in a single jolted mass and he felt Indian flesh pressed, for the space of an awkward second or two, against his own.

'I see a rickshaw,' he said, extending his neck. 'We may be lucky.'

Looking round to see if Crane was listening he was horrified to see him standing side by side with the Hindu girl, not listening at all.

'Mr Crane, Mr Crane,' he said, 'I think I see a rickshaw.'

'We need two, surely?' Crane said.

'You could ride. I can walk. I am used to it.'

As he turned to say these words he looked over his shoulder and saw Crane with a cigarette in his mouth. The cigarette was not lighted. Crane was patting the pockets of his suit for matches or lighter and presently in a moment of fresh revulsion Father Simpson saw Crane bending down to take a light from the cigarette held up by the impossibly silvered, reddened fingers of the Hindu girl. For a second they were very close to each other and it was almost, he thought, as if their lips were touching.

The impulse of this awful thought shot him off the raft into the dust of the jetty. He began to shout at the rickshaw. But the boy, taking one look, turned with flat indifference and walked away.

Father Simpson turned to find Crane and almost shouted, his voice squeaking:

'They are always the same. They are incorrigible louts! They simply don't want to. They are absolutely the most –'

'I like a walk,' Crane said. 'Let me have the suitcase. It will do us good.'

'No, no.' Grasping the suitcase, he shook his flabby cheeks and was overwhelmed, in a black moment of self-reproach, by the way he had shouted. It was a grievous mistake; he felt ashamed; he hoped no one had heard. He turned to reassure himself and was just in time to see the Hindu girl folding herself like a yellow and orange moth into the black husk of the rickshaw.

He puffed forward against the dusty track that wound upwards between thickets of plane and bamboo and flowerless rhododendrons, glad that no one had noticed him and glad at last to be free.

'You really don't mind walking, Mr Crane, you honestly don't mind?'

'I love it.'

'I really ought to walk more. I really ought. The country is very beautiful. It's atrocious the way one gets out of the habit of it.'

'You play chess?'

'No, no, I don't play chess.'

'What fish have you got here?'

'Fish? What fish? I'm awfully afraid I can't say. You mean in the river? You must ask Colonel Mathieson about that.'

He turned again, looking down the hill, partly in nervousness, partly prompted by some instinctive curiosity to see if the rickshaw carrying the girl had departed. To his horror and anger it was coming up the hill.

'Do you know Colonel Mathieson?' He spoke swiftly, bubbling with embarrassment. 'He is the most awfully nice man. He was something or other in Intelligence in Delhi.'

'Was he?'

'I think he still dabbles that way a bit. He has really come here to retire and grow raspberries.'

'That is what Intelligence officers were meant to do.'

There did not seem to be anything amusing in this remark to Father Simpson, who in a flashing moment of nervousness remembered what it was Colonel Mathieson had told him the day before. Or rather of course it was Mrs Mathieson. She could have got it from no one else but the Colonel and in consequence the remark about raspberries and intelligence seemed a little unfair.

'You know if you don't mind my saying so you ought not to pre-judge Mathieson in quite that way.'

'I'm sure he's a very nice fellow.'

'He is indeed. And he is not old. He is not a Blimp. I think he had some ghastly assignment or other in Chungking. Mrs

Mathieson is frightfully nice too. They're expecting a baby.'

Crane did not say anything; and now Father Simpson could hear the rickshaw coming close behind them up the hill. The sound renewed his nervous fear that Crane, hearing it too, would somehow re-involve himself with the girl.

He blurted out:

'Do you think there will be great trouble here? There are the most terrible riots and things, aren't there, I mean? Not that it would touch us, here at the Mission. But there are awful rumours. There was something Colonel Mathieson, or rather Mrs Mathieson, heard only yesterday.'

Crane threw away his half-finished cigarette and forty paces behind him the rickshaw boy, who had been waiting for that, increased his pace so that he could pick it up.

'You really ought not to pre-judge situations by rumours you hear from the wives of Intelligence officers,' Crane said.

Father Simpson smiled. That of course was really rather good. He had laid himself open for that. It was his reward for the vanity of trying to be clever, of trying to judge others. Judge not that ye be not judged: he must be careful to guard against that.

'Anyway,' Crane said, 'what did Mrs Mathieson say?'

At that moment the rickshaw boy, having gained speed through rushing hungrily forward for the cigarette, drew level with the priest and Crane. He had stubbed out the cigarette and put it behind his ear. It gave him an appearance of cockiness, a certain scornfulness, that seemed for a moment to be shared by the girl behind. The priest saw her jewelled feet pouting forward from under the orange-yellow folds of the sari, the toenails painted scarlet like the nails of her hands. Under her left eye she had five or six pockmarks and as he saw them he winced a little. He could never escape the feeling that these marks had been branded there. And yet they gave her, he thought, as they always did give these creatures, a queer attractiveness. He saw her turn her head very slightly as she passed. It seemed for a moment as if she were going to give a sign of recognition, perhaps a smile, but nothing happened. She seemed to be staring beyond the rickshaw boy at some fixed point up the hill, dark sullen eyes so lightless that they might have been drugged, and suddenly Father Simpson thought:

'Gracious goodness, the camp. The camp, of course. Why ever didn't I think of that?'

The rickshaw went past and up the hill; and in a few seconds there was nothing to be seen of the Hindu girl except her left hand, dark and scarlet, hanging over the side.

'She is going to the camp,' he said to Crane, but Crane was looking back over the brown river, pleasantly flowing between skeletoned avenues of plane and willow, wondering if he could hire a house-boat after the Kashmir fashion, instead of living with a collection of dreary priests at the Mission. He would inquire about it. He could fish and write in peace and it would be rather fun.

'I didn't think of it before and of course it's obvious,' Father Simpson said.

'What is?'

'The camp. She is going to hang about the camp,' he said.

'Is there a camp? Where?'

'Behind the trees there. You see the road. I think there are two platoons there or something like that. You will see the tents in a moment or two.'

'What about house-boats?' Crane said. 'Can you hire them now?'

'I rather fancy they are awfully difficult. Most of their owners have gone. Colonel Mathieson has been looking for one but of course there's this upheaval now and he is living with us at the Mission until —'

He stopped speaking. Staring at the small sandy road that wound off the main hill road between scrubby and dusty bushes he pulled himself up sharply, waving podgy hands.

'But that's absolutely the most extraordinary thing.' He set down the suitcase.

'What is?'

'The camp isn't there.'

He stood on the dusty road, in the sunlight, turning first to Crane and then to the woodland, scarred between the trees by tyre-marks and rings of ashes.

Thoughtfully Crane waited. A Kashmiri boy in khaki shorts was wandering idly about the spent fires and Father Simpson called across to him, asking about the camp.

The boy, lifting his head and opening his mouth, darkly staring, did not answer.

'They were here yesterday,' the priest said. 'Last night. I saw their lights.'

'Bang goes your theory about camp followers.'

'I suppose so. Yes.'

Crane picked up the suitcase. Father Simpson did not notice it and they went on together up the hill. Already it was quite hot and Father Simpson breathed with gentle pain through his mouth, with the regular hiss of an expiring valve.

It was three or four minutes later when Crane realized that the rickshaw too had gone. It seemed to occur to Father Simpson at the same moment and he stopped again in the road.

'They have evidently –' he spoke with difficulty, breathing hard, and Crane, very tired and thirsty and realizing for the first time that he had not breakfasted, thought, 'Here we go again,' but Father Simpson said:

'That is the road round to the nuns' quarters. There. Past the cypresses.'

'I see.'

'We have fifteen or sixteen nuns. The school is there too. We teach the local children. The Assistant Mother Superior is Spanish. We are a very mixed lot.'

About a hundred and fifty yards away the big wooden gates of the Mission were open under a high archway of cream plaster. Seen from the low angle of the road the arch seemed to float above the mass of buildings behind it, like a large bleached bone curved in blue air. It gave Crane, for the space of a second or two, a curious sensation. Hungry and empty and tired, he felt uplifted. He seemed to be swimming gently to the top of the world.

'Are you a Catholic?' Father Simpson said.

'No.'

'I always ask because it saves complications.'

'I'm not anything.'

'Just so.' He spoke gravely; and then in an immediate moment of gaiety he smiled. 'That's all right. Don't think of it. We are quite used to it. We are the most frightfully cosmopolitan lot you ever saw.'

Crane did not answer and they walked the rest of the way to the gates in silence except for a moment when Father Simpson insisted on taking the suitcase back again 'because,' he said, 'Father Anstey would never forgive me otherwise.' Crane did not argue and his sense of being uplifted remained with him for some time longer, taking him through the little avenue of cypresses and so under the archway and beyond the gate.

In that moment Father Simpson saw Father Anstey running down the path between the hospital and the gardens. He was so astonished that he stopped at once. He had never seen Father Anstey running before. It was an unimaginable thing. It was as if the Assistant Mother Superior had begun to dance with castanets. It was an inexplicable and excitable fantasy that did not belong to the realm of the Mission at all.

And seeing it he felt himself stiffen. He did not go forward to meet Father Anstey. He felt extraordinarily calm. The mental flabbiness that Father Simpson sometimes called mystic irrationality because he could think of nothing better fell suddenly away from him like a loose and discarded skin. He knew that something important, perhaps even something very wicked and very terrible had happened. He remembered as he stood stiffly there how Father Anstey had pulled his leg about the rabbits escaping and how it had hurt him and frightened him at the time. It did not touch him now. He rather pitied Father Anstey for so childish a trick. It seemed suddenly to be, in its triviality and its untruth, one with Mr Crane's rather ironic rebuke about listening to rumours spread by former Intelligence officers. And now, in his compressed and stiffened state of mind, it all connected up. He knew that Father Anstey's running and the deserted camp down the hill had something to do with each other. He remembered what Colonel Mathieson – no, Mrs Mathieson – had told him yesterday. It had something to do with Pathans butchering an entire village in the hills –

'Father, Father Simpson. I thought you were never coming – I –'

'Mr Crane wanted to walk. In any case there was no rickshaw.'

'Mr Crane.' Father Anstey looked for a moment sick with running. The solid Yorkshire calm of his face, the old eyes colourless and watery now with the distress of exertion, had evaporated, leaving it momentarily as flabby as Father Simpson's had been from his own crude exertions among the potatoes.

'What is it?' Crane said. Out of the corner of his eye he had a glimpse of Father Simpson, drawn up, his lips tightened with calm.

'There has been an invasion by Pathans in the north,' Father Anstey said. 'They are coming down. Butchering everywhere.'

Crane felt himself tingle, sharply and suddenly, with excitement. No longer tired, he exulted so immensely for a moment in what Father Anstey had said that he forgot to ask whether it was rumour or fact.

In that moment, before he could speak again, Father Simpson looked at him with great calm. He seemed to have drawn himself up and Crane realized, for the first time, seeing him beside the crinkled and depressed figure of Father Anstey, that he was very tall. He began to walk steadily forward, holding Father Anstey with one arm, carrying the suitcase with the other. And for a moment Crane, his mind still weaving about with exultation, did not follow.

And seeing it Father Simpson turned, a second later, and smiled. It was an extraordinary smile. It too had a strange muscular and ironic exultation.

'Bang goes your house-boat, Mr Crane,' he said.

3

At four-thirty in the afternoon Crane stood in the small orchard of apples that ran the full length of the one-storeyed hospital building, staring at a trench. Colonel Mathieson, who had turned out to be a man of thirty-two, of pleasantly bantering temperament, with a fair moustache, stood at the far end of the trench, in nothing but a pair of khaki shorts that were now dusted crimson, like the rest of his body, with a thick powder of thrown-up soil. It occurred to Crane for the seventh or eighth time that afternoon that he might ask him if he played chess but for the seventh or eighth time also the thought was blown out of his mind by the figure of Father Simpson, standing in the centre of the trench, leaning on a spade that had much the appearance, against his stripped corpulence, of a spoon.

The trench was about thirty feet long and about knee deep and not quite wide enough to contain the body of Father Simpson, Crane thought, at the widest part. It did not seem long enough either. It could never possibly contain, he thought, all who might want to shelter there: the Franciscan nuns, the men, the forty or fifty refugees, jibbing and scared and laden with squeaking children, who had been coming up the hill all afternoon, bringing with them some of the wailing and jostling and stench of the bazaars, and were still coming now.

'What do you think?' he called. He leaned on his spade and called to Colonel Mathieson. 'Is it long enough?'

'Length is not everything,' Colonel Mathieson said. 'Is it wide enough? Will it take Father Simpson?'

'It was a thought that was in my mind.'

'What do you think? Shall we let a little out at the waist? For Father Simpson's sake?'

'It is for the Father to say.'

'Of course. Father: what do you say?'

Father Simpson smiled; he was growing quite used to it. Since the moment of his small but exquisite triumph about the house-boat he had even began to like it. It had kept the day going; it had helped to insulate him, as he believed it had also helped to insulate Mathieson and Crane, from a multiplicity of the deadliest fears.

'There's only about half an hour before dark,' Colonel Mathieson said. 'Shall it be length or width, Father? What do you say?'

'It was not my intention to come down to the trench,' Father Simpson said.

'Check-mate,' Crane said, and it seemed another excellent opportunity to ask Colonel Mathieson if he played chess but Colonel Mathieson said:

'Come and bring me out of my misery. I am slain in the high places.'

Father Simpson smiled, shyly but with confidence, and said:

'Upon thy high places. Tell it not in Gath.'

'Hasn't the exercise done us all a power of good?' Crane said. 'By the way, Father, what happened to the daughter of the Philistines coming up the hill?'

'She is here.'

'Who is here?' Colonel Mathieson said. 'What daughter of what Philistines? Is she someone delicious?'

'She is a bad girl. Isn't that so, Father?' Crane said. 'She is a bad girl?'

'Colonel Mathieson knows her,' the priest said.

'Colonel, Colonel,' Crane said.

'It is only Kaushalya,' the priest said.

'She is a sister of one of the Kashmiri Christians,' Colonel Mathieson said. 'She pays a visit now and then. She was a dancer in Bombay.'

'There is no truth in the word was and none in the word dancer,' the priest said. 'Don't talk of her.'

Colonel Mathieson came up out of the trench. The sun had gone down beyond the hill, above the river; the rock that had so perturbed Father Anstey in the morning hung out over the brown water, with its line of leopard trunks that were plane-trees, like a gargoyle of bronze. Cooling breaths of evening wind threw yellow apple leaves into the trench and Crane could smell autumn, watery and thick with the odour of crushed apples, coming up from the river. Once again the trench seemed, in the twilight, very small. In twenty minutes darkness would fall and Mathieson said:

'It's just about adequate. We can whack in tomorrow.'

'Isn't there a moon?' Father Simpson said. 'We could dig by that. I am ready to go on. I'm not tired.' He looked up and down the trench that seemed, against his pale and sturdy corpulence, much smaller than it was. 'It isn't big enough. There are forty or fifty people here now. By morning there will be seventy or eighty. Perhaps more.'

'I'm game. I forgot the moon,' Crane said.

'The nuns will dig,' the priest said. 'Everyone will dig.'

'Where is Maxted?' Colonel Mathieson said. 'I forgot Maxted. Isn't he here?'

'No,' the priest said. 'Maxted is in Lahore. He went on Thursday. He is fixing up his air passage. Mrs Maxted and Julie are here. They were going home.'

'How accurate you are with your tenses, Father,' the Colonel said. In his moment of reprisal he drove his spade into the grass about the trench, embittered to new and personal ironies, irate and tired.

'I am sorry,' the priest said. 'It was thoughtless of me. I should not have said that.'

He began to put on his shirt. It seemed like an act of contrition and the shirt hung about him like a surplice, very white in the shadow under the apple-trees.

'We all need a drink,' the Colonel said. 'It will help us kid ourselves a bit more. It will help with our tenses.'

The priest did not speak. He stood tucking his shirt in his trousers, reflecting once again on how his tongue, his spasms of nervous vanity, trapped him into these moments of pain, with their aftermath of salted, sickening self-condemnation. He had enjoyed the digging so much: all the banter, the male-

26

ness, and the laughter. And now – it was terribly sad about the Maxteds; for Mrs Maxted, for the girl especially. She was very young; she had been born here, actually up here in the Mission confinement ward, and had been eight or nine, he couldn't remember exactly, at the beginning of the war. She had been going home so many times, then and afterwards and now, but she had never gone. She had never seen England. He knew that she longed to go and he could not bear to think of it. Cries of the wretchedest self-reproach pricked his heart like little jets of fire without making their physical escape into tears; and he was very glad when Crane, who had put on his shirt too, said:

'We're all a bit tired. A drink will do us good.'

The priest heaved himself up from the trench. It was a little difficult and Colonel Mathieson, leaning down, gave him a hand.

'Will you have a drink, Father?'

'Thank you.'

'We'll go to my room. Will Father Anstey come?'

'Not for the drink.'

'Perhaps we can find Mrs Maxted and Julie,' the Colonel said. 'My wife will be there.'

'They are probably helping in the wards. It's absolutely chaotic. There are forty or fifty beds to make up and food to get' – he said quickly, words expunging his guilt, his remorse at his stupid blunders with words – 'the sweeper woman is here by the way – Meran – you know – the little creature –'

'And all nine children?'

'There will be ten by tomorrow,' the priest said.

'There was never such a fruitful father,' Colonel Mathieson said. 'I must find his secret formula –'

'Already dead five years and still a new baby every year,' the priest explained.

As they all laughed Father Simpson felt the last of his self-reproaches die and Crane remembered, too late again, that he must ask the Colonel about chess.

They went up the steps of the Mission and through the central hall, a high white room, towards Mathieson's room in the corridor beyond. About thirty Indian women and half a dozen nuns were making floor-beds along the walls on either side of the hall. As the priest and Mathieson and Crane went through Crane saw, among the beds, an English girl of nineteen or twenty folding a blanket. The blanket was grey and she held it flat against her body; above it he could see nothing but her dark eyes and darker fringe of hair. She finished folding the blanket as Crane went past and as it slipped down her body it gave him the impression, with pricking swiftness, and only for a second or two, that she had taken off her dress. The flat grey blanket fell away like the dead shell of a nut, revealing the smoothed white kernel of her ward-smock below.

Colonel Mathieson called out: 'Julie, where is your mother? I want to talk to you too,' and Crane was not aware of what she said in answer.

She did not seem to be looking at Mathieson either, but at Crane. And in a curious way she seemed, Crane thought, to be annoyed with him. She seemed to have guessed what he was thinking about the ward-smock and the blanket.

'Find your mother and come along to our room,' Colonel Mathieson said, and then: 'Oh! I forgot. This is Mr Crane.'

From another corner of the room there was a burst of children's voices, in shrieking little storms of laughter, and the girl pretended not to hear.

'Mr Who?'

'Crane. From Bombay.'

'Oh! from Bombay.'

The small irony, like a pin scratch, filled Crane with impatient irritation as he walked on. Another of those cool and stuck-up mem-sahibs, he thought, and did not know why such a casual exchange of glances, in which he had not spoken a word, should suddenly roughen his entire feelings, souring him like the bite of acid fruit. He felt slighted and on edge. The immediate effect of it was to make him turn and look back. At once he felt intensely stupid for having done so. Just as before, with another blanket, the girl was standing there and as before it was like a flat grey husk held in front of a body; and as before she was looking straight at him. The blanket was about to be folded and her white smocked body was about to be revealed and she knew what he was thinking. But now he could not make up his mind whether it was some oblique and ironic invitation to repeat the thought or simply some kind of virgin obstinacy. He felt it was not only that she resented in him the discovery of that sort of thought. It was as if she wanted him specifically, from that very first moment, to dislike her.

He still felt on edge, roughened with annoyance, as he went into Colonel Mathieson's room, following Father Simpson. He was angry with himself for turning and looking at her the second time. It was not only what she had wanted; it was what she had expected. It was a trap.

Some moments later he was aggravated into a fresh burst of irritation by Mathieson, who brought him whisky. He did not like whisky; he was revolted by its after-breath corruption and it made him, in quantity, very sick. He wanted more than anything a long cold gin, with fresh limes and ice and a spoon. Now instead the whisky was lukewarm and he was angry and revolted because it was whisky and because Mathieson had not had the sense of decency to ask him what he preferred.

All the irritations India had ever bred in him pranced like devils in his mind in another moment as Colonel Mathieson said, loudly:

'Ah! here are the mem-sahibs. Come in, come in.'

Crane looked up to see Mrs Mathieson, a pretty woman of about thirty, whom he had met at lunch, coming in with a fair-haired woman of fifty-five or so wearing a jumper of red and blue cross-stripes and grey trousers. His dislike of women in trousers was added instantly to his dislike of whisky. He hated that word mem-sahib too. Mrs Mathieson, tired, her pregnancy not yet noticeable, was small and quiet, inoffensively decent, he thought, but Mrs Maxted, introduced, said loudly:

'Ah! yes Mr Crane, I saw you disporting yourself in the trenches. Real trenches! It's wonderful.'

Colonel Mathieson's room was nothing more than an enlarged cell with an army camp bed and a long chair and a pile of heavy leather trunks in one corner, and now Mrs Maxted seemed to fill it like a booming aggressive fly.

'And you in the trenches too, Father Simpson. You looked absolutely terrific.'

Father Simpson smiled shyly and looked down into his glass.

'It was really his idea,' Colonel Mathieson said. 'He thinks of everything.'

'Oh! no, I simply –'

'Don't be so modest, Father!' Mrs Maxted said. 'It doesn't become you.'

'I simply like digging,' Father Simpson said. He blushed slightly, very nervous again, searching frantically for some change of subject, and said: 'Where is Julie? I thought Julie was coming in?'

'You know I believe he's the most frightful ladies' man!' Mrs Maxted said.

Father Simpson smiled, blushing a little, but did not speak.

'Isn't he, Mrs Mathieson? Don't you think that? Where *is* Julie anyway? Do you know our Kashmir, Mr Crane? Is it your first time here?'

'She went to wash,' Mrs Mathieson said.

'Is it true we're to have a black-out?' Mrs Maxted said. 'Somebody said we were. Are we?'

'As far as we can,' Colonel Mathieson said.

'I'm sure Father Simpson thought of that too, didn't you, Father?'

Father Simpson smiled.

'Did he, Mr Crane, did he? Where have you come up from? Bombay? Did they have black-outs there? In the war, I meant?'

'I'm hungry,' the Colonel said.

'Don't say the word,' Mrs Maxted said. 'I feel like a wolf.'

Colonel Mathieson had walked to the window of the little room and now stood there with his whisky, staring out at the compound of grass, bordered by rows of cypress interplanted with yellowing maples, that lay between the main building, and the hospital annexe thirty yards away. It was almost dark but Crane, as he joined him, could hear groups of Indian children, like puppies, squealing and laughing under the cypress branches, among fallen maple leaves. Some of his anger evaporated and he said:

'Do we black-out really? Or was it a gag?'

The Colonel had not time to reply before Mrs Maxted shouted, 'Julie! Here you are at last – aren't you *dead*?'

The Colonel moved away to get something for the girl to drink. Mrs Maxted made a laughing remark about Father Simpson and his brain-wave for a black-out, and Crane stood steadily gazing out of the window, listening to the squealing voices of the children he could not see, determined this time not to turn.

But suddenly behind him Mrs Mathieson switched on a light and the Colonel called to him:

'Better pull the curtains, Crane. Just as well.'

The curtains of the high windows, of thick blue material, like linen, were perhaps a remnant, he thought, of that half black-out India had imposed on itself, in martyrdom, during the years of war. They were controlled by a double cord that hung at the side. He pulled jerkily at the shorter cord but nothing happened; and then more savagely, first at the short cord and then the long one; but the curtains did not move. Then he seized the curtains themselves, trying to pull them with his hands, but they would not slide and behind him he heard Mrs Maxted laughing too and he made a final attack of impatient savagery on the shorter cord. A splintering crack in the upper fittings brought Mrs Maxted running:

'I'll do it, I'll do it! Leave it! Leave it, you silly man. You'll have the whole thing down.'

She took the cords one in either hand and pulled with light efficiency. The curtains closed with ease and her voice rattled with triumph:

'Isn't it astounding how men can never do these things? A simple thing like pulling a curtain and before you know it they have the whole house down.'

Crane did not speak. He turned, temporarily dazzled by the small electric bulb nakedly blazing above the Colonel's bed. He could not look at Mrs Maxted, loudly acclaiming his stupid male inefficiency, or at the daughter. Blistered by complex and impotent hatreds, he felt himself on the point of walking out, and then Mrs Maxted said:

'What *is* happening, Colonel? Does anyone know? Do we really have to go to the trenches? I hope not. The damp brings on my asthma, it always brings it on.'

'Colonel, the supper-bell has gone,' the priest said. 'I think we ought to go in.'

The Colonel, grinning at Crane, held open the door for his wife and Julie Maxted. After they had gone through he waited for some seconds for Mrs Maxted, but in her inconsequent way she had become interested in Crane and was saying loudly, as the young priest waited too:

'Are you Catholic, Mr Crane?'

'No,' Crane said.

'Good, good. Cheers. Nor am I.' The priest stood aside quietly, unoffended, waiting. 'My husband is. But Father Simpson is always trying to convert me – aren't you, Father, aren't you?'

'I never try to convert anyone.'

'Oh! – hark at that, Mr Crane, hark at that. Did you hear that? Rome never trying to *convert*! Doesn't that take the biscuit?'

With downcast eyes the priest went to the door and held it open. Beyond it there were revealed, in long confused rows, thirty or forty improvised beds on the stone floor of the central hall. With a burst of laughter children from the compound came running down the aisle between them, once again like dark puppies, Crane thought, and Mrs Maxted said:

'I feel I shall shriek with all these children careering round. You can't hear yourself think any more. Do they *have* to?'

'We have nowhere else for them,' the priest said.

After he had closed the door behind Crane, Mrs Maxted and the three of them walked down the aisle between the beds. On the walls a few electric light bulbs had been shaded with cones of brown paper. Light was thrown whitely down on dark bodies, on nuns, on children, on bundles, and on scrambled bedding in a series of stark and narrow tubes.

Under one of these tubes, smoking a cigarette and staring steadily beyond the smoke of it at the corresponding tube of light on the opposite wall, sat the Hindu girl in the saffron-orange sari who had come up that morning from the boat. She did not move as the three of them went past, but Crane, turning at the end of the row of beds, saw Father Simpson look at her. He heard him speak a word or two as he went past, without stopping, and as if she knew it were something he wanted to appear casual and unimportant, as not worth elaboration or an answer, the girl did not move. To what Father Simpson said she had no answer. She went on staring into the cigarette smoke, at the tubes of light on the wall, her face like a smoky mask in the downward cone of light. It was only when Father Simpson had gone past that Mrs Maxted said:

'There you are, Mr Crane, there you are. Did you see? Did you hear? And he wants us to believe he never converts anyone!'

The priest had already hurried past them so that he could hold open the door leading into the refectory beyond the hall. Now he held it open, smiling gently at Crane.

Mrs Maxted sailed jauntily into the lighter blacked-out room beyond, saying loudly:

'Look out, Mr Crane. The approaches are awfully subtle.'

The priest smiled again and closed the door. Mrs Maxted began to say something about the Jesuits but remembered herself in time. Colonel Mathieson and his wife and Miss Maxted were standing at the long supper table, with Father Anstey waiting at the far end. Dr Baretta, a slim Eurasian girl, perhaps twenty-nine or thirty, stood next to Father Anstey with her husband, also a Eurasian, a man of bluish chiselled lips and almond yellow face and hands; and Mrs Maxted said, seeing them all:

'Are we frightfully late? Are you waiting?'

No one spoke. Father Simpson took up his place at the end of the table opposite Father Anstey, with Crane and Mrs Maxted on either side. Father Anstey said a benediction and Father Simpson answered Amen, with a straggling chorus from the others.

'You did nobly with the trench, Mr Crane,' Father Anstey said. 'Is it finished?'

'Not quite.'

'We are digging again tonight,' Father Simpson said. 'By moon.'

'What trench?' Mrs Maxted said. 'Oh yes, of course. The trench. Air-raids and that sort of thing?'

Her voice seemed to flutter about the high white room, up and down the table, over the bread and soup, and wooden dishes of fruit, the green carafes of water, the plates of raw red beetroot, with the precipitant aimless dashes of a bat trapped and dazzled by light. It had on Crane a mesmeric effect, so that he was through the soup and was cutting away at a plate of cold rather fat mutton and potatoes before he fully realized that Miss Maxted was next to him.

'How do you like it up here after Bombay, Mr Crane?'

'I'm not from Bombay.'

'I thought Colonel Mathieson said Bombay when you came through the hall.'

'I came up from Bombay.' He felt weary and trapped by the pettiness of explanations. 'But I'm not from Bombay. I'm not from anywhere.'

'Oh,' she said. 'Could it be some fault of mine?'

'I don't think so.'

'That's a relief. It sounded awfully like one of those personal matters.'

'Did it?' He stared at his plate, not caring, all his feelings set on edge once again by her oblique and tiresome ironies, the loud bat-like vapourings of her mother, the atmosphere of tedious parochialism. He hated suddenly the tasteless mutton as if it were some sort of composite expression of these things and then from the far end of the table Father Anstey called.

'You're not eating, Mr Crane. You must eat, you diggers. Give Mr Crane some more meat, Father. He'll need it. It's early yet.'

Father Simpson piled slices of cold fat mutton on to Crane's plate and when Crane protested Miss Maxted said:

'Eat it up, Mr Crane. The diggers need all their strength. It's good for you.'

'Have you enough, Mr Crane?' Father Simpson said.

'Plenty, Father, thank you. Quite enough.'

'Another potato, Mr Crane?' The girl held the dish and its wooden spoon across the table, about the level of her breast, mocking him. 'Two potatoes? Yes?' He felt himself teased between that line of sight and another, five or six inches above the edge of the wooden dish of potatoes, at the level of her eyes. He knew that now he was being teased as he and Colonel Mathieson had teased Father Simpson, with many tireless and rather cruel irritations to which Father Simpson had responded with that slow and gentle smile of forbearance that was like the smile of someone emerging from a cat-nap or a dream. He knew that it was fantastically and stupidly puerile of himself to take notice of these things. He knew that sooner or later he must not take notice; that he must speak to her with decent normality, without infuriating tangents of meaning that charged ordinary gossip with malice; but suddenly the two potatoes, and then another, were on his plate, the dark eyes were mocking him with fresh flashes of surprised innocence, as if it were all an accident, and her voice with a sort of milky acidity was apologizing, 'Oh! I'm sorry – so sorry – so silly of me – they just slipped –' so that he felt himself petrified into a moment of frigid protest:

'I said no potatoes, thank you.'

He picked up the spoon from the potato dish. He lifted the potatoes, in a crushed cold mess, from his plate. She was laughing at him: not with her mouth but with her eyes and underneath her eyes and behind them, and he wanted for a single moment to sling the potatoes in her face. She was growing up to be another nice infuriating superior English mem-sahib, he thought, like her mother and ten thousand pukka mem-sahibs before her from all the bridge clubs and tennis clubs and swimming clubs and gossip clubs, from Bombay to Calcutta, Delhi and Darjeeling, and wherever else they clanned together. She was another one who had flounced her way through the war with no other wounds but the sores on her finger-tips from

35

tying Red Cross parcels. She was another one who fancied herself in the high places. She was another daughter of the Philistines: except that it was another sort of philistinism, another sort of prostitution, the sort at which the colonial female was as always more deadly than the male. Give me the lady in the sari, he thought, I've had enough.

Thinking all this, still holding the potatoes, he was unaware of silence in the room. He was unaware of Father Simpson, frantically searching in another moment of pained embarrassment for a change of subject that would clear the air.

The priest sat with his nervous podgy hands elastically locking and unlocking themselves. He looked with diffident anxiety from Crane to Miss Maxted and then down to his plate. It was another of those lamentable moments of misconception that somehow had to be changed or frustrated. He sought frantically for solutions as he had sought for them when the girl Kaushalya had flaunted herself before him on the boat.

And then in a moment more fervid than the rest it came to him. It was so terrible and so ridiculous and yet to him so important that it seemed to inflate his entire body. It seemed to pump him, jellified with anxiety, to his feet.

'Father, forgive me!' he said. 'Excuse me! I didn't shut the rabbits up – they will be out – just as you said –'

His hands stopped their podgy elastic fiddling and a second later he dashed out of the room. Crane dropped the potatoes on to his own plate and Mrs Maxted, hitting the flanks of her trousered thighs with her flat hands, rocked backwards and forwards with hideous shrieks of laughter.

4

As Crane walked up and down the terrace below the apple-
trees, smoking nervously, intensely irritated with himself, waiting for the moon to come up and the digging to begin, he saw
the main door of the Mission building open and the figure of a
woman stand darkly in the lighted doorway. He heard a voice
from inside shout. 'Black-out! Black-out!' and then heard the
woman running down the steps. In a wild moment he thought,
'If it's the mem-sahib come to apologize, I'm out,' and began to
stride quickly away across the grass towards the wall of
cypresses that stood up like rows of black swords, rigid in the
dead night air.

A moment or two later he heard the voice of the woman
calling:

'Mr Crane, Mr Crane! Is it you? Are y' there?'

It was neither the voice of Miss Maxted nor a voice he
remembered hearing before; and he called back:

'Yes; it's me. I'm here. Who wants me?'

He saw the figure of a girl in nurse's uniform running down
the terrace and across the grass. He heard something that
sounded very much like 'Damn the trench', and then she was
there before him, much smaller even than she had seemed when
coming down the steps, no more than five feet five inches high
and panting with running:

'Ah! there y'are, Mr Crane. I've been looking all over the
shop for you.'

'Something wrong?'

'You remember me? McAlister? I took you to your room.'

'Oh! yes.'

'Once seen never forgotten,' she said. 'From Glasgow. You
remember you guessed the first time?'

He had not remembered.

'Mr Crane,' she said, 'the Mother Superior sent me to tell you we're so bunged out that we have to change your room.'

'That's all right,' he said.

'Will you come to see it? We've had to put Miss Maxted and Mrs Maxted together with Mrs Mathieson, and you and Colonial Mathieson in another room. It's a wee titty bit of a room but it's nice.'

'Separating the cats and dogs,' he said.

'That's it.'

His cigarette was almost finished. He lighted another from it and pulled at it hungrily. She watched him with a pair of small keen grey eyes that were fiery for a moment in the heightened glow of the new cigarette.

'Will you come to see it?' she said.

'No. I trust you.'

'It's time someone did,' she said.

She gave a great sigh, pressing her hair back from her face with both hands. He asked her if she were tired and she said, her hands still pressed against the sides of her head:

'A wee bit. It's been a hell of a day.'

He laughed and she said:

'There I go again. Pure habit. I'll never break myself.'

'It's the good old Glasgow,' he said.

'That's it.'

He smoked greedily for a moment or two and she watched, keen small eyes hungry too.

'All the damns and bloodies and hells in the world don't mean a thing to me. They're just like frightfully and awfully – just superlatives –'

He laughed again and she said:

'What d'ye think's goin' to happen? I mean here – you know?'

'Anything,' he said. 'Perhaps nothing.'

'Whatever it is it'll be no worse than Rangers and Celtic, that's sure, or my father beatin' my mother's brains out with a brick every Saturday.'

He smoked rapidly and she watched him again in silence, saying at last:

'I'm a great brick-heaver myself. I learned it young.'

'Been here long?'

'Two years. I came to India with the Queen's Nurses. Then after I got back from Burma I had –' She stopped.

'Yes?' he said.

'I had a nervous breakdown –'

'War?'

'No,' she said.

'What then?' he said.

'Oh! what do women have nervous breakdowns about?' she said.

Not answering, he stood absently letting the cigarette burn away in his hands, staring at the glow of green-orange that had now begun to light up the horizon beyond the folded crust of hill forest across the river.

'I must go back,' she said.

Watching the rising glow of moonlight, seeing the gentleness of it slowly diffuse, deeper orange every moment, into the blue-black sky, he had not really heard. He felt an immeasurable glow of calmness spreading upwards into himself as the light was spreading up into the sky and it did not for a moment occur to him that it might be because of her.

When he turned from looking at the glow of light it was to see her once again gazing, with that tired pinched stare of hunger, at his wasting cigarette, and suddenly he knew what it was she wanted.

He held it out to her without a word.

'No,' she said. 'No.' He held it an inch or two nearer her hands and she snatched at it swiftly. 'No,' she said. 'No, I shouldn't.' He could see her fingers trembling, the red light quivering on the white stalk of paper. 'No,' she said. 'No, I'm sort of on trial – I might take vows –'

'You can say ten thousand Hail Marys and it will be all right.'

'It makes it worse,' she said. 'That's blasphemy and you know it.'

'You can even say the Joyful Mysteries.'

'It's the first for fifteen months – is it terrible? – shall I? – I've got to, it's been a hell of a day.'

She put the cigarette in her mouth and pulled at it with one long savage breath, shutting her eyes. It was like an act to which she had been frantically driven by hunger and thirst and she stood for some seconds holding the smoke before she let it go, slowly and exquisitely, covering herself with a little cloud.

She gave the cigarette back to him, a second later, as suddenly and savagely as she had taken it. In the doorway of the Mission there was a crack of light and Crane heard the voice of Colonel Mathieson saying something to Father Simpson and then Father Simpson's voice, higher and almost squeaky, in reply. He remembered in that moment that now, at last, since he was to share a room with Mathieson, it might be possible for them to play chess together.

He lifted his cigarette to his mouth. In the act of doing so he felt the nurse, whom he had forgotten in the pleasant reflection of the Colonel and the prospect of chess, snatch the cigarette from his hands. 'I'm a terrible person,' she said, 'terrible, terrible,' and whenever he thought of her long afterwards it was as she stood there in the eager and almost terrified tension of that moment, gasping at the cigarette, her small grey eyes tired and glittering hungrily and at last calmed and assuaged, saying, 'Terrible, God forgive me, terrible, terrible,' before she dropped the cigarette out of sheer nervousness of frightened guilt and ran away.

He put his foot on the cigarette and under the apple-trees came Mathieson and Father Simpson, the priest carrying his spade. Crane remembered about chess, but Father Simpson, turning in the rising moonlight to look back up the terrace, said:

'Who was that? Running.'

'Nurse McAlister,' Crane said. 'She came to tell me about the room.'

'Ah yes. That reminds me – Father Anstey would like you to meet the Mother Superior. And the Assistant Mother Superior too. She is Spanish. Before you go to bed.'

'Shall we go to bed?'

'Oh! I hope so. I think so.'

'What do you think, Colonel?'

'No damn Pathan tribesman is going to keep me out of bed. Or anybody else,' the Colonel said.

'That's the spirit,' Crane said. 'Up the die-hards.'

Father Simpson laughed; and Crane saw the flaccid cheeks of his face flopping up and down, boyish and yet old in their fatness. The banter had begun. Over the hills, bluish and steely at the extreme fat line, indigo and black in the intervening valleys below, the moon came up like a scarlet balloon in slow ascent, three-quarters full, casting ripe and bloody light, extinguishing immediately the green flash of lower stars. The trench under the apple-trees became, in this intense and brilliant glare, thinning to orange, the gash of a yellow stream in fruit-strewn grass, and Father Simpson, brown habit floating, jumped into it like a joyful penitent into a holy river.

'Belly-flopper,' the Colonel called, and Crane said:

'You're sure the rabbits are shut up before we begin?'

'Every one asleep,' the priest said.

He began to attack the end of the trench with rushing extravagant lashes of his spade, grunting. 'Grunt, Father, grunt,' the Colonel said, 'fetch it up. Get rid of it,' and the priest replied by heaving himself upright in a moment of open-mouthed relief, splendidly belching.

The surprise was so great that Crane for some moments could not speak for laughing. The final irritations of the day, festering into stupid moments of annoyance with Miss Maxted, dissipated themselves down cool moonlit terraces of vine and peach, now pale green and ruby in the day-like glare of moon, like the echoes of Father Simpson's belching. He felt suddenly that he had been an awful fool; that he ought to apologize; and that tomorrow he would make some sort of attempt, however humiliating, to expunge all the stupidities that seemed to have been begun by his staring at the girl as she folded the blanket and by Mathieson's casual remark that he came from Bombay.

A moment later Mathieson said: 'A splendid effort, Father. Is everything allowed?'

'Everything,' the priest said, and belched with horn-like noises again, relieving himself of new gaseous burdens of mutton and potatoes.

This time Crane found himself not laughing. The extravagant belch of the priest seemed to hit, far across the valley, a wall of rock among the forest. It seemed to leap gutturally back. It seemed to him he caught in it a sinister sort of shout: partly animal, partly like the staunched yell of a man wounded in the guts. It died away so quickly that he could not be sure of it; and then as he turned to remark on it to Father Simpson and the Colonel he saw that both of them were digging heartily at the trench-end and that they had not heard.

Later, in moments of competitive wind-raising, he paused and listened again. Leaning on his spade, he looked through white moonlight into a valley that was dead. The projecting elbow of rock that had so disturbed Father Anstey that morning hung above the river now with the poised ferocity of a bone skinned of flesh; the river below it had a frozen glacial beauty, quite colourless, moon-frozen under its ebonized wall of rock. The echoed cry did not repeat itself; he put it down to the chance yell of a night animal or perhaps a bird that had synchronized oddly with Father Simpson's belching. Once the main door of the Mission opened again and he found himself uneasily looking up, thinking instantly that it might be Miss Maxted, walking out for a final breath of air, but as with the echo across the valley nothing happened and she did not come.

The effect of both these things made him uneasy rather in the way that Father Anstey had been uneasy; it was like a haunting ache in the bone. He dug strenuously, liking it, helping to lengthen the trench just before midnight to another twelve or fourteen feet. 'Enough to take the nuns and Father Simpson,' the Colonel teased. All night the physical bantering jokes had gone on; the Colonel on several occasions made water noisily against a tree. It was very like the life of a Mess, Crane thought. Tonight it seems funny; it is very hearty and wonderful; it protects us and tomorrow it will grow thin. It was exactly as he remembered it once with a squadron of fighter pilots: all the physical heartiness, underlined by fear of death, all the jolly exultation in little things, above the ache in the bone.

'If the Colonel has quite finished,' Father Simpson said finally, 'I think we could call it a day.'

'I have quite finished,' the Colonel said. 'It is simply the cold weather.'

'Perhaps there will be cocoa to warm you,' the priest said.

Up in the Mission, in the main hall, Father Anstey was walking between the two lines of beds with two nuns.

Above the beds all but two of the cones of light had been extinguished, so that it was almost dark in the hall except for a blue-bulbed light over the doorway leading to the refectory.

In this strange blue light the two nuns appeared as if carved in starch. Crane stood before them and bowed slightly and Father Anstey said:

'This is our Mother Superior, Mr Crane. You have not met before.'

'No,' he said. 'I am delighted now.'

She smiled slightly in a way that was less a smile than the gentle relaxing of carved pale muscles, ageless and neutrally sweet.

'And this the Assistant Mother Superior. Sister Teresalina. From Spain.'

She had, he saw, one of those twisted Spanish faces that seemed to have been put in a clamp, crushing development. It gave her the effect of being prematurely shrunken, already neutralized and old. He felt that, like the Mother Superior, she could not speak and he found himself involuntarily looking for Miss Maxted, but suddenly she said:

'Do you know Spain?'

'Yes. I was in Barcelona for a year.'

'That is not Spain,' she said. 'That is Catalonia. Another country.'

'I am sorry,' he said.

'Sister Teresalina is from Sevilla,' Father Anstey said.

'That is Spain,' she said.

Their voices were indeterminate, not much more than whispers, in the darkened ward. Someone walked down the aisle between the beds. Crane looked beyond the two starched

43

and anonymous figures, in the blue light, for a possible glimpse of Miss Maxted, but it was only Kaushalya, still smoking, walking back to bed.

He saw her lie down under the cone of light and begin again, as if she had never left off, the dead stare at the opposite wall, dark except for another light now; and Father Anstey said:

'Is it quiet outside?'

'Very quiet, Father.' It was Father Simpson who spoke, gently, with decorum, all trace of banter discreetly buried away.

'How is the trench?'

'We have finished it, Father. It is much bigger. It will take forty or fifty. Perhaps more.'

'I call it very noble of you, Mr Crane and Colonel,' Father Anstey said.

'We did nothing,' the Colonel said.

'It is Father Simpson's baby,' Crane said.

The thought of Father Simpson and a baby made even the Mother Superior smile; and Sister Teresalina said:

'Don't talk of babies. There will be at least one on our hands before tomorrow.'

'I think we could get some sleep,' Father Anstey said. 'What do you say, Colonel?'

'I think so.'

Five or six good nights were whispered before the two nuns floated away under the blue light. Crane and Mathieson went down the ward between the beds, leaving Father Simpson and Father Anstey alone. Crane looked at Kaushalya sitting under the white cone of light, smoking still, not looking at him or at Mathieson or the two Fathers, or even at anything, and he thought again that she seemed to be waiting for something. It recalled for him the guttural and echoed cry, following Father Simpson's belchings, across the valley; and he thought anxiously, with abrupt and unreasonable tension, of Miss Maxted. He would have to see her, somehow, first thing tomorrow.

In the small room he and Mathieson were to share he undressed by moonlight. His feet were cold and he did not take off his socks. Undressing, he stood most of the time by the window, looking out at the cypresses, black under the moon. Dew was falling on the grass where the Indian children had played, and in the moonlight it sparkled like the multiplied reflection of the few colourless and undiminished stars.

When he turned again he saw that Mathieson was in bed. They had not bothered to switch on a light and now suddenly he recalled what it was, all day, he had planned to say to Mathieson, and for one reason and another never had.

'I meant to ask you if you played chess, Colonel,' he said.

'Used to play by correspondence,' the Colonel said.

'We must play some time.'

'Some time,' the Colonel said.

He said good night suddenly and then did not speak again. It was very quiet except for a stretching of the canvas on the Colonel's camp-bed and for some time longer Crane lay awake in the silence, on his back, smoking, hardly drawing his breath, listening for sounds that never came.

5

He woke with the moon full on his face, in a vivid nightmare of a screaming child, not knowing where he was. This screaming was not simply an agony of somebody running frightened down the corridors of his dream. It was an order, telling him to get up. After some moments it came to him that this was not the screaming of a single child but a whole mob of children, in panic, frenzied with terror. It was not simply a nightmare of sleep, but a nightmare that was real; it was not only the screaming of children, telling him to get up, but the voice of Colonel Mathieson, yelling madly at him from above the bed.

He leaped up in time to see the Colonel rushing out of the door. Beyond the door a corridor, momentarily blue-lit then dark, was for a single second longer a fusion of reality and dream, and then he heard a shot. He heard the rifle-bullet whine across the hill outside, spending itself in air. This clean harmless flight sounded so solitary and woke him to such calmness that he got out of bed and began to put on his trousers. It was only then that he realized he was very cold. His legs felt stiff and bloodless as they touched the cloth of his trousers and his fingers were so clumsy and dead that he could not do up the buttons. He stood fumbling stupidly with these buttons for some seconds longer as if for some reason it were necessary and very important to be correctly dressed and then the rifle-bullet came back. It seemed to have described an elliptical course across the hill outside. It sounded extraordinarily like an infuriated mosquito. He was just thinking this, still obsessed with the main notion that he ought to do up the last of his trouser buttons circumspectly, when the bullet smashed the window above his head.

When he rushed out into the corridor, only realizing at that moment that his feet, still without shoes, were even colder than the rest of his body, he at once fell down. It did not occur to him until much later that this was a purely instinctive thing. A whole volley of rifle-fire was sweeping through the Mission and fifty children seemed to be screaming for every shot. It was dark and he did not know where he was. He heard the wild yelling of a man's voice, and he shouted, 'Is that you, Colonel? For Christ's sake what's happening?' but the only answer was another yell that seemed to set off, somewhere in the direction of the main ward, another volley of fire with another trail of screams.

All this time he was lying on his face. He lay there for perhaps fifteen seconds or so, but it seemed, between the two sets of screams, like a terribly long time. He lay thinking, 'I ought to go back for my shoes. It's important. I ought to have them. I shall need them. The floors are dirty and I shall get foot-worms.' And then he was running. His stockinged feet on the stone floor of the corridor were numb and he could not feel them.

At the end of the corridor a door was banging on its lock, as if someone had just gone through. He pushed it open. He fell immediately over the body of an Indian woman lying face upwards in the room beyond. His feet touched her face but she did not move or groan. His revulsion at this sensation of his shoeless feet touching the dead face was so great that it impelled him forward in a slobbering burst of panic.

'Colonel! For Christ's sake where are you, Colonel?' he shouted. 'Colonel! where are you?'

To his astonishment the Colonel answered from fifteen or twenty feet away.

'Crane!' he yelled. 'I can't find my wife and Mrs Maxted. I can't find them!'

A fresh burst of rifle-fire, with women and children screaming in frenzy, came from the main part of the building, and Crane said, abruptly calmed by the voice of the Colonel:

'They're probably in the trenches.'

'Will you look there? I'll go to the main hall.'

'Where are we?' Crane said, 'I haven't the vaguest —'

'We're behind the refectory!' the Colonel shouted. 'There's a door here – you can go this way. Outside.'

Crane began to speak again but he heard the banging of another door and he knew a moment later, in the darkness that was now acridly shot with smoke, that the Colonel was not there.

He groped his way through the refectory, feeling with his hands along the table where he had gone through the appallingly trivial affair of the potatoes with Miss Maxted. The windows had been hurriedly blacked-out with what seemed to be old Franciscan habits of Father Anstey and Father Simpson, so that the moonlight came through as a brown burnt glow. He snatched one of them down. Moonlight flowed in with white brilliance so that he could find his way through the door at the far end. Just as he had reached it he remembered the brown habit he had left on the floor. A burst of firing and a new torrent of screams came from the middle of the building as he picked it up. It would come in useful, he thought; he could wrap someone in it, perhaps a child; and as he reached the door this thought prompted another: the notion, for some reason, that it might even give him immunity.

Then as he walked out into the full glare of moonlight he remembered his own words to Father Simpson:

'Nowadays they make targets of anything.'

In that moment, with that thought, in the moonlight that was like day, he felt his mind really clear. He walked across the terrace, folding the brown Franciscan habit in his hands. The eastern end of the building was on fire, pouring smoke down the lower terraces in grey clouds, under the line of moon. He remembered the trench. He scrambled down the bank below the terrace, feeling the dew through his socks as he landed on the flat grass below. He remembered Mrs Maxted and Miss Maxted and Mrs Mathieson.

In that moment an Indian woman ran screaming from the door of the hospital, halting thirty or forty yards away from him, seeing him in the moonlight. He wanted to shout at her that it was all right, that she must go to the trench, that nothing would happen, but he remembered suddenly how the words he would shout in English would be to her only strange words, the foreign idiom simply a new sort of terror. Even as he thought it he opened his mouth and in the same moment two Mahsuds, the first Pathans he had seen, ran down from the hospital building, swinging rifles.

He heard her scream as she turned to run. He saw her run backwards a little, and then sideways, caught in the trap of the two Mahsuds charging down on her. She looked like a little dark rabbit, terrified and blinded by light, not knowing which way to run. He heard her scream again and he saw her put up her hands.

He heard the sickening blow of the Mahsud rifle-butt as it hit her across the skull. He felt the bone break in it as if it were his own bone, her final frantic whimpering, as if it were his own heart crying. He stood for a second or two in sickness, his horror draining coldly down to his cold feet. Then they picked her up. They stood her on her feet as a child stands a doll. He knew that she was dead as she stood there for a fraction of another second before she began to fall down. Then as she fell down one Mahsud seized her clothing, pulling her upright; but she had fallen too far and now her bodice ripped away. He heard it slit down and saw its whiteness parting as if it were a skin, slitting away and showing her brown body beneath. He saw all of her brown dead figure in the second before it fell for the last time, the two Mahsuds on top of her.

He stood watching for a few moments longer and then it was all over and he walked down to the trench. The sourness of fallen apples was mingled with the odour of fire, the one crushed and musty and acid, the other choking and dry, so that he was forced to stand still for a moment, under the skeleton apple-boughs, because he wanted to be sick.

When he could be sick no longer he went on to the trench. He felt already that no one could be there. The rape on the terrace would have set them screaming, he thought. Then as he got to the trench he was astonished to see it full of upturned faces, moon-pale and terrorized and waiting in silence for him to come. They looked, with their dead-dark eyes, like a long grave of skulls.

'Who's here?' he said. 'Is Mrs Mathieson here?'

'Oh! Mother of God, Mr Crane. It's me, McAlister.'

'Who's with you?'

'Myself with seven or eight of the nuns. And about twenty women.'

'Isn't Mrs Mathieson here? Or Mrs Maxted?'

'No.'

'Nor Miss Maxted?'

'No.'

Women were crying and whimpering. A nun nursing a child farther down the trench said:

'There are more nuns and some women in the vines.'

'I'll go and look there,' he said. 'Are you all right, Miss Mc-Alister?'

'Fine,' she said. 'We're fine.'

'Good.'

'It's no worse than Saturday night in Glasgow,' she said, and laughed.

With the echo of this incredible sound in his mind he walked down to the second of the terraces, where the vines made long grey-blue alleys in the moonlight. He stood on the path and called gently, almost in a whisper:

'Is Mrs Mathieson there? Mrs Maxted?'

A figure, startlingly white, came up the path. It was Miss Maxted. She seemed to look right past him: as if beyond him there were countless other figures, more important, among whom she was searching.

'I can't find my mother. I can't see my mother.'

She suddenly broke into running, her head held desperately forward, her breath sobbing. She actually ran a yard or two past him before it came to him that she was really running up to the Mission. He held her back by the hands and she said:

'She's absolutely no good alone. She's so awfully helpless.'

Violently she pulled herself free. He let her go for another yard without protest. Her long springy hands slid out of his own coldly. At that same moment a Pathan rushed across the top terrace, firing his rifle at the moon, awaking in Crane an

50

abrupt and curious emotion against the figure he had let go. It took the form of a hard and protective kind of rage, making him leap again after her, partly knocking her down.

She did not seem at all surprised at this clumsy rush at her and she did not speak. In the moment of knocking her down he heard a woman shrieking. It was partly as if the girl herself had shrieked, partly as if the woman he had seen raped on the terrace had come to life again and had renewed her own hideous shrieking too. A flame shot out of the smoke in the burning eastern wing of the Mission and he threw Miss Maxted into the vines, slapping his hand across her mouth. He struck his head against one of the bamboo poles on which the vines were trained and the pole cracked off at the base like an echo of the rifle-shot, bringing down several yards of vines flatly, like a skeined curtain that fell on top of them.

He did not know how long they lay there, covered by vines, and his only sensation came to him very slowly. It was a dull paralysis of his entire right hand. It took him some time to realize that his hand had been rigidly bitten and held by her mouth from the moment he had slapped it there and knocked her down.

Some time later he felt her mouth open loosely, in relief, letting his hand go free. He suddenly felt exhausted. He had not the strength to move his hand away from her face. He simply let it lie there for a few moments longer against her wet mouth until finally she took it in both her own hands and moved it away.

It was only when he kicked the section of fallen vines free with his feet that he felt himself at last mentally and physically free. The sour dregs of his sickness filled his mouth. For a last second or two he lay staring at the moon before the ghastly impact of all he had seen and heard hit him into full wakefulness.

'Where was your mother? Wasn't she with you? Where did you last see her?'

'She went back for her shawl –'

'With Mrs Mathieson?'

'I think so: yes. I remember now. They were together.'

While speaking he pulled himself up to his knees. He squatted on his heels, looking at her face. It was very white in the moonlight; she seemed suddenly much younger than he had thought she was. She looked simply like a scared child, stunned by impalpable terrors. 'Good Christ,' he thought, 'what did I say to her?' He tried to recall, in a vain and ridiculous moment, something of what it was he had done up at the Mission, in Colonel Mathieson's room, and then afterwards, at supper. Something about potatoes, about a curtain that would not pull – he could not remember what it was that had made him so distraught. The confused and enraging trivialities of a few hours before mocked him. He felt cut with shame, miserably, as after a puerile joke; and as if to make it sharper he vividly and involuntarily remembered Father Simpson.

A child began crying, dryly and thinly, in the vines. He said something hastily about keeping the children quiet and the girl said:

'It's probably the Meran woman. She was having the baby when I walked up and met you.'

The thought of Father Simpson, renewed, filled him with an even sharper concern than the crying child. It affected him as the disappearance of her mother had affected the girl. 'She's so awfully helpless.' The priest was so like a lumbering dream that he would probably stumble into a gang of murdering Pathans rather as he would walk into the convent sewing-class, and so get himself promptly and fiendishly carved up.

There now seemed to be less firing in the Mission, and the smoke in the eastern part was dying down. Recalling Father Simpson, he remembered Father Anstey too. The Yorkshireman had struck him as being rather like the ghost of a carthorse. The sinews had dried up; perhaps he was too old for the job. Crane had sensed a certain lack of authority, he thought, as between the once sturdy elderly priest, now dried up, and the younger, flabbier, dreamier man. Neither of them, he thought, would get very far.

And then he remembered Mathieson. The thought of the Colonel brought him some relief. The Colonel was experienced and dependable. He rather liked the Colonel; he had been a little hasty about the Intelligence and the raspberries; and suddenly he thought:

'What in hell am I waiting here for? I came to look for Mrs Mathieson – that's what I came for –'

He remembered the Colonel's horrified and desperate cry. 'I can't find them!' as he got to his feet. The girl was sitting up, absently clutching the brown habit he had snatched from the windows of the refectory, and now she said:

'You haven't got your shoes on. You came out in your socks.'

She looked up at him, distracted because he was not listening.

'What are you going to do? Your feet are cold. They're wet and cold. Where are your shoes?'

She touched his feet with her hands and he was vaguely aware of her kneeling there, wrapping them in the priest's habit. But he was still not listening, and she was already speaking again, saying something more about his shoes, before he took his eyes off the figures crowding about the main door of the Mission. The fire had sprung up freshly again; the roof of the eastern end of the building was burning in a triangle of black and orange. In the light of it he could see ten or a dozen Pathans raging about the steps, swinging rifles like clubs, shouting with bloody falsetto yells, and he could not get out of his mind the notion that they were butchering Father Simpson and Father Anstey.

His emotion behind this was a sort of enraged affection. He knew suddenly that he had grown very fond of the shy and gentle priest who had dug with himself and the Colonel all afternoon under the apple-trees and had taken their banterings with such dignity and amused grace. Over in the far end of the Mission a roof-timber split and fell in the fire, raising a redder spout of flame, and in it he thought he saw the Pathans disperse.

He was about to walk out on the path when he thought of his feet, covered with the priest's habit, and he bent down to move it away from them.

'Where are you going?' she said. 'What are you going to do?'

'Lie down,' he said. 'Cover yourself up. Get farther in the vines.'

53

'What are you –'

'Farther in,' he said. 'Farther. Farther still.'

He made her crawl twenty or thirty yards into the alleyway between the vines. 'Lie down,' he said, 'as far under as you can,' and she lay down close under the lower leaves of the vines and he covered her with the habit, pulling it up to her chin, so that only her face was free.

She looked in that moment very much as she had looked when he had first come into the central improvised ward that afternoon, and he said:

'I'm sorry we got off on the wrong foot – this afternoon – you remember, when I came in and looked at you.'

'It doesn't matter. It never happened.'

'It was silly of me and I'm sorry you hated me.'

'I didn't hate you,' she said.

'That's something anyway.'

'I didn't hate you, but I hate Bombay, and when they said you came from Bombay –'

'I didn't come from Bombay, and I hate it too,' he said.

'It just shows you,' she said. 'I'm terribly sorry too, and I wanted to say so.'

She spoke tenderly; he wanted to do nothing but lie down with her, crawling under the habit. It would have been wonderful to lie and warm his feet there and let what was happening up at the Mission happen, and let day come. He spread his hands across her shoulders, smoothing the habit like a blanket.

'Stay here,' he said, 'for God's sake don't move.' He was overwhelmed with a hungry weariness to lie down with her again, his mind and body bludgeoned with sickness and horror. 'Whatever happens stay here. For Christ's sake – you understand – stay here –'

'I'll stay,' she said.

He touched her face, not speaking because he was overwhelmed again by the misery of leaving her there, very young and rigid and almost, it struck him, like a corpse under the brown habit; and then he crawled out from among the vines.

He had walked thirty or forty yards up the path before he saw that a new and more awful thing had happened. He stopped

54

dead in the middle of the path. Up on the terrace, in front of the Mission, nothing seemed to be happening now. There were no howling Pathan figures and nothing was moving except the drifting woollen smoke of fire.

Instead a small crowd of yelling Pathans were under the apple-trees. There were eight or ten of them. And as he stood there the women began to file, some of the nuns carrying children, out of the trench. He thought he heard the voice of McAlister calling them, as she might have called a class of children, to keep together. Behind him the child cried dryly and almost inhumanly again in the vines, like a little dog, and up in the Mission a single rifle fired, the shot smashing through glass, the sound splintering with weird whinings across the valley.

He thought for a moment of going back to quieten the child; and then he remembered that it was new-born, that it had to cry, that there was no way of stopping it. He thought of Colonel Mathieson and Mrs Mathieson and the unborn child. There was nothing he could do. They were going to butcher the whole lot of them before morning anyway. It might as well be now as later; and he followed the women up the hill.

6

When Father Simpson heard the first shot his immediate thought was not for Mrs Mathieson or Mrs Maxted or Julie, or even the patients in the hospital ward, but for Father Anstey. He was perfectly sure also that Father Anstey would not be thinking of him, but of the Mother Superior, the Indian women and children, the patients and the nuns. He had not thought of going to bed. He was still in the little room that was called a library, though it was not much more than a high pantry-like cell with a dozen shelves of books, and he was writing his bi-weekly letter to his mother at Richmond in England. The letter was not going very well; partly because he was really listening for something like the rifle-shot that when it came broke the eastern window by the chapel and helped to start the fire; partly because he was thinking of Mathieson and Crane. They were such worldly, assured, and likeable fellows; and the long day with them, for all its anxieties, had excited and jerked him out of himself. It had been wonderful to make friends. Except for occasional visitors who spent a night at the Mission because they preferred it to the ordinary rest-houses, he hardly saw any men. His upholstered world, made up of work and devotion, introspection and professional triviality, was never rippled or roughened by such splendid nonsense as had gone on in the trench that evening and afternoon. He was more than glad of it. The damp shyness of his mind made him very rusty sometimes, and now Crane and Mathieson had steeled and brightened him up.

In consequence, when the first shot smashed the chapel windows almost next door to him, he was neither frightened nor confused. He even folded up the letter to his mother and put it in its envelope and tucked it in the drawer of the desk.

The thought that he could finish it when he came back made him also look at his watch. The time was half past one. Then he reflected quite casually that if anything disastrous should occur outside it might mean that his watch would be smashed, and he took it off his wrist and put that in the drawer too.

All this took two or three minutes. Some instinct told him that Father Anstey would be in the chapel. By the time he had opened the door and had begun to walk down the corridor, lit by a small yellow wall-bulb at the far end, the first serious volley of fire smashed most of the windows in the south chapel wall. It was this volley that made Crane fall flat on his face and lie there for some time worrying about his shoes.

Father Simpson had no instinct to fall down; his feet, large and rather flat, were perfectly warm in his thick shoes. He planted them down with a stout and heavy firmness as he walked down the passage and into the chapel. The chapel had never been lit by electricity; Father Anstey felt keenly that it was not, in some way, a proper thing. All its illumination came from old-fashioned pedestal oil-lamps of Benares brass and two more that burned perpetually in the east window behind the altar. Now one of these lamps, hit by bullets, had fallen down, and its oil, spilling and running about the floor, was burning the altar cloth.

Father Simpson, coming into the chapel, strode heavily forward and began to flap at the flames with his sleeves. At any small exertion, as in digging potatoes, his breath came in flurried blowing gasps and now he rushed at the flames in a series of pig-like charges, grunting as he had done at the potatoes and the trench. In this way the flames were fanned and it was some moments before he realized that the simplest thing would be to take off his habit and smother the fire with that.

He was so preoccupied with slapping and smothering the flames about the altar that he hardly heard the second volley and its subsequent torrent of screams from the main ward. Deprived of his habit, revealed in trousers, braces, and a thick flannel vest on which his crucifix hung like an identity disc, he did not look so fat. He had something of the appearance of a

57

muscular publican, in his shirt-sleeves, mopping up the bar.

When he had succeeded in damping down the fire he left his habit spread about the floor where the worst of the flames had been. His eyes were full of paraffin smoke, and fragments of moonlight, shot with bits of flame, helped to blind him a little more.

In this half-blind fashion, stabbing his podgy fingers into his eyes, he staggered heavily back up the aisle. He was a little less than half-way down when the door swung back and a small Mahsud, swinging a rifle, came blundering in, crazily shouting.

This figure intensely annoyed Father Simpson. He felt enraged with shock. He did not stop walking and the Mahsud blundered down the aisle. The sensation of outrage flared up in Father Simpson so furiously that he lumbered forward in a ponderous charge and a second later knocked the Mahsud down.

His immediate point of contact was the rifle barrel. He saw it aiming straight at his chest and he seized it at the moment the Mahsud fired. He felt the blast of the shot go past his left hip, in a hot tearing flame that singed his vest, and this annoyed him too.

He remembered something also about bringing his knee up on these occasions and as he thundered against the Mahsud he brought the full weight of his fat thigh, feeling annoyed and outraged and yet in a grim way quite calm, against the Mahsud's crutch. The Mahsud fell with the full weight of Father Simpson on top of him, winded and sick, letting go the rifle so that the priest, in the final moment of the fall, had it in his hands.

It was still in his hands as he lumbered out of the chapel, the Mahsud groaning and sick on the floor behind him. The light in the corridor had gone out but he was not dismayed. He had an advantage over both Crane and Mathieson in knowing the Mission in every detail and of knowing exactly where he was going and where he was.

His intuition now was that Father Anstey would be in the hospital ward. Most of the shooting and almost all the shrieking of women and children was coming from the central ward where the beds were. He decided to make his way round the

58

back of it, past the room where the three Englishwomen had slept, and through the kitchens.

At the junction of the long corridor a figure rushed past him and instinctively, for the first time, he raised the rifle. To his relief it was only Colonel Mathieson, who had run past without a flash of recognition or belief in the incredible figure with rifle, vest, and trousers.

Excited and distraught, the Colonel came back, grabbing the barrel of the rifle.

'I can't find my wife, Father! Have you seen her for God's sake? Where have you come from? I can't find her, I can't find her –'

'From the chapel – it was burning –'

'Give me that.' The Colonel took the rifle out of Father Simpson's hands, and the priest gladly let it go. The Colonel rushed away up the corridor, towards the shrieking central ward, and Father Simpson called after him:

'She is probably in the trench! I'll go down!'

'Crane's already gone to look there!' the Colonel yelled and a moment later was gone.

Relieved of the rifle, Father Simpson fell into his natural posture when walking, folding his hands. But without his habit he had nowhere to put his hands except on the bulge of his stomach and because of this he did not fold them completely. Instead he clenched his fists, holding the triangles of his braces just above the buttons, and in this way he reached the kitchens.

It was quieter there and to his astonishment two nuns were working by the light of an oil-lamp on the stove. There was a thick smell of boiling cocoa and one of the nuns, the younger, seeing him in vest and braces, laughed.

'Oh! Father –'

'Where is Father Anstey?'

'He is in the little ward.'

He strode on through the kitchens, hearing the younger nun laugh once more as the back view of him was revealed. He was glad of her cheerfulness and she, as if to cover it up, called after him:

'Will you be having cocoa, Father? We are making it –'

'Yes, I'll have some,' he called. 'No sugar.'

To his intense relief there were lights in the small hospital ward. Eight regular beds, with four more improvised down the centre, filled the ward so that his large body could hardly squeeze its way down to where Father Anstey was talking to two sisters by a further bed. He recalled in that moment Crane's friendly jibe about his body being too large for the trench and then Father Anstey saw him coming down the ward.

'Oh! Father – bless you – God bless you –'

Father Anstey embraced him, pressing the fat of his upper arms with tense fingers of steely bone.

'What's happening, Father? What have you seen?'

'Where is Mother Superior?' he said. He looked round at the beds. A child was crying softly in the bed next to him; there was blood in bright scarlet splashes across the blanket. There was no sign of Sister Teresalina. He heard an elderly man muttering in German at the far end of the ward and Father Anstey said:

'She came in with the Hindu child here and then went back. The child was shot –'

'Went back? Where? Where did she go back?'

'The child was wounded in the central ward and there was another there, not so badly hurt.'

'I should never have given up the rifle,' Father Simpson said. He looked round the ward at the beds, lamp-lit, dark with scared figures like staring dolls. Father Anstey did not understand this remark and said, 'What, Father, what did you say?' but Father Simpson did not answer. A consuming and ferocious anger, springing from shock, greater than when the Mahsud had rushed into the chapel, had the effect of making his body rigid in its outrage. At the same time his face seemed perceptibly to have shrunk; and for a second or two, yellowish pink in the lamplight, the curve of his cheek-bones was revealed smooth as ivory, taut under stretching flesh.

He strode back down the ward. The Hindu child cried as he went past, beating the air with small dark hands. He hardly noticed her and he had reached the door of the ward before he realized that Father Anstey was still talking to him.

'Where are you going, Father? Be careful. One of the nuns heard Kashmiri voices – perhaps it means –'

'Kashmiri voices? It can't be Kashmiris who are doing this. I saw Mahsuds – if there are Kashmiris too it means a battle –'

He opened the door. Anger and outrage impelled him through it so blindly and obviously that he did not hear Father Anstey call briefly after him and he did not hear the child crying again as he let the door fly out of his hands.

He simply strode forward down the central corridor, towards the central ward, enormous and ponderous, blowing from exertion, his hands clenched across his braces.

7

As Janet McAlister helped the last of the women out of the trench she thought: 'Well, this is it. This is your punishment. This is what you get for your damn transgressions,' and then remembered herself, thinking so little of the podgy rose-black Hindu woman trying to scramble up the vertical wall of dry earth that she let her slither backwards. Dry lumps of earth and rock were shaken free and the Indian woman clawed with her hands, whimpering thinly. Panic was beginning to bubble up in her throat as her head slipped back, letting her underchin strike the raw corrugations left by Father Simpson's spade. Half knocked out, crying and frightened, she fell backwards into the trench and lay there, huddled up, in blubbing surrender. 'Always holler before they're hurt,' the girl thought, vexed but patient, 'always give up. No backbone,' and then jumped down into the trench herself, saying, 'Come on now, come on. *Juldi, juldi* now, *juldi*,' and lugged the woman to her feet.

For some moments longer, pushing the woman up the side of the trench, first by her thick sloppy thighs that had no resilience or reaction in them, and then from underneath her, by her flabby backside, she forgot about her transgressions. As she pushed upward the woman fell forward, head on the orchard grass that was wet with dew, so that her clawing hands slipped backwards. With the last heave or two more stones came down, bringing a stream of powdery earth into the girl's face and hair. This angered her so much more than all the feeble flabby struggles that she gave the woman a final gigantic push and sent her sprawling and free.

The impetus of this push, spending itself on nothing, overbalanced her. Her hands slapped against earth and rock, which showered on her feet, angering her again. A Mahsud swore loudly at a woman somewhere in the orchard; and she was surprised, not quite consciously, to hear the voice already quite far away. In this fusion of surprise and anger she was not aware that she had cut her hands on a rock or that she had wrenched the rock from the side of the trench and was carrying it in her hands.

'Come on now, *juldi, juldi.*' She scrambled up from the trench, dragging the woman up from where she still knelt on the grass, blubbing softly, her head beating up and down on her knees.

'Come on, *juldi, juldi* now. Get a move on, *juldi* now,' and then suddenly she looked up.

Across the orchard the last of the driven line of women had reached the terrace above. In the moonlight she could see them quite clearly. They were fifty or sixty yards away and she thought:

'Why the devil should we *juldi*? Why should we?' and then: 'There I go again, forgive me, let me be forgiven, mercy forgive me just this time,' and then a second later she knocked the Hindu woman down.

They lay on the ground for some seconds, the girl with her hand over the woman's mouth so that she could not scream, and thinking at the same time:

'I'm *juldi*-ing for no Pathan or Mahsud or Moslem or Hindu or Pakistani or anybody else. I'm *juldi*-ing for nobody.'

She held the woman's mouth for some moments longer with one hand, grasping the rock with the other.

'Lie still,' she kept saying, 'lie still, keep down, you must keep down.'

She became aware, after some time, of the rock in her hand. It made her laugh and she thought of her father: whisky-wild every Saturday night, throwing bricks in the yard of the tenements, or at Ibrox Park on New Year's Day, throwing bottles at the damn Protestants, drunk again. Everybody who wasn't a Catholic was a damn Protestant, just as everybody who wasn't Celtic must be Rangers, and that included all the damn Hindus and Moslems and Sikhs and whatever they are, she thought, and whatever they're fighting for. If everybody was Catholic, she thought, there'd be no Protestants and there'd be no fighting.

Presently she remembered the women hiding among the vines. She tried to get the woman to her feet and at the same time, and for the first time, she remembered Crane.

He was driven from her mind a moment later by a volley of firing from inside the Mission, the bullets whining briefly and then screaming away, joining the yells and wails of the Pathans and the women. The prostrate Hindu woman began blubbing; and McAlister, angered again, lugged her at last to her feet and began to run.

It took them less than a minute to reach the vines. McAlister, thin and wiry, ran some yards in front of the Hindu woman, pulling her by one hand, clenching the rock in the other. And when they finally fell down, the Hindu woman on top of her, sickly panting in terrorized gulps of breath, she thought:

'Well, that's over. That's the end of that.'

For a second or two she felt exhilarated. It was a little victory; somebody had been cheated. Then she was annoyed. The Hindu woman, previously flabby with fear, now sprawled over her like a tense and hysterical cow, moaning loudly.

McAlister could not get up. It annoyed her intensely that she could not get up and she was about to swear again when she remembered herself in time. Four times in three months she had been before the Mother Superior; once before Sister Teresalini. The fourth time the Mother Superior had despaired: 'Sometimes I think you will never be a good Catholic. Sometimes I really think so, I despair,' and McAlister had said: 'Sometimes I think so too. It's just a habit with me.'

'That is it,' the Mother Superior said. 'There you have it. Your faith cannot be like eating and drinking. It cannot be simply a habit. It must be conscious. It cannot be simply a habit mixed up with other habits –'

'I am headstrong, Reverend Mother. That was partly the cause of my nervous breakdown. I never think.'

'Thought is simply an accessory to the spirit. It is the spirit that you must have. When you have the spirit right then the thought will be right.'

'It's my father,' she said. 'I think my father put the devil in me.'

'Then,' the Mother Superior said with gentleness, 'we must put the devil out of you. Will you try? We will pray for you, child, and that will help you.'

'I will try and I will pray too,' McAlister said.

The recollection of all this, smoothing out her annoyance about the Indian woman lying on her half-suffocatingly, in rising hysterics, cleared her mind. She was simply vexed with herself: first for her own impatience, then because she had selfishly thought that, by hiding in the vines, she had herself escaped and was free.

She gave the Indian woman another push and then got up, kneeling for a moment or two to straighten her hair.

Kneeling, she was torn between action and prayer. She thought of the Mother Superior, of her own inadequacy, of the need for a positive and conscious putting out of the devil. She ought to stay with the women in the vines: pray for them, succour them, exorcize herself. She had been guilty of a very terrible thing with Mr Crane: not simply the smoking, but something else – luckily it was purely mental and even he hadn't seen it – and nothing would be right until she had put it out by herself, like the devil, by penance and penitence and prayer.

But the devil, in the shape of her father, kept creeping in. The recollection of the women being marched by the Pathans out of the trench, probably to be raped and mutilated and shot, made her think furiously:

'Prayer won't help them now. I've got to get up there. 'Prayer won't save them – perhaps it will, though, perhaps it could, though – but whether it will or won't I've got to get up there, somehow, and damn quick.'

She got up off her knees and began to run angrily up the path. Her mind was a confusion of compromise between the devil that had to be cast out and the devil that was always creeping back in the shape of her father, and she thought:

'Oh! God, I don't know whether I'm coming or going – Oh;

there I go again. I'd better pray a bit while I'm running.'

Swinging the rock in her right hand, clenching it hard and yet not knowing she still had it, she prayed in snatches as she ran up the path and on to the terrace. The women seemed to be going to the eastern end of the Mission, towards the chapel. 'I'm praying like a bit off the scrag-end,' she thought. She pulled herself together and began praying separately for Mother Superior, for Sister Teresalina, for Father Anstey, and for Father Simpson, but she was more than half-way along the terrace before she had prayed as far as Father Simpson, and she thought, half-winded:

'Oh! Lord, I'll never do it. Oh! Holy Mother, it'll ha' to be a collective do.'

In the first second of collective prayer she saw the line of women break. An Indian girl of fourteen or fifteen sprang hysterically out of it and began to run back.

Instinctively she opened her arms. She called something wildly and felt an intense desire to succour and protect the child who was running. A second later a Pathan took four or five strides after the girl, curling a long dark arm about her like a whip. He reached her as McAlister, in a moment of energetic outrage, that was the devil of her father coming back, shouted for the second time.

The Pathan heard the shout and stopped. Letting the girl go, he saw McAlister. She must have seemed to him an extraordinary figure coming across the terrace, swinging her arms, shouting, her white nurse's head-dress askew, because he stood still for a moment, laughing.

McAlister, seeing it, felt anger and the devil mingle in new fury, and thought:

'Laugh, you big clot. I'll make you laugh the other side o' your neck!'

She saw him stride forward, still laughing. Like the Japs, she thought. They laughed too much. Even the wounded in Burma had had that sickly damn laugh on their flat faces.

She had walked another ten or fifteen paces before she realized that the Pathan was really coming straight for her.

Still laughing, he came the last eight or ten yards in a single cold rubbery sort of bound. At the end of it he took a terrific swing at her face, flatly, with his right hand. It was exactly the sort of swing her father had aimed at her every Saturday night, year in, year out, or whenever he wanted to bang a little sense or respect in her, and she ducked instinctively, like a boxer.

As she ducked she saw the Pathan lurch blackly across the moon. She was blinded for a second or two by the dazzle of darkness and light. She heard the Pathan grunting and the slap of his hand on his rifle stock as he lugged it off his shoulders. She saw the world of moon and mountain skyline behind him twist violently and she knew, somehow, he was about to swing that rifle-butt at her. She ducked again but this time he was too near and she saw the skyline twist again and she was falling down.

As she fell the Pathan, for some reason she could not immediately understand, let the rifle go. A second or two later she knew that it was because he wanted both his hands to be free. She felt them rip with great violence at the front of her cloak, skinning her like an animal. She felt the entire naked front of her body from her neck down to her thighs quiver with cold and shock. She swung her arms frenziedly and her head struck the dusty grit of the terrace. Her breasts were small and tight, and at home, in Glasgow, her sister Jeannie had sometimes laughed at them but now suddenly they seemed very large and there was no way of hiding them as she fell. The fury roused in her by this was increased suddenly by the Pathan biting her neck. She felt his mouth clot with warm spittle just above her shoulder. Her small breasts were crushed so that she could not breathe, and in agony, suffocated, she swung the rock.

She felt the rock hit the Pathan between the left ear and eye. It seemed to skid from the bone of the forehead and crush the eye-ball, like jelly. He gave one long tearing scream of pain. She hit him again, this time into the cup of bone about the eye. This cup was wet with blood and the Pathan, shrieking, hit her wildly with his left hand, across the face, knocking her free.

She hit him, once with the rifle-butt, as he staggered blindly into the moonlight, his face running with fresh blood, the eye-socket a blinded and glittering mess of blackened jelly, and twice as he lay on the ground. As she struck the rifle-butt into his face the third time she heard a volley of firing from somewhere behind the chapel and it frightened her so much more than the things she had seen and done that she began running.

Along the terrace Crane had heard it too. He had come up from the vines by way of the patch of ground where Father Simpson kept his rabbits. Terrified by rifle-fire, the rabbits were bounding about in their small hutches like ghostly clockwork toys. They had affected Crane for a few moments more than all the shrieking of the women, and as he reached the terrace, their white ghostly terror still troubling him, it seemed for a moment that one of them had escaped and was dashing towards him. He realized a moment later that it was McAlister. She called his name.

It was only when she had finished calling his name that he realized how silent that end of the terrace had suddenly become. His painful recollection of the imprisoned, bumping, terrified rabbits came back. McAlister stopped running, making frantic efforts to cover up her naked body, drawing her blue cloak about her breasts, and then he realized that from behind the chapel there was no longer any shrieking. The last volley of shooting had killed it altogether.

8

About the same time an Afridi Tribal Officer, Sikander Shah, a tall high-cheekboned young man with brilliant intelligent eyes, from the Bara valley, was lying on the road below the Mission. He had become separated from the main invading forces but had managed, with discipline, to keep his men together. There were twenty-three of them and he was resting them in a boat-yard.

The main body of broken Kashmiri forces had retreated farther down the river. Two stray companies, reduced to rather less than the strength of one by Pathan flank attacks ten or twelve miles to the north-west as early as eight o'clock, had straggled out alone on a disorderly detour across rice-fields. In patterns of black and straw-white rectangles, dry and dusty after the heat of summer, these rice-fields gave no cover under the moon. Both companies had lost an officer and there was some quarrelling from time to time as to who could rightly claim the only Sten-gun, relic of the British, that had not fired for a week owing to careless reassembly and was now carried by a Mahomedan corporal as a point of senior pride. This corporal had put himself in charge and now showed a more ferocious keenness to fight for the Sten-gun than for anything to do with Kashmir. The company was very noisy as it came blundering along, out by the open rice-fields, into a country of big deodars and plane-trees by the river. Their voices, split on walls of rock, were magnified as they came back over water to join the swishing echoes of their feet in the big fallen plane leaves. These sounds were eventually heard by the Afridi officer who sat wondering what to do about the Mission, now on fire.

In twenty minutes he had laid ambush, killing fourteen

Kashmiris, taking five prisoners and relieving the corporal of the Sten-gun. It took him another half an hour with his sergeant to strip the Sten-gun and put it in working order. and it was after two o'clock by the time he was going up the hill to the Mission with his sergeant, the Sten-gun, and ten men.

The young officer was proud of a long descent from kings and after the fashion of Afridis distrusted everybody, especially the British, who had usurped his country, but still more the Kashmiris, who were simply timid or lying fools. His grandfather had been killed by the British in the Tirah Campaign of 1897, leaving his mother as a girl of five to be brought up in an English convent school on the borders of Peshawar. She had married, repressed and unusually gentle, very late, and he had grown up with tender memories of her and the convent school to which she had sent him later. He had learned kindness and very good English there; and the result, in an adult officer, was a curious conflict. Traditional fiery hatreds, going back beyond the Campbell raids of 1850 into ordinary tribal furies, and fired always by the pride of royal blood, were continually at war in him with irreconcilable creeds like forgiveness of sin and love thy neighbour as thyself. Instinct and intelligence, the old India and the new, clashed in him as they had begun to do everywhere, in all Indian youth, making them joyful because the old British devil was going out at last and fearful and bewildered because some new devil was coming in. His mother had not only been very proud of his descent from kings, of his fine, Semitic, true Afridi nose, but also very proud of his fine, convent-taught, intelligent English, and the two things were symbols of all the things that were in conflict within him.

And now as he went up the hill where Crane and Father Simpson had followed the rickshaw in the morning he was far from happy. He had killed several Kashmiris; he had captured a very good Sten-gun; but the Mission was clearly on fire and he had been listening for a long time to rifle-fire whining all over the hill. And it was not right that the Mission should be on fire; his mother would have been horrified. He was very uneasy because of it himself: not simply because there were

70

innocent and inoffensive people there who could be killed, but because he knew that tribal warfare and modern warfare had nothing to do with each other. All his real training had come, oddly enough, from the British during the war with Japan, and from active service on the Manipur Road. Tribal distractions like looting monasteries, shooting priests, and butchering women and children after stripping and raping them were not in his book. They had no place in scientific warfare, which was simply the process of destroying the enemy efficiently, unemotionally, and without pleasure. Diversions like loot and rape and murder could simply amount to sabotage. He recalled as an example of it the fact that the Mahomedan corporal and another Kashmiri had still been quarrelling about the right of the Sten-gun at the moment when his own revolver bullet had hit the corporal in the belly. That was the way actions were lost, by emotional distractions and feuds.

He got to the gates of the Mission just before three o'clock. Firing was still wild in the compound behind the chapel and he could hear women screaming everywhere. In the moonlight a wounded Kashmiri came running out of the gates, holding his stomach with both hands – broken and jibbering under pressure, he thought, as they always were – and he promptly shot him at three yards range.

The presence of stray enemies made him decide to leave six men at the gate. He went into the front compound through a patch of cabbages, by a smaller garden gate farther up the hill, with the sergeant, the Sten-gun, and the rest of his men.

Across the compound, in the central body of the Mission building, there was such fantastic screaming that he did not know where to begin. This screaming, coming from a convent, recalled his mother so sharply that he felt a ghastly curdling of his blood. The cabbages had wetted his boots and his feet were cold. His prompt shooting of the jibbering and wounded Kashmiri and earlier of the quarrelling corporal had given him considerable satisfaction. With the British he had extended his English, embracing new terms of war; and the shooting of the Kashmiri had been, he thought, a bloody good show. But now suddenly he felt terribly and guiltily sick, his veins alternately hot and wet and cold; and there were no words for how he felt in his new British vocabulary.

He led the sergeant and his three men towards the Mission building, slowing himself down, trying to pull himself together. He was a little less than three-quarters of the way across the compound when the figure of a man, shirt-sleeved and white in the moonlight, ran from the back of the Mission, under the windows of the refectory.

Trembling, the young Afridi officer shot at it over-promptly. From twenty-three yards range he missed very badly but he felt much better.

He heard the bullet ricochet off the wall and saw the figure fall instinctively and smartly on his face. He began running up to it, ready to shoot again, when Crane, turning on his back and seeing the officer's uniform, shouted madly:

'Put that bloody thing away and come and stop your bastards before they butcher everybody in the place!'

Sikander Shah stopped dead. He was not so astonished as relieved. These were the sort of words he understood; they were the plain and simple words of a man who understood warfare; and with them his sickness, which had receded, now thickened hotly and came back. With terrible guilt he thought of his mother again as Crane shouted:

'For Christ's sake get a move on, man. They've got everybody stuck up against a wall.'

9

As Father Simpson went out of the hospital ward and along the corridor, not knowing what he was going to do but simply impelled forward by a purely physical and godless sort of rage, he remembered for some reason the cocoa that was being made by the two very young nuns in the kitchen behind the ward. It had the effect of calming him down. At the same moment he felt very thirsty. His mouth, cut on the inside from the fall with the Mahsud, was salty and wet with blood. For about forty seconds he stopped to staunch the bleeding with his handkerchief, jabbing at his mouth and gradually calming down.

These forty seconds saved him from being shot by the same Mahsud he had knocked down in the chapel. He had gone staggering and roaming round darkened corridors looking for Father Simpson. At the very moment Father Simpson was dabbing his bleeding mouth and thinking of cocoa he had reached the passage behind the main ward by the room occupied by Mrs Mathieson, Julie, and Mrs Maxted. In the confusion Mrs Maxted had lost touch with Julie and had now come to take another look in the room the three women had left together. She had lost Mrs Mathieson too and she was standing there, flattened against the doorway, terrified and constricted, as the Mahsud came along.

The Mahsud shot her where she stood and then went on, through the main ward and out on to the front terrace, to look for Father Simpson.

When Father Simpson reached Mrs Maxted she was sitting down at the foot of the door. The Mahsud's shot had gone through her left shoulder, under the blade. It had passed through the wooden door and into the bedroom, where Crane found it three days later, while looking for cigarettes, in the straw palliasse where Julie would have been sleeping. Mrs Maxted was not only conscious but was talking about her asthma.

'All right, Mrs Maxted. Don't talk. Don't talk now –'

He bent down, put one arm under her legs and the other about her shoulders, picking her up, and she said with astonishing lightness:

'I suddenly get the most awful attacks and then I simply can't breathe –'

He picked her up and carried her into the central ward.

Afterwards he felt he would never have got into that room, more than ever now like a casualty ward with its two rows of jumbled bedding and groaning women that he could hardly see in the light of candles stuck into tin-lids on the floor, if it had not been for Mrs Maxted.

He laid Mrs Maxted down on an empty bed, under the wall. From all about him the terror of the night seemed to narrow down, crystallized into the tiny area of candlelight about her face. Unreal and unbelievable for so long, it now achieved reality in sudden and singular statements about her health. She seemed to have been saving them up for him:

'I walk round the kitchen sometimes in the morning, talking to the *chaprassi*, and I have to hang on to the chairs – I simply can't stand up.'

An enamel bowl of warm water was standing by the bed. He unbuttoned Mrs Maxted's pink pyjama-jacket. Some distance up the ward, a woman cried in a series of regular bubbles of pain, the sound like the boiling of a pot. A nun murmured words of comfort. a candle moved tree-like shadows down the walls. Father Simpson dipped a square of flannel into the warm water and washed Mrs Maxted's blood from her shoulder. He saw nothing of what was happening behind him in the ward. Mentally only the picture formed, and he was not afraid of it. He smelt antiseptic, clean and astringent, in the bowl, and Mrs Maxted said:

'I had some awful doctor in Bombay who tried to make out the whole thing wasn't physical at all – it was just mental and all that –'

At least there's no bullet, Father Simpson thought. He squeezed the bloodied flannel into the bowl like a pressed orange, with one hand, smoothing her forehead with the other.

'Men's hands are so much warmer than women's I always notice,' Mrs Maxted said. 'Feel mine. I've always had the most frightful circulation –'

She raised her hands to put them against his. For a moment he did not notice it very much. 'I ought not to let her talk,' he thought, and then he saw that she could not raise her hands more than a few inches from the bed.

She held them flatly outstretched. At the same moment he smelt cigarette smoke in the air, a little thin perfumed smoki-ness creeping in out of the general odour of fire, but he did not notice that much either. He noticed only that Mrs Maxted's hands hung as if paralysed in air. At last he took them in his own and laid them gently back on the bed.

'You mustn't wave your hands about,' he said. Her chest was heaving desperately in the candlelight. On the wound there was a little viscous blood, liver-coloured, about the size of a bean. Exactly as with asthma, she struggled for breath, her mouth beating darkly at the air.

He turned to reach again for the bowl of water. It did not surprise him to find that it had gone. In its place was a tray, neatly covered with a white huckaback towel. He removed the towel and found underneath it an orderly collection of band-ages and gauze, with adhesive plaster and scissors and a medi-cine bottle of antiseptic and a second smaller bowl of water. He moved neatly among these things, efficiently selecting what he wanted. All that he did now was accomplished delicately. His air of minute concentration about the tray did not recall the blundering figure attacking the trench and the potatoes.

In great gasps of breath Mrs Maxted managed to achieve a remark about the doctor in Bombay:

'I told him he was mental – I believe half the time they just don't know –'

Not answering, he moved the candle in its tin-lid holder a foot or so nearer the tray. It almost fell over. He unrolled the pink sausage of lint, and then the cotton wool. Across his mind strayed the thought that he could never remember which was the correct side for the lint to go on. Mrs Maxted breathed painfully again and he could once again smell cigarette smoke in the air.

Cutting the lint, he could not see the impregnated side very well in the candlelight, and once again he moved the candle. For a second time it almost fell over.

'Father – Father Simpson,' Mrs Maxted said, 'did someone knock me down?'

'You must be quiet' – he turned his face, solid and taut in the candlelight, and he saw her moving on the bed – 'No, you must not get up,' he said, 'no, not now.'

'Somebody knocked me down,' Mrs Maxted said.

Turning back to the tray, he was aware of a curious and illuminating difference there. The candle, that had almost fallen twice, seemed now to have a row of scarlet beads underneath it, along the edge of the tin-lid.

He cut the lint, turning it over. He could see better now. He remembered which was the right side. A single shot outside the Mission startled him, waking him to the fact that the row of beads on the tin-lid were fingernails.

His appreciation of this simple fact, joined to the fact of the cigarette smoke, the movements of the candle, the interchange of bowl and tray, came to him slowly. It was some time before he looked over his shoulder and saw the Hindu girl, Kaushalya, squatting on the floor behind the tray, her hand holding the candle.

Even then he did not look at her face. She seemed to be holding it far back from him. It was not until he saw the candle-light pressed forward, in sharper concentration, that he grasped the significance of it all. Moving to lay the pad on Mrs Maxted's chest he saw the candlelight advance across the bed. He turned then and saw that she was holding a second tray in front of her face. Swiftly he saw the dark eyes above it; the little screen of cigarette smoke; the big blue circle of turquoise about the ears; the scarlet mark of lips on dark skin.

On the bed Mrs Maxted smiled. Her forearms, brushed by his own as he laid the pad on her chest, were very cold. He was startled by them into self-condemnation. He was distressed by his own inadequacy. It was very wrong of him, and very stupid. He ought to have covered her up.

In that moment he realized that he had never covered her up because there was no blanket. He looked about him, seeing almost for the first time the ward with its beds and little candles, the dark figures on the beds; the floating nuns, scroll-like, anonymous, between; the three rectangles of moonlight at the end, one of them an open door through which the raging Mahsuds had come and gone.

Out of all this, from another bed, came the Hindu girl with a blanket. She laid it over Mrs Maxted's feet, the lower part of her body, and up to her chest. And having laid it there she sat on the far side of the bed, so that Father Simpson could see her.

Not really thinking, he found himself glad of it. He was not disturbed, as he had been in the morning with Crane, by her presence. That special and indescribable feeling of physical discomfort, so acute when Crane had stood close to her taking the light for his cigarette, had gone. It seemed rather silly. He almost ascribed it to Crane. They were rather odd birds, newspapermen, rather free. Of course in a way they had to be, it was their job, they dealt with all sorts of people. They were not like himself, exclusive, detached, in a cocoon.

'Somebody knocked me down,' Mrs Maxted said. Upturned, her eyes searched for Kaushalya. She smiled. But the girl did not understand and Mrs Maxted said:

'Doesn't she understand? Doesn't she speak English?'

Father Simpson, cutting strips of adhesive plaster, his tongue out, his teeth on edge at the spongy touch of scissors on the material, spoke in Hindustani, asking the girl whether she spoke English or not.

Her lips did not move in answer. She gave instead that strange twist of the head, half sideways, curiously melancholy, that he could never decide was either negative or positive, and Mrs Maxted said:

'Doesn't she?'

'No,' he said. 'I think not.'

'It's queer how they sometimes never do,' she said.

He wondered why it was queer. He laid the pad more closely on Mrs Maxted's chest. In the candlelight the faces of the two women and himself seemed to join, for the first time, in a wonderful moment of triangular accord. Speech was not an affair of tongues, he thought, but something more of heart, of eyes, of silences. It was very quiet now as he stuck the ribbons of plaster across Mrs Maxted's chest and shoulder. Perhaps it's all over, perhaps they have gone, he thought, perhaps it's all right. Mrs Maxted, actually smiling, as if for a moment sensing some such relief in the air, stared up at the Hindu girl letting her cigarette burn away from her beaded scarlet nails, and said, yet again:

'Somebody knocked me down. You understand? No? Somebody knocked me down.'

A moment later, with the final strip of plaster about to be pressed over Mrs Maxted's chest, the middle rectangle of moonlight at the far end of the ward was shattered by a mob of raging Pathans, howling with hoarse frenzy as they moved down the ward.

Father Simpson stood up. He became clearly aware, for the first time, of the ward and its moonlit figures, ghoulish and stark. Women were shrieking everywhere. A Pathan, spectral, ahead of the rest, was slicing the air with a knife. The floor was a mass of distorted limbs, of feet crushing splinters of moon.

Kaushalya did not get up. Mrs Maxted, aware of new terrors, opened her mouth as if to begin shrieking and he actually heard the thin peep of her voice before the Hindu girl crushed it out with her hand.

This tiny sound brought him fully to himself. He bent down by Mrs Maxted, holding the blanket.

'I am going to cover your face,' he said. He heard women in panic crushing and falling against floor and walls at the far end of the ward, like soft ninepins kicked in a corner, but he went on: 'I'm going to cover you right over. Don't move. Don't do anything. Pretend –'

Her eyes were scared, bright above the lifted blanket.

'I am sorry for the things I said about Catholics,' she said. 'I didn't mean –'

'It's nothing – it's not important –'

He covered her face gently but swiftly. His crucifix was entangled with his vest and it was some moments before he could get it from under his shirt. Two Pathans leapt at the Hindu girl, one at each arm, flinging her fifteen feet up the aisle between the beds. The crucifix came up at last from under Father Simpson's shirt, warm from the heat of his body, and he crossed himself twice and laid the crucifix on Mrs Maxted's chest.

When he turned again there was no one at that end of the ward except the Hindu girl, lying on the floor where the Pathans had left her, and Mrs Maxted and himself. He crawled from between the beds, on his hands and knees, to where Kaushalya lay.

She was lying flat on her face, staring up the ward, at the level of the floor. He could not tell if she lay there in terror or paralysis or because she was wounded. Her body was so stiff when he tried to turn it that finally he picked her up as she lay, face downwards, his hands under her breasts and thighs.

'Are you hurt? Are you all right?' he said, using first English and then Hindustani. She turned her head towards him, when he had laid her on the floor next to Mrs Maxted, just as the two Pathans came rushing back down the aisle.

One kicked him in the small of the back, pitching him forward, and when he got to his knees again Kaushalya had gone. He glanced swiftly at Mrs Maxted. She had not moved, he thought, and was glad; and then he saw that his crucifix was not there. He was momentarily distressed; it was a precious thing: his younger sister had given it him; and then he saw that she must have taken it under the blanket.

He forgave her, then, the things she had said to him. He had never really liked her. She was a very silly woman, with a shallow, thoughtless, stupid tongue. He had resented, without he hoped the faintest outward show of distress, her idiotic chatterings about his faith. But now between them, he thought, there was no longer a breath of contention; and he felt quite happy.

It was not until he was on his feet again, nearly a minute

later, that he became aware that there was now at the far end of the ward a sudden horrifying order in everything. Most of the women had stopped shrieking. They were huddled together, along the wall by the open doors, like a crowd of whimpering beaten dogs.

It came to him that they were about to be shot. In this sudden regimentation there was new terror. He strode down the ward. Half-way down a Pathan rose from a bed and ran leaping like a hurdler across the divisions separating the beds. On the bed a woman, naked from the waist down, writhed, rocking from side to side, desperately beating the air about her with dark hands.

He looked instinctively at her face, remembering Kaushalya. But it was not Kaushalya, and the woman, seeing him pass, was freshly embarrassed and terrified and in panic drew a blanket up over her body.

He went on up the ward and some seconds later he saw Kaushalya. Four or five Pathans were pushing the women into a single line along the wall and she was at the end of the line. He saw the red glow of her cigarette as it moved in her hands.

As he reached her there was a moment of disturbance on the steps beyond the central door. A man shouted something in English and a Pathan fired wildly at him as he ran. It occurred to the priest that it was Colonel Mathieson. Strange that he hadn't seen Mathieson all evening, nor Crane. And suddenly, alone there with the huddled women, he remembered them both, with a pleasant start of affection, as they had been that day. Excellent fellows, he thought, friendly, excellent fellows.

What was it Crane had said? Is the trench wide enough for Father Simpson? – something like that. It will hardly matter now, he thought.

A Pathan hit him about the waist with a rifle-stock, pushing him up against the wall. He fell against Kaushalya. She was in the act of putting the cigarette in her mouth and as he knocked against her a shower of ash fell from her hands.

He felt for his crucifix. Momentarily, not finding it there, he was lost. He felt vaguely across his chest with his large hands.

His flabby helplessness, so marked in the earlier day, came back. Deprived of the crucifix, he longed for something to touch and hold, securely and strongly, as he had held his braces when striding from the hospital ward.

Struggling flabbily with himself, he was aware again of Kaushalya's cigarette. He wavered terribly: if he could not smoke then he had to pray and for an instant he shut his eyes, opening them at once again, bitter at his own cowardice. He looked down at the cigarette, burning away in her hand. In another moment a flash or two from the Pathan rifles would disperse, for ever, all that he felt on earth and was. It could not matter and yet he could not ask her. It was like asking a woman if he could kiss her, and he could not ask that.

She put the cigarette to her mouth, pulling at it slowly, pressing her head back against the wall, as if quite calm. It seemed an age to him before her hand came down. Following it instinctively, he trembled, and then, in another moment, he took it and held it, gripping it hard.

She did not look at him. He pressed his head against the wall, staring in front of him, calmed now and unafraid. He thought of several people, steadily, one by one: of Colonel Mathieson, of Crane, of Father Anstey – and then, most unexpectedly, of someone he had not seen all day and yet had seen, he felt, somewhere that night, in one of his moments of unresolved nightmare.

'Dr Baretta,' he thought. 'Where is she? Odd I should think of her.' He was disturbed by shadowy recollections and thought: 'I saw her somewhere. After all I did see her. Dr Greta' – the fine gentle Anglo-Indian face struggled out of the darkness, troubling him – 'I did see her somewhere – yes, I did –'

A moment later he looked round and saw, unastonished now because he remembered it all, that she was standing beside him.

'They have shot my husband,' she said. 'I saw them –'

The ward seemed to splinter into fragments before his eyes at her words, joined now to the more bitter and terrible of his recollections. He gripped the young doctor's hand in his left hand, holding Kaushalya's in his right, and said in a loud and confident voice, in English, surprising himself by his own calm:

'I propose to give Absolution – to all of you – no matter who you are – even if you do not understand –'

A Pathan came raging down the line and hit him in the mouth. He stood very still, gripping the hand of the Hindu girl on the one side of him and of the Anglo-Indian on the other, feeling an intense love for both of them extend itself quietly, in profound waves through his body. He began again, stubbornly, resolutely, and in the same loud clear voice, 'Oh, Father – Oh God, our Father,' and the Pathan hit him in the mouth again, and then again, on the rebound, as his head came back from the wall.

He began to speak once again, steadily and clearly, gripping the hands of the two women on either side of him, but a woman's screams and the smooth manipulations of rifle-bolts across the ward smothered his voice.

When he tried to speak for the fourth time he was aware of Dr Baretta crying. He lifted his arms and held both her and Kaushalya by the shoulders. The Hindu girl was not crying and he was very glad. He exulted for a moment in tenderness for them both and then began, in a fine clear voice, to speak for the fifth time.

In that moment he was astonished to see Crane in the doorway. Another figure, strange to him, too tall for Colonel Mathieson, lifted a revolver and to the priest's intense astonishment shot down a Pathan who was hitting a woman in the face.

Fearful and glad at the same time he shouted: 'Don't come in, Mr Crane, don't come in, they will shoot you,' and at his side Kaushalya let fall her cigarette, crushing it slowly on the floor with her foot, blowing the last cloud of smoke against the light of the moon.

10

Father Simpson picked up one of the Meran children, an Untouchable, and folded her to his breast. He saw Crane running out of the door, into the moonlight. He called after him so loudly that the child began crying, wailing with a monotone of warm wet sobs into his shoulder. Crane did not hear and someone among the women, hearing the Untouchable child wailing against the priest, was relieved enough to laugh. Hearing the laughter, as if it were a signal, the child cried a little louder, and then another woman laughed and the child cried a little louder still. Dr Baretta said, 'Let me hold her,' but at that moment Sikander Shah came up and said, 'Are you the priest? I am going to lock these people away. Have you somewhere they can go? For safety?'

'Yes,' Father Simpson said. 'This way.'

Leading the way to the small ward, holding the weeping child in his arms, he went through one of those spasmodic lapses of memory for which Father Anstey had so often reproached him but that was now more relief than forgetfulness, and in consequence forgot completely what it was he had wanted to call to Crane.

Crane ran across the terrace and, still in his stockinged feet, down the path towards the vines. Under the apple-trees the trench gaped like a yellow mouth in the moon, empty. Across grey pleats of hills, now that the moon had turned, snow was visible on high peaks like white crusts of starch. Down below, in the village, on the other side of the river, half a dozen fires started by the raiders were burning smokelessly, bright orange.

Some distance before he came to the vines he began calling Miss Maxted, using her Christian name, saying 'Julie! Julie!

It's all right. Julie!' He had sent McAlister for safety there and it was McAlister who replied:

'She went to find you, Mr Crane. Didn't you see her? She went –'

'For God's sake!' he said. 'When?'

The nurse appeared up the path, small and anxious, running. 'It was after you sent me down. She was worried about her mother.'

He felt the coldness of his feet for the first time. It seemed to solidify into two perpendicular bars of deathly sharpness that robbed his legs of strength. In the relief of finding Sikander Shah, of stopping the general massacre inside the ward, he had experienced wild relief. It was all over: the Mathiesons were all right; Mrs Maxted and the girl were all right; the shooting and the screaming had stopped at last. In an idiotically jubilant moment he felt the whole lunatic dream had shattered.

Now he was aware that he had never seen the Colonel since the moment they had first clashed against each other in the darkness; that he had not seen Mrs Mathieson or Mrs Maxted at all. In his legs the solidified bars of coldness, more weariness than pain, broke and seemed to dissolve to water.

He remembered the last volley of shooting far behind the hospital and how, with astonishing abruptness, it had frozen into brutal silence.

He said: 'I'm going to look for her. Get the women into the hospital ward. Quickly. It's all right.'

It was only in the moment of turning to run back towards the terrace that he realized he had spoken to her from a distance; that he had yelled all these things at her while she was still coming up the path. Now she called after him some remonstration, in her sharp Glasgow accent, about his shoeless feet. He hardly knew what she was talking about and simply yelled back:

'Have you seen Colonel Mathieson?'

He had already reached the steps of the terrace by the time he shouted, and he never knew what she answered. A stray shot in the valley made an exceptional flight of sound, singing across from one escarpment to another like a steely mosquito,

84

and then dying out as he came within twenty or thirty yards of the chapel. It made him realize how silent everything was; that the terrace, except for the solitary woman who had been clubbed down in the centre of it, was quite deserted.

He was brought momentarily to his senses by a notion that the entire frontal façade of the Mission, with a moonlit deadness and the little smoke from the burning chapel, was a fake. Deprived of its hideous raging figures, of McAlister nakedly running, of women being beaten to death, it was not real. It made him stop for a moment, gasping and exhausted. Why the hell was he running up here? What was here? 'Mathieson!' he shouted. He did not know why he should have shouted Colonel Mathieson's name in that sudden way unless simply as a way of smashing the silence about him, of restoring reality to the fake dead walls.

A figure replied by groaning from the path that went down behind the chapel. Between the thick double rows of cypresses the groaning had only a partially intelligible quality that eluded him. A moment later a young nun came out of the path, her head almost completely wrapped in her hood, babbling German.

He was so delighted to see this living figure that he began to run towards it. Seeing him, she stopped and stood shrieking. She shrieked with her teeth closed, so that her mouth, oval and white and stretched in the moonlight, flashed like a glittering spoon.

This single partly imprisoned scream, more dreadful than if she had opened her mouth, finally cleared his brain.

'Have you see Miss Maxted?' he shouted. He took her by the shoulders, shaking her. 'Have you seen Miss Maxted for God's sake – Miss Maxted!'

Her shrieking became a kind of paralysed hissing. He realized that she could not open her mouth. The bared, spoon-like oval of teeth was locked in terror. Her face was skull-like under its hood, stiff as dead bone.

He ran on past her, along the path between the cypresses.

The moon had fallen westward and a long segment of shadow under the chapel was empty. He ran thirty or forty yards down the path before he saw what it was that had made the little German nun shriek between her locked teeth.

He saw the dark faces, the dark arms and ankles, of ten or a dozen Indian women lying before him on the path. He remembered the final burst of shooting. In the moonlight the dead bore the queerest resemblance to piles of ejected laundry, ready for washing, and in his mind a wild flickering of disjointed fragments of experience and fear now became whole and clear.

Among the dark faces, at the far end, was a single white face. He saw it upturned. It was hideously like something he knew. He discovered presently that the face was the face of Mrs Mathieson. Relief calmed him for a moment until he realized that under this face was another, also white. He began to drag Mrs Mathieson free. In his demented clumsiness he fell down, sprawling against other bodies. Finally the second body was free and he saw the face of it.

It was the face of a nun he did not know. He let it fall and got up, staggering and falling over the accumulated bundles of the dead. At the same moment the little German nun appeared beside him on the path.

She was articulate and sane again; her hood had fallen from her face. 'It was Sister Meyer,' she said. 'She was from Alsace. I am from near Alsace too, on the German side. She is my cousin. We came together.' She talked, released now, very fast, simply, informatively. 'We were together. We were cousins and we were together. The lady stood in front of me. We were here and she stood in front of me.'

'Come on,' he said.

He took her by the hand and walked away with her up the path. She did not cry. Her hand was very small and she walked with her head down, talking.

'You have no shoes. Where are your shoes? Have you lost your shoes? We must find your shoes,' she said. 'It's awful walking without shoes.'

'We have to find Miss Maxted,' he said.

'Miss who? Miss who?'

She walked beside him like a child. 'The lady stood in front of me. Who was the lady who stood in front of me?' He could not speak in answer and simply dragged her along.

At the door of the Mission, on the top step, stood a figure with a rifle. He felt the hand of the little German nun quiver in his own. She stopped speaking and he thought, 'Let the bastard stand there. We're going in. We've got to go in. She's in there somewhere. Christ, if only the sun would get up – God, if only it would get light –'

From the steps the figure with the rifle advanced to meet him. He saw the rifle swing back. He began to shout, caring no longer, his mind crazy in his truculence, 'Get out of the way, you bastard!' when some familiar line of the figure, more clearly evoked by the slant of moonlight, filled him with joy. It came to him in a moment that he was shouting at Mathieson.

The Colonel stood still on the steps, saying simply: 'Where is she, Crane? I can't find her. Nobody can find her.'

'Where's Julie?' Crane said. 'She may be with –'

The Colonel shouted with unexpected fury, so that the German nun gripped Crane's hand like a frightened child: 'What do you keep asking about Julie for? She's inside somewhere. They're all inside. What I want to know is where – oh! for Jesus' sake – where is she?'

Crane could not speak. He felt his lips idiotically quivering, and then the German nun said:

'The lady stood in front of me. She stood in front of me.'

'What lady?' the Colonel said. He was moved by new and more ferocious agonies to blunder down the steps. 'What lady? What are you talking about?'

'There was a lady –'

'What lady? Where? What did she do? Where was she?'

'She was there. She is over there. She is with my cousin. We were cousins. We were together.'

'Show me!' the Colonel said. 'Show me!'

He gripped the little German nun by the flesh of her arm, above the elbow. He lifted her in a single movement down the steps. Crane saw his face flash past as if the nun had pulled him down. He could not speak and in his mind there was neither need nor inclination to stop him. He let him go on, down the steps. He watched him blunder on across the terrace, partly lifting, partly driving the little nun along. After ten or fifteen seconds of it he walked up the steps himself, dazed and feeling curiously lost without the small hand of the German nun in his own, without her curious constricted voice repeating its solemn recitation of Mrs Mathieson, her cousin, and the dead.

A moment of agony for Mathieson halted him at the doorway. It dejected him; he felt suddenly filled with dribbling cowardice. He had let the Colonel go to look on the most awful things without a scrap of condolence or help. 'I can't do it,' he thought, and in the same moment remembered Julie Maxted.

Between these two agonies he walked back down the steps. Despair at not knowing whether to go one way or the other kept him indecisively alone in the middle of the terrace, staring in the moonlight at the starchy crusts that were high far snows. He heard voices. Somewhere in the direction of the main Mission gates he saw a fire; and he realized that the Pathans, having drawn off at last, were camping.

He turned to follow Colonel Mathieson. Immediately, across the terrace, he saw figures. In the man he recognized the shape of Father Simpson, massive in shirt and braces, but he did not recognize the figure of the nun hurrying beside him until he remembered the brown habit he had thrown over Julie Maxted in the vines.

He called their names. 'Father! Julie. Father Maxted!' In his release from distress he mixed the names three times, unaware of it. 'Father Maxted! Father Maxted!'

Standing beside them, panting, he saw the girl's face. It was wrapped about by the hood of the big brown habit, cool and white and in some way anonymous, staring at him. His relief at seeing her was so great that for a second or so he could not speak and Father Simpson said:

'Everyone is to be locked inside, Mr Crane. We lost you.'

'Colonel Mathieson is round by the chapel,' Crane said. 'I found a nun there. She is from Alsace —'

88

'Meyer?'

'Yes. I'll fetch them.'

'I will go,' Father Simpson said. 'Take Miss Maxted to her mother. She is at the end of the big ward. Unless they have taken her to the hospital!'

He strode away, hands locked across his braces, huge but not pompous; the big belly was thrust forward, not loosely but tautly, aggressively. A fire woke again across the valley with shots of pink and orange flame. The front walls of the Mission reflected it; the steps up which Crane and Julie Maxted hurried without speaking were turned for a moment to the colour of fresh brick.

Inside the central ward two wall lamps had been re-lit, and under them the long lines of bedding lay disordered, just as they were left.

Under the first of these lamps Crane saw a vaguely familiar figure kneeling down, probing with delicate calligraphic thrusts at an Afridi's wounded thigh. It was Dr Baretta. It was as if she were drawing with a silver pencil, under intense concentration, microscopic pictures on the dark skin. She did not look up and the Afridi had the appearance, silent and numbly carved, the face only partially disclosed under a mass of long black hair and carving-knife moustaches, of a warrior in bronze, laid on the tomb of a church.

Under the wall light he could see only Kaushalya, squatting in the extreme corner of the ward, smoking, her sari folded up now so that it covered her head. There was no sign of Mrs Maxted. The Hindu girl loosened her sari slightly, revealing her face. There was nothing in its passive and sullen delicacy that had changed, he thought, since the first moment he had seen her on the boat that morning. It was as if nothing had happened to her or near her or to anyone about her.

He heard Julie Maxted say, some paces ahead of him now, distressed: 'She is not here – they have taken her –' and he turned to speak to Dr Baretta. In the act of turning he saw Kaushalya stretch out her hands and disclose, under the blanket by the corner bed, Mrs Maxted's face. The Hindu girl, so that her hands could be free, laid her cigarette on the floor and now the smoke of it was burning greyly upwards, under the small wall lamp, between her passive averted face with its touches of worn scarlet and the face of Mrs Maxted on the floor.

To his relief the girl did not cry out. He felt calmed and in some way cleanly and intensely relieved by this revelation. His calmness increased as he saw Julie Maxted turn and wildly look about her for a moment before beating her hands on the wall.

He stood by the wall and held her for a long time, not speaking. She stood against him, burying her face in the fold of his arms. Down the ward Dr Baretta continued to operate on the Afridi with the minute and impartial concentration of someone engraving a design with a point of silver. Beyond her a slow ridge of purpled rose, a rising reflection of fires in the valley, spread across the window.

Some time later Crane saw that Kaushalya had covered Mrs Maxted's face. He realized that she had put out the lamp too. It was only when he looked up the ward and saw that Dr Baretta had disappeared that it came to him that he had been asleep there, where he stood.

'Julie,' he said. He spoke only once but she did not answer and he did not speak again. She was breathing softly and regularly; he could feel the warmth of her breath, comforting and moist, against his throat. Tired out, his brain clotted with sleep and the need for sleep, he let his mouth rest against the side of her face. Waves of fatigue kept pulling down the lids of his eyes with the mechanical regularity of smooth shutters. Some long time later he realized that what he had thought were the purple-rose reflections of new fires were really the first signs of breaking day.

'Where are we? What's happened?' said Julie.

'You slept for a bit.'

'It's very quiet.'

'We have to get out of here,' he said.

She moved her body, trying to ease its stiffness. Moving her legs she felt his feet, still shoeless and now very cold. As she felt them she began crying for the first time, in terrible gulping

sobs and then in a continuous murmur, choking her mouth by
biting the sleeve of her habit.

Down the ward the wounded Afridi stirred on the bed. 'We
have to get out of here,' Crane said again. He watched the
Afridi get up, stagger clumsily about for a moment or two,
testing his wounded leg. There was a threshing, brassy jangle
of tribal accoutrements. It struck Crane suddenly that the
Afridi looked extraordinarily like a stage soldier, fantastically
over-cloaked, over-brassed, unreal. The Afridi staggered about
and walked down the ward, swinging the wounded leg. He
reached the door and pushed it open with violent clashings and
Crane saw him for a moment standing on the terrace beyond,
wiping a black hand across barbaric moustaches, in the glare
of rising sun, before hobbling away.

Crane felt himself breathe with involuntary relief and said
again : 'We have to get out of here. Tell Kaushalya.'

'You have to get something on your feet,' the girl said. 'It's
terribly silly.'

'Kaushalya,' he said. He tried to frame in his mind a few
words of Hindustani but he was very tired and fagged and
they would not come.

'Kaushalya,' he said and then he realized that she was not
listening to him. She had thrown back her head and was looking up and he realized in the same second that she was really
listening to something else. Julie Maxted had stopped crying
and was listening too.

A plane was roaring up the valley, spluttering cannon-fire. He
prepared instinctively to fall but the roaring arc of sound swept
away and retreated, beating staccato embroideries like a vast
sewing machine on the gorge of rock below.

When it was over he thought : 'Who the hell is flying
Tempests? Not the Pathans. They've got no air force. Only the
Indian Air Force have Tempests –'

He heard the plane roaring back.

'Get down !' he shouted.

Lying on the floor, arms outstretched, one across Julie
Maxted's shoulders, the other on the bed where Mrs Maxted
lay, he waited for the plane to roar with its flattening beat of

91

obliteration over the Mission. When it had gone and he got to his feet he noticed that Kaushalya had not moved; and he said, curtly, with annoyance and yet in a way that sounded incredibly stupid when he found the words:

'Come on. That was a Tempest. Come on!'

He opened the door for Julie Maxted, shouting again for Kaushalya to come too. Was? he thought. What the hell am I thinking about? Which side are we on? Was? Where are we? He remembered the banter of the Colonel and Father Simpson: how accurate you are with your tenses, Father; the thought of Julie going home. Up the valley he heard the Tempest coming back. He went back and lugged Kaushalya to her feet. To his intense amazement she smiled: bravely, superciliously, with a slow revelation of white teeth, for the first time. He called to Julie, 'Run, for God's sake! Get down!' but she shouted back, 'I'll wait, I can't go without you!' and a moment later the three of them were running down the corridor, in half darkness, towards the smaller hospital ward.

The Tempest came flat over the Mission for the third time, drowning the flat flannel-like slappings of his wet shoeless feet on the corridor. Was – not was, he thought – is – this is it – for God's sake, this is it! – and then for the third time the plane was over.

Only when it had gone was he aware of reverberations of silence broken, presently, by the sound of children singing, and on the cold dawn air a smell of cocoa.

11

If Father Simpson experienced a feeling of exultation as the sun came through the windows of the hospital ward it was not so much because the night was over and horror might be lessened after its transition through light, but because the children were singing. It was better to count the living, he thought, than the dead – still better to hear the living as they sang – and he was actually counting them as Crane came into the ward with Kaushalya and Julie Maxted.

It was then, as he saw the girl wrapped in the priest's habit, beaten about by grief and tiredness, that his lapse of memory ended. His mind in a single shocking jerk went back to Mrs Maxted. He remembered how he had left her, face covered, on the bed. A spasm of nervous self-reproach threw him forward half a pace, and then that, too, ended. It was succeeded by a wave of that sickening self-condemnation, salty and repulsive, that had overcome him in the trench, when he had made his thoughtless mistake about the tenses. He knew suddenly that Mrs Maxted was dead. He saw the dried blue bruise of grief on the girl's face, across the eyes. His joy at the children's singing – it had been his idea to start it and he had put a young Italian nun, Carlotta, in charge – ran out of him, leaving him empty and arrested where he stood. In the crowded ward, that was now with its over-populated confusion of bundled and squatting bodies, beds and charpoys, like a section of any Indian street at dawn, he stood foolish and helpless, not knowing what to do or say or how to redeem or expiate the terrible sin of omission that had left Mrs Maxted to die, without comfort or succour, alone.

All the strength that had been released in him by physical action went suddenly dead. He wiped one hand across his face:

he needed a shave; his beard seemed to be growing, grisly and miserable, as far up as the wrinkles in the fat under his eyes. After a night of pure thoughtless release in action his thoughts came rushing back in the form of hammering and twisting reproaches. His face, frizzled and frowsy with sleeplessness and its day's growth of beard, was weak and grim.

He was relieved to see Father Anstey cutting across the line of Julie Maxted's approach. He heard something about cocoa; he saw McAlister taking Julie away to the kitchen, where breakfast of a sort was being made. From the other end of the ward the children laughed because the hymn they had been singing had ended. They liked it and were pleased with themselves. The nun Carlotta began singing another hymn, the voice warm and throaty but clear and reed-like at the same time. The children, multi-lingual, unfrightened, mixing Hindustani with bits of English and Italian and syllables of dialect he did not understand, joined in, and some of his strength came back.

By the time Crane and Father Anstey came over to him he had pulled himself together. He was in fact the first to speak and said with nervous quickness:

'Colonel Mathieson is in the kitchen, Mr Crane. There's some breakfast of a sort –'

'Not quite ready for it,' Crane said.

It seemed to Crane there were two hundred people in the ward. It reminded him, with its singing, its huddled beds and bodies, of a London tube-shelter during war. Another of those pleasant cosy international scenes, he thought, that are now getting so familiar to all of us, and then Father Anstey said:

'We have lost our dear Mother Superior. She died of her wounds. And we cannot find Sister Teresalina.'

'But she was here – out there – in the ward –'

'We know that. She tried to protect our dear Mother. She was seen. It was about the time Dr Baretta's husband disappeared. They seemed to go together.'

In anguish Father Simpson felt for his crucifix. It was not there. His large hands quivered like swollen sausages about his empty chest.

'Have we had a check?' Crane said.

94

He saw the younger priest's mouth twitch with nervous concentration, and then almost bark out, with recited accuracy:

'We've forty-five adults and twenty children – that includes the two new-born ones. Seventeen Hindu and Sikh families. Thirteen nuns. Four men.'

'Thank you, Father.'

'What have we lost?' Crane said.

'I can't tell yet. I don't know if Mrs Maxted – or Dr Baretta's husband –'

'Dr Baretta has looked everywhere,' Father Anstey said. 'It seems they took him out somewhere. He was not really Hindu – like Greta he was only half-Indian – no one knows what happened.'

'What can we do?' Crane said.

'There is this young Afridi officer. He seems intelligent. He has put himself in charge. I think we must do whatever he says.'

Crane stared down the crowded floor of the ward.

'Not much room.'

'We shall straighten out.'

From the end of the ward the voice of the nun Carlotta broke reedily and freshly above the children's voices, and Father Simpson looked startled.

'Was Mrs Maxted? – was she? – I mean, did you find her?'

'Kaushalya was with her,' Crane said.

'When she died?'

'I think so.'

'I'm glad to know it – one makes the most hideous misjudgements –'

His fat lips began to tremble loosely; he looked as ineffectual and indeterminate as when Father Anstey had first frightened him in the garden, as jellified with alarm as when Crane had met him by the river; and suddenly Crane felt sorry for him, saying in a way that was warm with new affection:

'Anyway, Father, the rabbits are all right.'

'Oh! Mr Crane, really! – is that so? – I forgot all about them –'

'Probably need feeding.'

'Yes, yes. They must do. We must save scraps for them.'

'Won't you get breakfast, Mr Crane?' Father Anstey said. 'The children have had theirs.'

Down the ward a young Hindu woman stood up and began combing her hair. Crane was disturbed by the sight of it, black and uncoiled down her shoulders. Woken to a new preoccupation, his first fear, he thought of Julie; he remembered with bruising clarity the woman he had seen thrown and stripped on the terrace. We're a battle line, he thought. What if we don't get rid of these bastards? He watched the woman sweeping the comb with smooth bright lines through the black silk towel of hair. She was pretty, rather as Kaushalya was pretty, sullenly and darkly. Beyond her the young nun Carlotta looked fragile and white as egg-shell; he saw the lovely straight Italian line of the nose uplifted. We have forty women, he thought, and rape is international.

'You should get breakfast, Mr Crane,' Father Anstey said. 'You look all in.'

'Perhaps I will.'

'Speak to the Colonel. He is not a Catholic and it is not easy –'

'Do we have to be Catholics?' Crane said. The question of religion, arbitrarily imposed in a moment of tenuous weariness, struck him as being something of infuriatingly small account.

'I did not mean to imply distinctions, Mr Crane. We are all the same under God.' He spoke bluntly, with his high Yorkshire accent, forthrightly.

'Perhaps the Colonel will play chess with you,' Father Simpson said. Much of his composure had come back. He seemed eager to seize, from between Crane and Father Anstey, the moment of awkwardness, and break it up.

'Perhaps you will give me a hand after breakfast, Mr Crane,' he said. 'I should be grateful. We have another trench to dig. I can hardly ask the Colonel to do these things.'

At the end of the ward children ceased singing for a second or two; and then began again, led by the young throaty Italian voice; and Crane said:

'I'm sorry. Anything you say. I'll even feed the rabbits.'

Father Anstey laughed. 'That's champion.' The blue eyes, crinkled under pressure of laughter, seemed awake for the first time. Crane was glad. A moment later he saw them turn cross-wise to look at the kitchen door.

It had opened and Dr Baretta had come in. She looked without visible reaction beyond the three men, and as she came across to them, her eyes unbroken by light, she lifted her hands once and let them fall.

'I can't find him. They won't let me go out.'

She was very slim; the bones of her wrists were sharply delicate through the cream-yellow transparent skin, her eyes ash-coloured and sparkless as she stood unbuttoning the cuffs of her white blouse. They were stiff, crackling as she folded them back.

Father Simpson said: 'Don't look any more, my child. Mr Crane and I will look.'

'They are guarding the doors,' she said. 'A few of them. The rest have gone.'

'It can't be,' Crane said.

'I heard an Afridi say they were going to the front.'

'There is no front,' Crane said.

'He said they were going to the front,' she said.

'Perhaps it simply means they have pushed ahead some-where,' Father Anstey said. 'Mercifully I think the Kashmiris are no match for them. What do you think, Mr Crane?'

Crane remembered the Tempest flying over and said:

'They're probably mopping up in the village. They'll be back.'

'I'm very worried about the village,' Father Anstey said. 'Miss Jordan and Miss Shanks are down there. They never came back again.'

'Who are Miss Jordan and Miss Shanks?'

'They are English ladies,' Father Simpson said. 'They have a house-boat. They were here yesterday afternoon and then they left.'

'There were fires there all night,' Dr Baretta said, 'You can see them still burning now.'

Crane, worried, looking down the over-crowded ward, at the

children singing, at the mass of bundles and bodies, at the young Indian woman combing her hair, remembered his first view of the Mission, stuck nakedly like a cake decoration on the hill-top; his jibe about it, and Father Simpson's shocked reply to that unthinkable thing. He had been more right about it than he thought.

He felt he must talk to Colonel Mathieson. Dr Baretta had walked away, vaguely, her cuffs undone at last, her sleeves rolled up, her skinned-willow arms exceptionally frail and gleaming as she prepared, farther down the ward, to work among the beds. A new-born baby lying like a rose-brown hairless puppy with its Hindu mother cried with tiny dog-like howls as the doctor picked it up from the bed, and the mother smiled with a gleam of white teeth as the Anglo-Indian girl comforted it. Crane was left alone with Father Simpson, who said:

'You ought to get some breakfast. We have some digging to do.'

'I think no one ought to go outside until we have seen this Afridi officer fellow – what's his name?'

'Sikander Shah. I asked him.'

'He's the boss. We ought to wait for him.'

'The dead have to be buried and they are going to be buried, boss or no boss, officer or no officer.' The priest suddenly spoke with fanatical insistence, the corners of his lips thin-drawn until his mouth was almost fleshless. 'No one is going to dictate to me about these things.'

'It isn't a question of dictation. Just sense.'

'It isn't even a question of sense. It's a question simply of what is right and what has to be.'

'It would be better to wait a bit.'

'I am not waiting. I won't wait. The dead cannot be left about like dogs.' The priest, in these few moments, had regained the look of blindly outraged aggression that had caused him to blunder through the chapel, knocking the Mahsud down. He did not seem to see Crane, standing there before him, advancing what he felt to be the argument of common sense. Sweat in small white prickles broke out on the smooth boyish skin of his forehead and he spoke in an odd clenched whisper that seemed more furious because he kept it so low.

He pushed past Crane, brushing him with his heavy tautened stomach.

'I'm going out. We have to find Dr Baretta's husband. I shan't rest until we find him and Sister Teresalina.'

'She is probably with the rest behind the chapel.'

'Oh God! Oh God!'

Hanging his head, terribly shaken for a moment in the act of blundering away, he put both hands to his face and then recovered himself:

'It has to be done. One can't shirk it. It is very terrible but it has to be done.'

'Why don't you wait a bit?' Crane said.

'I will not wait.'

'One stray shot by some idiot and they'll bump you off.'

'Then let them bump me off.'

'That's no service to the dead and it's no service to the living,' Crane said.

'To me the dead are living.' He pushed past Crane, stomach blundering and taut, towards the door through which he had wandered out to the chapel during the night. And turning there he thrust out his fleshy chin and said:

'Talk to Mathieson. He needs it.'

'The dead are so much easier, aren't they?' Crane said. 'You don't have to explain to them.'

'I'm terribly sorry. I didn't mean that – I shouldn't have said such a thing –'

He stood helpless and weak again, trapped by his nervousness into a new moment of condemnatory pain. Sickening salted bitterness drained his face of colour, leaving it ghastly, the sallowness brightened by the dark sweaty beard.

Crane, upset by the moment of tension that could not now be broken by banter as in the orchard on the previous day, pulled himself together, thinking: 'The man's right. We're all a bit past it – I need breakfast – need my shoes on –' and said:

'All right, Father. You go. I'll get some breakfast. I'll come and find you.'

99

The priest nodded gently, nervous and diffident and friendly; the aftermath of his agonies grew about his face in lines of shadow.

'I won't be long,' Crane said. 'I'll bring a crust for the rabbits,' and the priest, in the moment before opening the door, smiled.

The children were still singing as Crane went out of the ward into the kitchen, where Colonel Mathieson was sitting at a centre table, trying to coax a Kashmiri boy of five or six to eat his breakfast of boiled millet and cocoa.

'I found your shoes,' the Colonel said. 'They're under the table. I brought your shaving things too. And some cigarettes.'

Tired, unsurprised at this thoughtfulness, Crane said 'Thanks' and sat down opposite the Colonel and began to put on his shoes.

'This is a naughty boy,' the Colonel said. 'He doesn't eat his breakfast.'

Dark-eyed, partly frightened, partly sleepy, the boy sat with his hands under the table, a tin plate of millet in front of him. With big oiled eyes he looked from the Colonel to Crane and slowly back again.

Three nuns were busy about the stove. One of them presently brought Crane a slice of bread and butter and a mug of cocoa.

'Look at the big man,' the Colonel said. Crane held the mug with both hands, drinking slowly, letting the steam bathe his tired face. 'He eats his breakfast. You see how big he is.'

The boy did not move. The millet was almost cold on the plate and the Colonel picked a little of it up in a spoon.

'Come on,' he said. 'Everybody feels better when they've had breakfast. Don't they, Crane?'

'Does he understand?'

'He understands. He speaks English. He goes to school with the nuns.'

Crane began to bite slowly at the bread and butter. The boy watched him, lifting his face with the slightest movement of shy response from the plate.

'He can sing like the others,' the Colonel said, 'only he didn't feel like singing.' He let the millet slide from the spoon back to the plate. 'He's hungry.'

The boy did not look at Mathieson but sat watching Crane instead. Crane ate slowly at the bread and butter. He smiled once but the boy had no response and after another drink Crane said:

'They say the Pathans have gone to the front. What do you make of that?'

'They went off in trucks. I heard them.'

'Could there be a front?'

'It ran through here last night. I know that. Yes: I suppose there could.'

At the table the boy looked from Crane to Mathieson. The Colonel smiled and moved closer to the boy, putting one hand across his shoulder and with the other picking up the spoon.

'Come on,' he said, but the boy did not move his blue-red moulded lips. 'Where is Father Simpson?'

'Gone to feed the rabbits,' Crane said.

'You see, the rabbits have breakfast,' the Colonel said, 'When do we start work?'

'You need some sleep.'

'There's a lot to be done. We can sleep afterwards. When do we start?'

'There's no need for you to do anything.'

'Some boys play football but they have to eat breakfast and drink cocoa,' the Colonel said. He let the spoon fall back gently into the boy's plate, taking up the mug of cocoa instead. The boy did not lift his eyes. 'The digging did us all a power of good yesterday. You said so yourself.'

'We can manage.'

'I want to come.'

He spoke simply, finally, so that Crane felt no need for argument. With a sort of absent tenderness the Colonel put his right hand on the boy's head, smoothing it down his hair. The children sang, a little louder than before, from the hospital ward. The boy, hearing it, lifted his face, slowly and flatly, in a movement that seemed to free him from the bondage of his cooling plate of millet, the untouched cocoa, and the gentle coaxing of a man he did not understand.

As he sat there, his face freed and clear, listening as it were with his eyes, all the response the Colonel had sought in him and had not woken came suddenly to life.

Big slow tears began to fall brightly and soundlessly from the eyes that had seemed oiled over and unawakened. The Colonel continued to smooth his hand down the dark hair, so that it seemed as if he were easing the tears in their fall. The boy did not cry out. From behind him the Colonel smiled at Crane, saying something disconnected about 'You see, he cannot find his sister – it was a little difficult –' his voice disjointed and broken because Crane saw, all at once, that he was crying too. His tears fell as suddenly as the child's and he let them fall in the same way, making no attempt to stop them, and now it was as if the Colonel were free of bondage too. It was almost a pleasure that at last the tears could fall; that now the game was over; and suddenly he picked the boy up in his arms and said:

'Get the spades. I'll be out there. We've a lot to do.'

He went through the kitchen door with the boy in his arms. Crane, remembering the rabbits, picked up his uneaten bread, and at that moment Father Simpson came in from the corridor.

'Sister Teresalina is not behind the chapel,' he said. His face was yellow under dark thorns of beard and his lips were shaking. 'She is not with the rest.'

12

By mid-afternoon Crane and Father Simpson and Colonel Mathieson had finished work on the new trench in the orchard, under the apple-trees. Across the gorge smoke from fires had drifted about in the autumn air and clung now to low sections of forest like feathered mould. On the river the house-boats seemed cut from white paper and far off, at immense distances cleared by cloud, the high snow-line sprang from rose-blown folds of dying forest like a flared white cockscomb.

About noon the Afridi tribal officer had appeared in a truck, driving it himself, bringing four wounded men. One of these men stood with leathery glare in the sunlight, holding what remained of a shattered forearm. Crane could see blue-white splinters of bone thrust like torn roots from earth-brown flesh. The Pathan stood summarily at attention by the bonnet of the truck, glaring inscrutably beyond the three Europeans, beyond the terraces, beyond the succeeding folds of tree and rock and rice-fields. Blood dripped from the smashed flesh of the arm and slowly down the fingers of the hand that held it, like a scarlet-leaking tap, but on the face above it, with its aggravated thrustful stare, there was no hint of pain.

The Afridi officer came down to the orchard, saluting with formality the three men who were digging the trench.

'I wish to offer my apologies to you for some incidents that took place last night.' His English had the succinct high accent, exaggerated by precise strong lips, of the Indian who has been carefully taught. 'I am very sorry.'

'Thank you for those few kind words,' Mathieson said. His face was very white. The skin had a sort of crustiness because he had not shaved.

'My men have no etiquette,' the Afridi officer said.

Even Mathieson laughed.

'Why do you laugh?'

'Etiquette is hardly the word for what your men have not got,' Father Simpson said.

'What should I say?'

They did not answer.

'My men are warriors. There is a war,' he said.

'Then let them get off to the damn war,' Mathieson said. 'For Christ's sake what are they doing murdering women in convents?'

'I agree.' The young Afridi, torn by conflicting memories of his mother, looked troubled. 'It was very stupid. It was not right.'

'It was not etiquette,' the Colonel said.

The Afridi officer, more than ever troubled, did not answer, and Father Simpson said:

'We were told you were leaving for the front. Are you? Is there a front?'

'No.' He was momentarily confused. 'I mean there is a front but we are not leaving.'

'If you are not leaving will you allow us to leave?'

'No.'

'Why not?'

'There is a war. The convent is in the line. It is very important. It is not possible –'

'It is not etiquette,' the Colonel said.

Father Simpson threw down his spade and came up, furious and blundering, out of the trench.

'With one truck you could evacuate us to the rest-house across the river. Most of us could walk if you gave us safe passage. It would not take a day.'

'I have no trucks.'

'What the bloody hell is that up there?' the Colonel shouted.

'It is for the wounded,' the Afridi said. 'I cannot spare it.'

'Why have you brought them back here?' Father Simpson said.

'This is my headquarters.'

'And your hospital?'

'Yes.'

'You have the callous effrontery to stand there and tell me that after the pain and misery and murder your men have done,' the priest raged, his body quivering fatly and terribly, sweat pricking out on his trembling face. 'You murder and rape half the women here and then come snivelling to be nursed by the rest –'

'Father, Father,' Colonel Mathieson said. 'It is not etiquette.'

'I am sorry.'

The priest, abruptly deflated, terribly pained, his anger gone, stood with hands limp at his sides, humbly and contritely staring at the grass. Just before him, almost under his feet, lay a yellow half-rotten apple, and slowly he crushed it with his right foot, as if crushing out the last of his bitterness.

'I am forgetting myself again.' He looked up at the young officer. 'It is not for me to refuse the use of this place to you or anyone else. What do you want?'

'I have one seriously wounded man.'

Crane stood watching the Afridi by the bonnet of the truck. The tap of blood was running a little faster and it seemed as if now, at any moment, the arm would break away and fall.

'He needs a doctor. You have a doctor. I saw her this morning.'

'Yes,' the Colonel said. 'Your men killed her husband and then raped her for good luck. Or was it etiquette? – you would know?'

'It is very hard not to be bitter,' the priest said, 'but she will not refuse you. She has no bitterness.'

'Thank you,' the young Afridi said.

'She has no anaesthetics either.'

'The Pathans are a brave people,' the Colonel said.

'I am very grateful,' the officer said. 'I thank you.'

Stiffly, unhappily, he turned to go.

'Always at your service,' the Colonel said. 'No charge.'

Father Simpson, anger flushing back into his face, called out too:

'Is there nothing we can expect in return?'

The Afridi officer came back.

'What do you mean?'

'Will you give some guarantee that the ghastly business of last night won't be repeated?'

'In war there is no guarantee about anything.'

'Only etiquette,' the Colonel said.

'How long will you be here?' Father Simpson said.

'Impossible to say. Who can tell?'

'Will you at least give us some immunity until we have buried the dead?'

'You may have until six tonight.'

'Thank you,' Father Simpson said. 'And after that?'

'Everything will depend on the course of the fighting.'

Crane, who had not spoken, came up from the trench.

'A Tempest came over this morning to have a look at you. I hope you saw it.'

'I saw it.'

'You know damn well you've got trucks,' Crane said. 'The Colonel saw them.'

'I have trucks : yes. But not for evacuation.'

'I was not thinking about that,' Crane said. 'I was thinking about the Tempests.'

'They are not our Tempests,' the Afridi said. 'I am not responsible for them.'

'He is only responsible for the boys having plenty of fun,' the Colonel said.

'The minute you start using this convent as a lorry park you're responsible,' Crane said.

'Who has said I am using it as a lorry park?'

'Well, aren't you?'

Up on the terrace the wounded Afridi seemed to grasp his arm a little tighter, his inscrutable dark stare broken by a fragment of pain for the first time, and the officer said :

'We are fighting for our existence,' and turned suddenly, with a curious proud finality, and walked away.

The Colonel bowed with bitter politeness.

'We thank you for ours,' he said.

Up on the terrace the wounded Afridi broke his attitude of frozen, pained attention, turning away to follow the officer in a curt movement that sprayed blood in a scarlet arc across his tribal robe. The shattered arm was held in position precariously, crookedly, like a cracked carrot. Swiftly Crane thought of Julie Maxted, the Tempest, the child who would not eat his breakfast of cooling millet, the tears of the Colonel that were the tears for a child of his own. Fear arising from these things took the form of a wild notion to rush instantly up to the ward, get hold of Julie and run away. He wanted intensely to be alone with her. The thought did not seem at all idiotic or impossible; and suddenly he felt a wave of unbearable tenderness for her stream up in him, waging bright new agonies of mind, so that he had actually taken a step or two across the orchard, in an involuntary rush of anxiety, before he heard the Colonel say:

'We've got a lot of work to do, Father. Come on.'

Standing with head slightly bowed, the priest said in a low voice:

'I know. I'll come in a moment. Carry on.'

Crane moved towards the trench, walking past the ungainly deflated figure of the priest, with its curious crumpled bagginess that simply heightened all its pain. At the edge of the trench, that was to be a common grave, the Colonel stood sardonically aside.

'After you, Crane,' he said. 'We must not forget our etiquette,' and Crane jumped in.

They buried the dead at five o'clock that afternoon. A few Pathans guarded the gate; some others did cooking in the wood beyond the orchard but the rest had not come back. The Afridi officer had driven the truck away to a front of whose exactness of line even he seemed a little uncertain. Blobs of smoke like puffballs sprang from escarpments of surrounding forest, congealing or slowly melting in the hot afternoon. A few detonations, occasional terse volleys of rifle-fire, barked about the hills. But for the most part the day had been quiet and under the apple-trees the air was ripe with fallen fruit, soft and hot with tender fungoid decay.

Crane stood with Julie Maxted and the Colonel ten or fifteen yards away from the grave they had dug that morning, below the steps, on the slope of trees. He had not wanted either of them to come. Their own insistence in coming had grown simply because he had spoken against it too much. By the grave, at one end, stood Father Anstey, with those nuns, seven altogether, including McAlister and the young Alsatian girl, who could be spared from the ward. One of these nuns, a German, was very old and Crane did not remember seeing her before. She had a face like a potato twisted by earth, its eyes flattened by age and time into lidless scars. Her hands were machines of bone, antiquated and yellow, sliding about her habit in swift manipulation, systematically making signs of the cross as if they were repeated patterns worked on a garment. He saw her mouth moving in dark swift gapes of tireless prayer, the head up and then down, the hands weaving in the pattern of supplication. It was so quiet that down among the vines a few minah-birds, raiding the last of the grapes, quarrelled with a curious human jumble of syllables, so that sometimes their chatterings were synchronized with the gaping lips of the nun and she seemed to be gabbling with a dozen bird-sharp voices.

At the other end of the grave Father Simpson stood with Dr Baretta. Her husband had not been found, and Crane could not see her face. She was simply a flag-like image of white revealed in occasional flaps of her hospital smock behind the immense frame of the priest, who had not been able to find his vestments and had rigged up for himself a stole of surgical bandages that flowed out from his enormous neck like a scarf. Behind them the sun threw across the hills an elongated and rising strip of light that seemed to be pushed upward by a colossal bar of shadow, towards the snow. Crane watched this bar of light, his mind drugged by the voices of the minah-birds, the intonations of Father Anstey, the curious militant sing-song of Father Simpson, the moan of the nuns' responses in reply, with a feeling of being hypnotized by its slow ascension, of being pulled drowsily upward to the extreme height of earth, to all the great high distances of India and the pinking, glittering snow. Tired out, bludgeoned by events, he discovered that he could not feel any longer. He could not think; he was being dragged away. He could not comfort Colonel Mathieson, immersed in the bitter charms of Pathan etiquette, or the girl. They had hardly been together for a moment since morning; all his thought for her had dried to powder. The last of it had seemed to dry and vaporize even as he stood there, blowing away like the smoke of stray fires that were still floating greyly about the hills. It was as if he were callous to all that was happening, or bored, or stupefied, as if he were falling asleep where he stood. The bar of shadow, blue-brown, had ascended so rapidly that above it only a thin ridge of rose ice remained. He watched with drugged satisfaction for the final moment when this ridge would be obliterated and he himself would have been drawn up to it and encompassed, like the snow, at last. He remembered hearing the voice of Father Simpson split in a moment of higher agony and rise sharply, killing the responsive mumble of the nuns. It seemed to hit him like a stone whining out of the quiet air. A moment later he knew that he was staggering forward, that he was really falling asleep where he stood. The sun at the same moment went off the ridge of snow, leaving it a vast ember, smouldering and fiercely blue, and he put out his hands and came to himself aware once again of the gaping mouth of the nun with a face like a potato.

His brain cleared abruptly and he looked round at his side for Julie Maxted. She was not there and the Colonel said:

'She went.'

'Where? – how long? –'

'Only a minute.' His mouth twisted; he seemed about to make, Crane thought, another of his quips about etiquette, and then smiled. It was painfully touching and Crane could not bear it.

'You don't mind?' he said, and remained only long enough to see the Colonel, still with that curious twisted smile on his mouth, looking grievously and bitterly young, shake his head.

Crane turned and went up the steps and across the terrace. He ran the last forty or fifty paces to the west side of the Mission. The run brought him to the place, between the building and the patch of cabbages, where he had first met the Afridi officer. At the edge of the cabbage-patch Father Simpson kept his rabbits in four stilted wooden hutches.

He saw Julie Maxted walking towards them, quite slowly,

along the path. He called after her: 'Julie.' She did not answer; but for some reason or other he knew that she had heard. She went on walking and he called again. This time she put out her left hand. She did not turn again and the outstretched hand, held there for him to take, had on him the same unbearable effect as the Colonel's smile.

'Oh! God,' he said, 'I was dreaming – standing there – I didn't even know you'd gone –'

'I didn't want you to know.' She stood bravely, not crying, talking in a whisper. 'It is over?'

'No.'

'I couldn't bear it. Will they mind? Will Father Simpson mind?'

'No.'

'He's always very sweet to me.'

He took the hand she had held out to him; he held it lightly as they walked. After some moments she took it away again, grasping his own instead.

'What's going to happen?' she said. He knew that she was talking almost purely for the sake of talking, and he said:

'I don't know. Nobody knows. When this Afridi officer comes back we shall be at him again.'

'Can he stop it? Can he get us out?'

'I don't know.'

She walked on as if thinking about that: a little ahead of him, still grasping his hand. They had reached the garden where the cabbages, in blue-green lines, like vast hard roses, had already a bloom on them in the evening air. A crisp and shattering burst of fire, quite close down the hillside, startled both of them. He felt her tighten her grasp on his hand and the sharpness drove out the last of the drugged sleepiness that had held him mesmerized, watching the sun.

Another burst of fire, a little closer, set the rabbits jumping and bounding about in their hutches, as he remembered he had heard them doing in the night. 'They probably need feeding,' he said, and began to break off cabbage leaves as he walked down the path. She broke off a few leaves also with her free hand. The sun had gone down completely. The wall of the

Mission, flat and windowless on that side, had suddenly the effect of cutting them off, almost imprisoning them, from all the world on the other side. He felt they were not merely alone but ejected into a curious isolation. In the confined, cut-off world of the cabbages, the gleaming white rabbits, pink-eyed and frightened behind frames of wire, they were separate and inviolate, screened from the dead. It struck him that they were like rabbits: not really human, only animal: locked up, pounding away in a twilight of rifle-shots, afraid. His thoughts about her, so difficult to frame in any case and now dustily dried and blown away all day by sheer exhaustion, would still not come to life again. There was no way of talking about love. It did not seem to belong to a day still so reverberating with violence that sometimes he could not believe it was a day at all, but only an explosive flash of reflected hideousness, and he was glad when she said:

'Open the door.' She stood by the hutches, letting his hand go at last, holding several big crinkled cabbage leaves against her body. He took the wooden peg from the iron staple of the door and said: 'He must have kept rabbits at home. As a boy.' He undid the door. 'I mean Father Simpson.' In the hutch the two rabbits retreated, pounding into dark corners. Crane stretched in his hand, catching smooth naked ears, and brought a rabbit out, holding it against his chest, smoothing the hard silky head with his free hand.

'Hold it,' he said. She lifted up her hands to take the rabbit from him; it felt a second of freedom and leapt, struggling, away from his chest. 'All right, hold it where it is,' he said, and she held it with her two hands just below her face. The rabbit, lifting its head, screened for a moment the lower part of her face, so that Crane remembered, with a startled and acute flash, the very first moment he had ever seen her, in something of that same attitude, bright black eyes only visible, watching him as she folded the blanket in the ward. That moment of his first glimpse of her seemed suddenly so real that all he had wanted to say to her and could not say came rushing out, with clumsy tenderness:

'I wanted to say something. There was nowhere to talk of it

and I wanted to say it all the time but somehow there was no-where – This is an awful place to fall in love –'

'It isn't bad.' She smiled. She had a way of smiling so that her lips were pressed outward in a long soft line. 'Not so bad. We're together. It's all right.'

He looked down at her. The rabbit had raised its head, covering her smile. She looked as if wrapped in a white fur. Only the black eyes were visible above it, warm and sparkling.

'I can't bear it,' he said. He felt all the life between them drawn out, thread-like, ready to snap. The tension of quietness in the air grew ominously sharper. She let her head drop side-ways, pressing her cheek against the rabbit's head, looking up at him, and he heard a truck grinding through its gears down the hill.

'Are you married?' she said.

He shook his head.

'Tell me if you are. Don't be afraid to tell me. It doesn't matter.'

'I'm not afraid. There's nothing to tell.'

'I'm awfully glad,' she said. 'I was going to pretend it didn't make any difference but somehow it does and it isn't the same.'

'I'd make a bad husband but I'd be a good co-respondent,' he said. 'You could always divorce me.'

He saw the cheapness of the joke reflected on her face. He was miserable and wished he had never spoken.

'That wasn't very nice and I'm terribly sorry,' he said.

'You haven't even kissed me and you talk about divorce,' she said. She smiled, this time slightly, wanly, not happy. 'You'd better begin now if you think like that.'

'I can't get near you because of the rabbit.'

'The rabbit can be moved,' she said. 'It needn't come between us.'

A moment later she bent down and put the rabbit on the path. When she stood up again it was again exactly as it had been when he had first seen her in the ward. The rabbit, like the blanket, had dropped away; all the front of her body was suddenly open and free. He shut his eyes, hearing the truck, now joined by another, grinding its gears up the hill.

He was still kissing her when he heard the Tempest coming up the valley. Her breasts and her mouth were warm. He felt himself shut out the Tempest, fiercely rejecting it, determined not to let it enter their screened isolated world, and then he heard it begin firing, the cannon-shell bursting with shocking nearness up the hill.

He struggled against its shattering intrusive roar a moment longer. He felt her fighting to break away. He opened his eyes and saw the truck-lights flashing down the hill; and then above them, in long orange pulses of fire that seemed curiously slow, tracer shell spitting out on the twilight air on its downward curving trajectory.

He actually heard a shell hit the wall of the Mission just beyond them as he threw the girl down on the path. Like a tiny echo of it he heard the rabbit squeak somewhere underneath the rows of cabbage leaves. The girl did not cry out and a second later the Tempest was over the garden, like a fantastically travelling lid, beating and flattening the two of them against the earth.

He did not know how long they lay there together after the plane had gone over, clattering and firing on down the valley, but when at last he turned to look at her it was still light enough to see her face.

As he stretched out his hands to touch her she gave a brave and painful smile. He saw the dark flash of her eyes. He smelled once again the fungoid and revolting breath of cabbage leaves, of raw earth, of the carved dry grave he had been digging all day, of death, ghastly and tangible and repellent, all about him.

He touched her face with both hands and she smiled again, still more brightly, so that he could not bear what he felt for her.

'You see what I mean,' she said. 'You kissed me once and it was nearly the last time,' and he felt all his body weeping bitterly.

13

McAlister lay awake on the floor of the ward, watching cold oblongs of moonlight at the windows, listening to the noise of truck-gears whining up the hill. Now and then across the ward a child stirred, making small noises of restlessness in its sleep: undertones for irregular bronchial coughing of the elderly German nun on night-duty by the door. Whenever McAlister turned and looked that way she could see her there: upright, her ugly patriarchal face so like a potato; her head pressed back against the wall in the light of the small brass night-light, coughing with brief discreet hacks into the palm of her hand.

The ward had never been so quiet since the Pathans, twenty-four hours before, had stormed up the hill. Exhaustion had gradually crept over it, thickly clotting over crowded bodies, drugging them. There was no bed for McAlister to sleep on. She lay on bare boards with her spare underclothes stuffed in a pillow-case under her head, her body covered with a torn priest's habit found for her by Crane. There was nothing remarkable for her in these discomforts and it struck her sometimes that it was extraordinarily like home. She had often slept on the floor there; and sometimes after a bad bout of her father's, when the bedclothes had to be popped for a day or two, or on New Year's Eve, when her uncles and aunts and cousins came down in a jubilant horde from Arbroath, she had slept with nothing but her mackintosh for a blanket, on the same sort of crowded fuggy floor, listening to the crackling bark of her grandmother coughing through the night just as the German nun was coughing now.

She had learned to sleep then by curling her body to the shape of her sister Jeannie's and turning in the night, instinctively, when she turned. She had grown so used to it that she was aware now of a curious sort of emptiness on the floor about her. Whenever she turned she was troubled because there was no one there. She had a strange and discomforting sense of sleeping nakedly, of needing another body to shelter her own.

Her thoughts in this way were re-focused on Crane. Crane, whenever he could spare a moment from Miss Maxted or Father Simpson or Colonel Mathieson in the task of digging in the orchard, had been distantly attentive. Her reaction to the moment when the Pathan had ripped her habit from her like a skin had been delayed. It had taken anger and terror a whole day to diffuse and filter down through her consciousness and crystallize quietly into the oddest sort of pleasure. The moment when she had run nakedly and with hysterical rage across the terrace and Crane had covered her body was still extraordinarily stark and vivid; but her terror had gone. There remained only a flame of her temper that every now and then sprang up again with viciousness at the thought of her humiliation. Whenever it passed the sensation of pleasure was left: a feeling of protective comfort, of another body sheltering and covering her own, that soothed and calmed her nerves.

Down the ward a child began to cry and before the German nun by the door could stir McAlister was picking her way through the lines of sleeping bodies. The child, a Hindu boy, lying on a bed with four others, looked up at her with black eyes half-clouded with sleep and the beginnings of tears. He groped into the air with his hands, not knowing where he was. She folded the hands down under the blanket, turning the child over, not speaking, pressing the small body back into the shape of the other three.

The child did not cry again but half-way up the ward McAlister heard, from somewhere beyond the terrace, a new outbreak of Pathan shouting. She felt a murmur like a shudder go through the ward and for some moments she stood still among the beds, angry, waiting for the children all about her to wake and cry. 'Once the children begin,' she thought, 'the women will start and then we'll have hell for the rest of the night.' She stood with clenched hands, tautly listening to the yelling argumentative voices outside. 'Damn and blast them,' she thought, 'damn and blast them.' She heard the gears of a truck crashed in, an engine revved to a roar. 'Blast you! Blast you!' she thought, all her rage of the previous night streaming furiously back. It made her recall, for some reason, Dr Baretta setting the smashed forearm of the Pathan brought in that morning: cleaning it, setting it, bandaging it, putting it in splints, tying the final sling: calmly, simply, inscrutably, efficiently, never speaking.

'Not me,' she thought, 'not me. Their arms can rot off. Let them walk about on stumps.' Down the ward the Hindu boy cried again.

Suddenly the roar of the truck engine stopped; the Hindu boy, as if shocked by the sudden quietness, gulped and seemed to swallow his own cry. She stood for a few moments waiting. Outside the building most of the shouting died and some of her temper, partly in relief, went with it. It was probably some damn quarrel about the motor, she thought, and then went on up the ward.

She was several yards beyond the place where she had been lying when she saw that Crane had come into the ward by the door through which Father Simpson had stormed the previous night. She knew that the three men were sleeping on the floor outside and it struck her in a moment that something was wrong.

Crane leaned by the wall, waiting for her.

'What is it, Mr Crane? Something the matter?'

'Nothing. It's all right.'

'What made you come in?'

'The noise, that's all. I wondered –'

'I'll make them damn well wonder,' she said. 'What the hell are they kicking up that racket for? – waking everybody up. We'll have the whole ward screaming again.'

'They're having fun,' he said.

'The next one that has fun with me can look out for himself,' she said. 'In the morning I'm finding a carving knife.'

Crane laughed. They had spoken in whispers and her voice had a low whistle of temper. 'You ought to get some sleep.'

'I slept this afternoon,' she said. 'What about yourself?'

'I'm all right. It's just the beds are a bit hard.'

She looked back down the ward; it was quieter now; the child was not crying. The German nun coughed into her hand by the middle door and McAlister said:

'I'll come outside and talk a bit. Do you mind?'

'No.'

In the corridor outside another small brass oil-lamp burned on the wall by the door of a small wash-room; at the farther end Father Simpson and Colonel Mathieson were asleep on the floor. Crane shut the door behind McAlister and leaned against the wall, listening. She flattened herself against the wall opposite him, by the oil light, small face tight-lipped, hard little Scottish chin thrust out and averted.

'Quieter now,' he said.

'I thought they'd wake the whole damn ward up.'

He stared across at her. The small fierce eyes moved relentlessly to and fro and would not look at him.

'You look tired. You ought to sleep,' he said.

'Somebody's got to keep awake.'

'Cigarette?' he said.

'No.' She looked across at him sharply, directly. 'You're not doing that to me again. Get thee behind me, Mr Crane.'

'You don't mind if I do?' he said.

'You know I'll mind,' she said.

He lit the cigarette with his petrol-lighter. He breathed out smoke in a long slow cloud, above his head. She did not speak. He put the lighter in his pocket and outside, noisily, too fast, a truck moved away over the gravel of the far terrace, and some voices shouted.

'Noisy brutes,' she said. The truck moved down the hill; the voices were quiet again. 'I'll give them one thing though.'

'What?'

'They've got guts.' She began talking of the Pathan with the smashed forearm. Except for her voice it was uncannily quiet in the stone passage; there was no sound at all from the ward or the terrace outside. 'He just lay on the bed and looked up while Dr Baretta probed for the bullet.' Crane watched her tired face; small beady brown eyes brilliant even in fatigue against the flat white wall. ' "Does it hurt?" Dr Baretta said, and all he said was : "I eat raw meat. I like it." '

She smiled slightly. He saw her right hand feel in a curious exploratory lost gesture along the bare wall. There was no venom in her face now; the creeping gesture of her hand along the wall seemed child-like and lonely. He blew smoke in the air and again there was no sound except his expiring breath.

He saw her head turn as if she were about to speak again. In the same moment there was a rush of voices in the adjoining corridor behind her. He heard a brassy jangle of tribal accoutrements as if Pathans were leaping down the corridor in great strides. Father Simpson stirred on the floor, throwing back his blankets, and Crane remembered, just in time, the little wash-room where the lamp burned. He took hold of McAlister's hand that was still creeping with its lonely exploratory patterns along the wall and pulled her in a single terrific bound across the corridor and pushed her into the wash-room, slamming the door.

The crash of the door shut out all other sound. When he turned back along the corridor he saw that four Pathans had come in by the door from the central ward. He had no time to speak or move again before Father Simpson, ponderous and blundering in trousers and vest, his braces tight across his fat body, strode past him.

The Pathans, carrying oil-lamps, swayed with theatrical fero-city down the corridor; and one shouted, swinging his lamp, in a curious stilted thin English :

'Where are your women? Where are they?'

'There are no women. You're drunk,' Father Simpson said. 'Get out.'

'We are here for women,' the Pathan said.

'You are drunk. There are no women. Where is Sikander Shah?'

'Who?' the Pathan said. 'Who? Who you say?'

'Your officer!' the priest roared.

'Officer! Officer! No officer! Where are the women?'

'There are no women,' the priest said slowly. He stood fatly, bravely, in the centre of the corridor. A Pathan swung his lantern in a half circle of excited rage and Colonel Mathieson said:

'The bastards will kill you, Father.'

The Colonel came up the corridor, putting his hands on the priest's shoulders. The priest did not move. The Pathan swung his lantern again and the priest held up his hands to protect himself. When the lantern struck his wrists he fell backwards by the wall. He rebounded from it with a tremendous shudder of rage to the centre of the corridor, bouncing and quivering there, shouting:

'There are no women. Get out, I tell you! Get out!'

The Pathan who spoke English hit him in the face. The priest did not stagger. Colonel Mathieson held him by the shoulders as if to steady him or hold him away but the priest shook himself free.

'Where is your officer? When does he come back? Where is Sikander Shah?'

In the ward a child cried and the Pathan hit the priest for the third time. The priest fell down. He made a wild and stupid lunge with both fists, overbalancing as he fell. He lay on the floor for a second or two until Colonel Mathieson and Crane went forward to help him up. The Pathan hit him again as he rose to his feet, the lantern striking him on the shoulder, the flame extinguished in an oily gush of smoke that exploded in his face, half-blinding him. He staggered about the corridor, groping, repeating savagely, over and over again: 'There are no women, there are no women. You're drunk. Get out! Get out!'

Half-blinded, he fell down again. He stretched out his hands; in the act of falling he struck his face against the door. His hands grasped the heavy brass knob of the door as he fell and the door opened under his weight, pitching him across the threshold. A woman began screaming and four Pathans surged in a spectral and savage rush through the opened door, yelling and laughing, trampling across the body of the fallen priest, crushing each other in a wild rush to break through to the ward.

Crane stood crazily in the corridor, thinking of Julie Maxted. His mind, stupidly deadened by the repetitive doll-like falling and bouncing of the priest, came to life in panic. He turned to shout something to Colonel Mathieson and saw that the Colonel too was lying on the floor trying to shield the priest with his body. In that moment he heard the shrill repeated blast of a whistle on the terrace outside and the noise of a truck engine starting up.

The returning rush of the four Pathans knocked him down. He heard the English-speaking voice shout: 'We come back!' and a second later four pairs of feet trampled across him, leaving him like the remnant of some crazy and half-theatrical football scrum, alone with Colonel Mathieson and Father Simpson on the floor.

He was the first to get up. The door of the main corridor was still open; he staggered across to shut it. On the terrace the whistle was still blowing and already trucks, roaring in low gear, were moving away down the hill.

He shut the door. He could hear children crying in the ward. He remembered McAlister, locked in the wash-room. When she came out a moment later Colonel Mathieson was already on his feet and between them they helped the priest stand up. His face, bruised, scorched by the gush of lamp-flame, had something of the look of a cherubic Negro minstrel, startled and enraged, eyes left white in rings of black; and he kept saying, furiously brushing his hands across his face:

'Where are they? Where are they? They shall not come in here! I will not have them in here like this! I will not have them!'

'They've gone, Father,' the Colonel said. 'Take it easy. Can you see?'

'I can see, yes. I am all right.'

He stood in the centre of the corridor, blinking like a ferocious minstrel, panting.

'How did they go? Why?'

'The sergeant whistled them up for parade,' the Colonel said.

'Damn and blast them!' McAlister said.

The priest, startled by this final moment of vehemence, came to life, pained.

'They are unnecessary words, my child,' he said and then, as if really seeing for the first time and not surprised. 'Oh! it's McAlister.'

'I am sorry, Father. I am terribly sorry. They slipped out.'

'Thank God,' he said.

'I am terribly sorry, Father,' she said. 'I will go to the ward. The children are crying.'

She moved to the door.

'Is there a key to the door?' he said.

'No, Father. There used to be – but not now –' She gave him a brief and nervous glance of humility and went through the door.

'A key won't help us,' the Colonel said.

'No: I am sorry for that,' the priest said. 'It was stupid – it was just a thought.' He looked down at his chest. 'My vest is torn.' His undershirt had been ripped across by Pathan feet, showing underneath the hairless, podgy flesh. 'My mother would have a fit.'

'Something has to be done,' Crane said. 'They'll be back.'

'I feel crazy. I feel I am not here,' the priest said. 'I can't think.' He stood by the wall, burying his face in his hands, shuddering.

'Come and lie down, Father,' the Colonel said.

'No,' he said. 'No. Crane is right. Something has to be done. I can't think –'

'You will think better if you lie down,' the Colonel said.

'No,' he said. 'No.' He stood with ferocious obstinacy by the wall, painfully struggling with himself, locking and unlocking his hands across his face. 'If I lie down I shall give way.' He trembled convulsively, his head shaken by involuntary shudders of shock. 'I am not going to give way. I am not going to give way. I will not give way to these beasts – these awful – these bastards –'

The shock of this fiercely ejected word suddenly calmed him

down. He let his hands fall from his face. Half-startled, half in shame, he looked up at Colonel Mathieson and Crane, blinking.

'What do you think? What shall we do?'

Colonel Mathieson swore softly, shaking his head. Crane, who could think of nothing to say, stood thinking of Julie Maxted. His preoccupation with attack by air had been shattered by the raid of Pathans crying for women. Now his body ached for her. In fear he recalled her impossible notions of escaping and then heard Father Simpson say:

'It's not the English women. Not the nuns. They won't touch them. It's the Indian women – the Hindus, the Sikhs. It's another part of the feud.'

'There's no hiding them,' the Colonel said.

Crane, absorbed by a memory of the woman combing, that morning, in the ward, her long black scarf of hair, did not speak. Impossible to hide them, as the Colonel said. He remembered Kaushalya: sometimes, inscrutable and sullen, in mute gravity, with fine-cut lips, very like a boy. That was something in common in India, he thought. Sometimes when young the men had a tender chiselled womanliness; the women a fleeting boyish masculinity. It was hard, sometimes, to tell one from the other.

'You ought to lie down, Father,' the Colonel said.

'No, no,' the priest said. 'No.' He walked distractedly up and down. The last of the trucks shot across the gravel outside. The lavatory door flapped on its catch. 'I'll wash my face.'

He blundered into the little wash-room. Crane handed the Colonel a cigarette but the Colonel, drawn, running his left hand through his hair, shook his head. Water ran into the washbasin in the lavatory and Father Simpson dashed it to his face with furious splutterings that were like groans.

'They'll be back. We have to think of something,' the Colonel said.

'Is he right about the English women?' Crane, worried once again about Julie Maxted, drew nervously at his cigarette. 'They practically raped McAlister.'

The Colonel did not speak. Desperately and miserably Crane wished he had never spoken, and said:

122

'I'm sorry. I didn't think – my brain is like jelly. I'm worried about Julie, that's all.'

'I know. I know.'

Father Simpson appeared at the door. Scrubbing his face with the lower end of his undershirt, he left black stains of smoke smeared across the cream wool. As he tucked the under-shirt into his trousers and wiped his hands first across his belly and then across his deadened, whitened face there was a certain puffy womanliness in the priest too, Crane thought. Father Simpson nervously pulled the vest tight across his chest and there was a momentary revelation of fat bosom before the wool sprang back and loosened itself again. Crane at the same moment recalled Kaushalya and the woman combing her long hair; and suddenly, in a twisted flash of sense that was so comic that for some seconds he could hardly speak of it to the Colonel or Father Simpson, the three things came together.

He leaned back against the wall, shutting his eyes. He drew hard at the cigarette, trying to press out and smooth the twists of his mind as he might flatten a warped board; and then said, slowly:

'We could cut off their hair.'

He saw the Colonel start, half in pain, half in amazement, and the priest said:

'Who? Who? Who do you mean?'

'The women,' Crane said. 'Cut off their hair. Pass them off as men.'

'Oh! no, no, no, no. It would never work. It wouldn't do. It would be the most dreadful sort of insult.'

'It would keep them alive,' Crane said. 'They might prefer it.'

The Colonel walked nervously up and down. On the wall the small oil-lamp, on its bracket, spat sparks from a wick not properly trimmed. He paused to take off the glass chimney, turning the lamp-screw at the same time.

Crane saw the nervously brittle face held for a moment above the naked flame; the hands trembled; and under a too-sharp turn of the screw the lamp went out. In the sudden darkness he heard the Colonel say 'Blast!' and then, clearly and quite casu-ally, as if without light it were something much easier to say:

'Dressing them as men wouldn't work. You couldn't do it. But you could cut their hair shorter and pass them as European. That might work. We could find my wife's clothes. There might be some of Mrs Maxted's too.'

The light did not reappear. Neither Crane nor Father Simpson said anything in reply. There was a smell of carbonized smoking wick and the Colonel said:

'It's awfully damn silly but I haven't any matches.'

Crane found his petrol-lighter and flicked it, holding it up above his face, the flame white. The Colonel smiled. Darkness seemed to have given him relief, to have broken the brittle nervous tension that had accidentally extinguished the lamp. Now light in turn had set free a wave of long-repressed gaiety, almost mischief, so that he actually grinned and said:

'I'd like to try it. It might fox them. Father, what do you say?'

Crane held his petrol-lighter to the lamp. The Colonel turned the screw, and the wick rose, burning brighter now. The priest, thoughtful, hands locked across his lower chest in the habitual pose of meditation, said:

'Yes: it might work. There are these ghastly taboos, though. They might resent it.'

'We will explain it to them,' the Colonel said. 'We'll tell them the alternatives.'

'We will tell them about the etiquette,' Crane said.

'Ah,' the Colonel said. 'Yes, I'd forgotten the etiquette. We will tell them about that.'

The Colonel put the glass chimney back on the lamp; the flame, drawn up, burned more whitely and his hand, steadier now, turned down the screw.

'What about the nuns and Julie?' Crane said. Nervously he had kept the petrol-lighter burning and now, in an incautious clumsy flick, he snapped it out.

'They will be all right,' the priest said. 'They won't touch them. After all the church, even here, gives a certain protection.'

'I hadn't noticed it,' Crane said and the Colonel, catching in the remark a fear that no ironies could conceal, smiled again and said:

'They may not come back. It may never happen.'

'Enough has happened,' the priest said.

'Yes: I know. I know. But it will end. There will be an ending.'

He walked suddenly into the wash-room, calling back:

'Isn't there a light in here? Crane, bring your lighter.'

Crane snapped the lighter open, into flame, and went into the wash-room, followed by Father Simpson. The room, about twelve feet by four, became so immediately congested by the three men standing there under the uplifted flame of Crane's petrol-lighter that Colonel Mathieson, turning round, pushed his elbow into the priest's belly, and said:

'Your pardon, Father.' The bantering ironies that had accompanied the digging of the trench came back. 'What do you think, Crane? Could we do it in here? Is it large enough to contain the Father too?'

The priest smiled shyly. He seemed glad, as he had been in the trench, of the return at last of the masculine ironic teasing prompted by the Colonel, and said:

'I shall ask leave of absence. I shall leave it to the ladies' men.'

A spasm of self-indictment, cruel and sharp, ran through him as the words flew out, unchecked, before he could stop them. Instinctively he looked for the pain on the face of the Colonel, but to his great joy and relief it was not there. His own pain seemed to translate itself in that moment physically. For the first time he felt his bruised face, where the lamp had struck between eye and cheek-bone, pulsing sharply under torn skin, swollen and raw.

Crane said hastily: 'Yes: we could do it here. They could come in one by one.'

'Crane and Mathieson. *Coiffeurs des dames*,' the Colonel said. 'You are a little long in the neck too, Father.' He ruffled the priest's hair and the priest smiled gently.

'Father Anstey usually cuts it,' he said. 'We usually do each other.'

'I forgot Father Anstey,' the Colonel said. 'We must tell him about this.'

'I will tell him,' the priest said.

Crane went out into the corridor and the priest followed, Colonel Mathieson coming out last and shutting the door. Too nervously Crane snapped out the lighter and dropped it.

'Now the bloody thing will never work again,' he said. He picked it up, sharply flicking it open, angry and taut. The flame shot out at once, startling him. It revealed in a single start all the anxious tension of his face. He shut the cap of the lighter down and in the moment of extinction the Colonel said:

'I think my wife had some trousers. Anyway Mrs Maxted had. We could dress Julie as a boy.'

'They like boys too,' Crane said. 'You know what they say up in the hills – find the boy –'

'I know, I know. It was just an idea. Perhaps we shall have another.' He held out his hand. 'Can I borrow the lighter? I'll go and get my wife's clothes.'

'I'll come with you,' Crane said.

'No,' the Colonel said. 'I'll go. I know where they are.'

Crane, not speaking again, gave him the lighter and the Colonel, followed by an abrupt nervous warning from Father Simpson – 'Be careful. They had guards at the other end' – went out of the door leading to the corridor. For a moment or two after he had gone Crane walked up and down. Thinking of Julie, he remembered the moment of shattering and almost extinguishing terror in the cabbage-patch, the moment of her brave and painful smile, the cruel idiocy of his joking. He longed hungrily for a cigarette. He put a cigarette in his mouth and felt in his pocket for his lighter. He remembered then how he had given it to the Colonel and abruptly from the other end of the corridor, the cigarette in his mouth, he turned to say to Father Simpson:

'Father, have you a lighter please? The Colonel has my lighter –'

The priest did not answer. Kneeling on his bed, face to the wall, his huge body very still except for a gentle beating up and down of his shoulders, he was praying hard.

14

Father Anstey got up at dawn, as he always did, and said his
own prayer on the little wooden prie-dieu by the side of his
mattress in the kitchen. The only place from which he could see
the colour of sunrise across the mountains was from the little
window in the projecting angle of wall above the sink. Even
that faced southward rather than eastward and all he could
really see from it was the lower and outer wings of cloud,
exquisitely heliotrope and rose, and the blue reflecting beads of
dew on the crinkled globes of cabbages. There was no sight of
the calamitous rock above the gorge.

Below and opposite him all the inhabited part of the valley
seemed to be on fire. Smoke from burning houses had fallen
among rock and trees, collecting in grey lakes across the gorge.
These lakes broke here and there to give him a glimpse of the
road and its bullock tracks exploding from the dust of several
army trucks slowly proceeding in ragged convoy under the
plane-trees. A house-boat seemed to be on fire, burning at one
end like a colossal white cigar. He thought of Miss Jordan and
Miss Shanks. They had come to tea on their promised afternoon, only the day before yesterday, and yet a million days
away, but the air had been too charged with doom for any
pleasantries like grape-jam under the prunus-tree. They had
gone away with firm and jolly resolutions to return on Sunday.
It was only late that day, after the night of shooting and terror,
that he even remembered it was Sunday. That absent-minded-
ness had distressed him terribly. Later he had done something
to expiate the sin of forgetfulness, the very thing with which he
was always charging Father Simpson, by having the piano
moved into the ward and playing it himself for a short service

before the children went to bed. His vestments were nowhere to be found but Father Simpson had had a brain-wave and they had made up all that was necessary from surgical bandages dipped in scarlet and indigo dye that the nuns had used for weaving.

Two Tempests and a Spitfire came eastwards up the valley, shooting up the convoy of trucks as he stood there by the window; but the world of aircraft was not his world and he had grown so used to wild and indiscriminate shooting of every kind that he hardly noticed it. Shooting of some sort had gone on with the crackle of fires all night. Now the drumming of cannon-shell and the whine of every sort of weapon from the valley in reply disturbed him so little that he remained at the window a little longer, thinking of Sister Teresalina and Dr Baretta's husband. It hurt him terribly that neither of them had been found.

Even as he stood there, all of himself coiled up into a tiny cleft of private distress, he saw distinctly below him, in gaps of smoke on road and bullock tracks, how the second of the two Tempests, on a return run, had hit the convoy of trucks with a line of cannon-shell as level as a row of dots from a typewriter. He saw two trucks, puffed aside by these dots, lurch off the road and pile up against each other on the lower track under the trees. Even this failed to wake him out of his private world; it simply held him fascinated in the same daze of mystic thought-lessness that had so often irritated him and sometimes infuriated him in Father Simpson. Terror and ghastliness all about him had succeeded only in destroying a final illusion of truth; he could not bring himself to believe in its reality. All of it was part of the toy-like nightmare that puffed the convoy of trucks off the road, sending men running from them like black ants escaping from little brown boxes of fire.

It was only when the Spitfire came back, directly over the Mission, that he really came to himself. He felt it was time to go into the ward. He walked calmly, thinking less of the Spitfire than of Sister Teresalina, crossing himself several times as he went. Sister Teresalina must be found, he thought. It could not go on; he could not bear the dread and distress of it. Like

Father Simpson he could not allow the dead to lie like dogs. He would speak to Father Simpson about it.

When he came into the ward the entire Mission seemed suddenly to be flattened by the direct overhead roar of the plane. He seemed to be the only person not shrieking. He heard windows in the eastern side of the building break with a sparkling and almost musical crackle under cannon-fire; and it recalled for him, in a wonderful moment of absolute waking, the piano.

He made a sliding sort of rush at it and began playing loudly, still standing up, his foot on the open pedal. He heard the young Italian nun Carlotta begin singing at the other end of the ward and presently the old heavy German nun who had been on night duty brought him a chair. It was only after a second or third run of the Spitfire, followed by one of the Tempests, that he realized that anyone but himself and Sister Carlotta was singing. Then he heard the mumbling grunt of the German nun beating, half in German, half in English, into his left ear, and he looked up to see a remarkable thing.

She was holding in her hand a bundle of her pink and white underclothes. He did not understand this odd phenomenon except to note that she held them in a frenzy of excitement and protection grimly, with clenched hands. The two of them were presently joined by McAlister holding an Indian baby. Between the singing of McAlister and the German nun and the crying baby he could not hear himself sing at all. It was only after he had looked a second and then a third time at the clenched bundle of underclothes that McAlister shouted into his ear:

'She's frightened the Pathans will get them. She sat on them all night. She adores the planes!'

He was cheered by these incongruities and found himself smiling for the first time since he had pulled Father Simpson's leg among the potatoes. He sang lustily, playing hymns with bold chords and once a verse or two of *Rule, Britannia*. He did not know how long he went on playing but the aircraft did not come back and presently three nuns came in from the kitchen with pails of cocoa and millet, boiled overnight, for breakfast.

He stood up to say a blessing. He began to speak in Latin and then thought how stupid it was to speak in Latin when only a fraction of the adults and none of the children could understand him. Then he remembered that practically the same thing was true of English, and he reverted to Latin at last, shutting his eyes and ending with *'In nomine Patris, et filii, et spiritus sancti, Amen'* and in the very middle of it remembering that he had so far not seen Father Simpson or Crane or Colonel Mathieson at all.

When he opened his eyes it was to see, at the end door, something that re-created in a terrible and startling moment the illusion that no part of what had been happening was true. Automatically he crossed himself and turned to speak to McAlister, but McAlister had moved away with the baby and was busy changing its napkin on the nearest bed.

What he saw was Father Simpson coming with Mrs Mathieson down the ward.

He was so pained and shaken by this illusion that he did not hear McAlister, taking a safety-pin from her mouth, say: 'For God's sake, in the name of the Father and all the saints –'

He, too, in that moment, beginning to walk down the ward with outstretched hands, knew that it could not be. He saw that Father Simpson was simply coming with a Hindu woman dressed as Mrs Mathieson. He remembered the dress, a white tennis-dress with crimson cuffs and lapels, because Mrs Mathieson had worn it on that doom-charged day when Miss Jordan and Miss Shanks had come to tea. The illusion of her return, the wild notion that nothing of all that had happened was true, lasted for another second or so. Then the woman went past him down the ward.

'Father, what is happening?' he said. Father Simpson stood sturdily between the beds, assessing the bewilderment of the elder priest with a faint smile. 'I thought for a moment –'

'We are cutting their hair. Dressing them as Europeans.'

'You are what?'

'We are cutting their hair. The Pathans came in last night, looking for women. It was the only way.'

Father Anstey, standing still, looking down, not speaking,

felt that the past had suddenly begun to divulge, in the form of woken ghosts, all the horror in which briefly he had not believed. On the bed beside him the baby cried again and Mc-Alister, nursing it high on her shoulder, took it away down the ward. Borne away, it stared back at Father Anstey from a face somehow touching and repellent in its bruised-brown wretchedness, and he remembered Sister Teresalina again.

'Is everyone all right? Were there any casualties?' he said.

'No.'

'We must find Dr Baretta's husband and Sister Teresalina somehow today.'

'I am going to find them myself,' Father Simpson said. 'I shall go out and speak to the Afridi officer and make it my business to find them.'

'Probably Mr Crane and the Colonel would go with you –'

'No; I shall go by myself. It will be a painful thing and I do not want Mathieson to go.' He smiled with dry, round charm. 'Besides, they are very busy in the *salon des dames*. The barber's shop.'

He went on down the ward and spoke to McAlister, who was giving the baby back to the Meran woman, the Untouchable, its mother. All about him, on the floor, children were eating breakfasts of millet and cocoa. There was a sickly fleshy fustiness in the air, an after-night odour of bodies, and he went to the extreme end of the ward and opened a window. He was not quite high enough to reach the catch and he stood on a chair. He waited for a moment or two, breathing new morning air that had in it a touch of snow from the mountains, staring over the vegetable garden and its dew-veined cabbages to the burning village across the gorge.

Beyond the arch of the Mission gate an army truck had stuck on the hill. He saw two Afridis wrestling with the starting handle. After a few moments they gave it up. He saw them go round to the back of the truck and presently three wounded men appeared, patched up with rags, followed by another carried by the two Afridis on a stretcher. The whole party began to struggle up the hill.

He went back up the ward, stopping to speak to Dr Baretta, who was taking a temperature, looking at the watch on her wrist with untroubled efficiency as she stood by the bed. He spoke to her of the wounded coming up the hill and then he saw that she was taking a pulse at the same time. She simply nodded and made no answer.

He called to McAlister to bring another woman to the wash-room. She followed him at once, bringing a young Sikh woman with a mass of intensely shining blue-black hair of great length coiled up on her head like bands of liquorice. She began to cry at once as she went into the wash-room and saw Crane and Colonel Mathieson waiting there. The Colonel was sitting in the chair and Crane had been clipping his moustache.

'Not the ends, you fool,' the Colonel said. 'Just the part where the drips hang.'

'It is an operation that calls for great delicacy,' Crane said.

'Then let's have some delicacy,' the Colonel said. 'I am not a haystack.'

Loudly, wailing, the young Sikh woman burst fully into tears. The Colonel got up out of the chair and Father Simpson said:

'They are bringing in wounded. They are coming up the hill.'

'Then let 'em come,' the Colonel said. A certain severity in the moustache-clipping had made him look sprucely fierce. 'I shall be happy to operate with scissors.'

McAlister comforted the Sikh woman, who sat sobbing in the chair, bowing her head so that it touched her breasts.

'We are overcrowded now,' the priest said. 'We can't do it. We can't have them here.'

McAlister unpinned the Sikh woman's hair so that it fell down like a glistening oily shawl, blackly hiding her face. In the corner by the wash-basin Mrs Mathieson's clothes were draped on a chair and a nurse went across and selected a blue-flowered dress, holding it against her body. The Colonel looked at her quickly, and said, flatly, the irony consequently sharpened:

'Wrong size, madam. You need a forty-eight.'

'A forty-eight what?' McAlister said.

'I haven't the least idea,' the Colonel said.

'Bust,' Crane said and McAlister angrily waved the dress as if she would hurl it at him.

'Please remember where you are,' Father Simpson said. Meekly McAlister turned away, leaving the Sikh woman to cry in shame, heart-brokenly, under the long canopy of hair. The Colonel stood stiff and spruce, his scissors over-precisely poised. Crane detected something murderous under these too elaborate ironies and Father Simpson looked nervous and worried.

'Sir,' the Colonel said, 'we are simply here to please,' and bowed.

'I am going out to talk to them,' the priest said. 'We cannot have Pathans and Afridis mixed up with the women in the ward. It's an absolutely monstrous situation. Moslem and Hindu and Sikh together in one ward. There'll be murder.'

'How accurate you always are with your tenses,' the Colonel said, and the priest, trapped again by nervousness into a remark of insupportable stupidity, simply bowed his head.

To Crane the little room, with its five figures, McAlister quiet and rebuked, the Sikh woman sobbing, the Colonel and the priest on edge, was suddenly a stifling little trap not large enough to contain them all. The charm of his few moments alone with the Colonel, clipping the moustache, had gone. He longed to get out.

'I'll come with you,' he said to Father Simpson.

'No.' All the defensive clumsy stubbornness of the priest came back. 'No: I will go alone. I will go myself. They cannot treat us like this.'

'You may not have much choice,' the Colonel said.

'The choice is simple –'

'Bargain with them,' the Colonel said. He was very serious now. 'They'll understand a bargain. Parley with them. Say you will leave the nuns and ourselves and Dr Baretta here as a hospital staff for the wounded if they will evacuate the women and children.'

'Under supervision,' Crane said.

The priest, indecisively fumbling across his vest for his missing crucifix, looked as if he could no longer bear the weeping of the Sikh woman about to lose her hair.

133

'Very well,' he said. 'I will do that. I will say that.' He turned, preparing to go. 'I have to find Sister Teresalina and Dr Baretta's husband.' He rushed out of the wash-room, too late to hear the Colonel call:

'Under supervision, remember!'

'Whose supervision?' McAlister said.

'I know, I know,' the Colonel said. 'Don't tell me!' The nun looked almost frightened by his abrupt severity. Partly to hide it, partly because the noise of weeping was beginning as it always did to get on her nerves, she bent down and looked through the thick black skein of hair into the dark face of the Sikh woman hiding in shame in the shadow beneath it.

'Come on, sweetheart, we have to get this over,' the Colonel said. He revealed, suddenly, a quality of gentleness that took the edge of pain off the first slicing, quivering cut of his scissors.

The Indian women, brought in by McAlister, came in one by one for the next two or three hours: going out again with shortened hair, to be dressed in the corridor in Mrs Mathieson's dresses. About nine o'clock the Untouchable woman came in, carrying her baby. The priest had not come back. The child, disturbed by new surroundings, cried a little for some moments and the Meran woman uncovered a brown, shining, milk-swollen breast to feed the child while Crane and the Colonel snipped with scissors above. At rest, soothed by suckling and the attention of the two men, the Meran woman dissolved into languorous grins, entranced. The Colonel gave her some refined touches of attention, clipping a fringe across the dusky forehead, holding the scissors at the level of his eyes, squinting over them with mockery.

'She is not to be trusted if you look at her like that,' McAlister said. 'She will be after you.'

'Her hands are full,' the Colonel said.

'She is a free lance,' McAlister said. 'She is never too busy.'

'I am shocked,' the Colonel said. 'I thought you were not supposed to know of these things.'

'I come from Glasgow,' she said.

The Meran woman, moving the child from one breast to another, preparing voluptuously to settle down again, grinned blandly, but everyone laughed and the Colonel called: 'Next please!'

When finally the Meran woman, still suckling the child as she walked, had gone out of the wash-room, grinning back at the Colonel for the last time, Crane said:

'It's odd Father Simpson isn't back.'

'I've been thinking about him. It's very odd.' He opened the door of the wash-room and put his head into the corridor and called: 'How many more hair-cuts?'

The Meran woman, naked to the waist, in the moment before trying on a dress, was charmed. She grinned again and did not hurry to cover herself as McAlister, who was holding the baby, called:

'I think it's the lot. I'll find out. There may be one more.'

'Find out and bring her in.' He gazed openly and directly at the Meran woman, who stood unconcerned. 'Splendid figure.'

'Go away!'

The Colonel went back into the wash-room and shut the door.

'There may be one more,' he said. 'Will you hang on while I go to find out about the Father?'

'Right.' As the Colonel went out there was a moment of charmed laughter from the corridor outside. McAlister put her head through the doorway and said: 'I must ask you to see that the Colonel controls himself. After all, this is a Mission.' She stood by the door, smiling with that unprompted gracious-ness, the virginal and neutral sweetness, that had been the common grace of every nun since the shooting had begun.

'Very tired?' she said.

'Hellish.'

A Spitfire, patrolling the valley some considerable distance away to the west, beat the air with its whistling engines, but he was too tired to listen to it, to care whether it came closer or not, and she said something about 'I used to have some sleeping tablets. Dr Baretta gave them to me,' and went suddenly away, shutting the door quietly as if it had been the door of a sick-room.

135

He sat down in the chair, feeling a great hunger for a cigarette. He put one into his mouth and then, feeling in his pocket, remembered that the Colonel had taken his lighter the night before and in the pressure of hair-cutting had never brought it back. He sat there with the cigarette in his mouth, head down, staring at the mass of black hair of all lengths that had accumulated on the floor. Its stale oily fragrance, slightly musty, filled the little room. He felt himself actually pitching and drooping forward into sleep as he sat there, no thought in his head at all, his senses too sluggish even to notice the Spitfire had fired at something in a brief burst farther down the valley and had turned away.

Finally the cigarette fell out of his mouth and lay there before him on the floor, among the mass of hair. Too drugged and weary to pick it up, he swayed about, half-asleep, until at last the door opened and he looked up, expecting to see the Colonel or McAlister.

It was Julie Maxted instead. She stooped down and kissed him before he could move or speak. In acceptance he let the tenderness of it cover him passively, simply moving his hands sleepily up and down her body. Then he remembered McAlister and said: 'McAlister will be coming back. She's gone to fetch the other body. Lock the door.'

'McAlister isn't coming,' she said. 'There aren't any more.'

'No?'

'Only Kaushalya. And she refuses.'

'I'd forgotten her.'

'You can hardly blame her,' she said. 'After all, when this is over –'

'When, when, when,' he said. 'God –' He groped about with his hands, sleepily and stupidly. She took them and put them round her body, up by her sides so that he could feel the breasts strained momentarily in the act of accepting him, and then up beyond her arms until they were folded across her back.

'Hold on to me,' she said. 'Keep there. Let me hold you there.'

Pressing his head against her body, shutting his eyes, he heard her voice as if from very far away quietly saying something about the wounded occupying the central ward. It seemed of little importance even when she said:

'The officer has been wounded too. Sikander Shah.'

'I couldn't care.'

'I think it's bad. They came to fetch Dr Baretta.'

'Let him rot,' he said. He remembered the scene in the orchard: no trucks, war is war, in war there are no guarantees about anything: only, as the Colonel said, etiquette. Now, he thought, the officer too knows what etiquette can be.

A door along the corridor opened and shut. He heard footsteps; the moment of privacy, so hard to get, was about to be broken. With hurried and painful tenderness she bent down and kissed him again. 'I love you so much,' she said. 'I can't bear it. I can't sleep for thinking of it –'

McAlister blundered in. 'Pardon!' she said, and went immediately out again, shutting the door.

'Come back!' he shouted.

McAlister, this time, knocked on the door. 'Come in,' he said.

She came in with a certain strained demureness, with bright pale eyes looking down.

'I came to bring the sleeping tablets and a message from Colonel Mathieson. He says please go along to the central ward.'

She held out the small white box of tablets. He stood up. 'Let Miss Maxted have the tablets,' he said. 'She hasn't been sleeping well.'

She gave the tablets to Miss Maxted, grinning with oblique demureness. 'Will I go or will I wait for her?'

'You will go,' he said.

'I heard you the first time,' she said and went out of the door with swift quietness, with a sliding neutrality that had in it a hint of mockery.

'I want you to see that she gets some sleep!' he called.

But the door closed and from beyond it there was no answer; nor the sound of footsteps. He looked down at the girl, smiling. 'She's probably on guard, waiting,' he said, but she simply parted her lips, holding them for him. 'I could sleep with you here, like this,' he said and held her with rigid weariness against the shape of his body.

'Don't,' she said. 'I can't bear it. It's no place to talk of such things –'

'Please get some sleep, anyhow,' he said.

'I'm not tired,' she said. 'I'm really not tired.' She tried to smile and succeeded only in weeping with enormous soundless tears. 'Only terribly empty sometimes – terribly, awfully empty inside.'

'Oh! my God,' he said.

He kissed her again and it was like kissing a person partly asleep already. He felt her tears on his face. McAlister coughed in the corridor outside. He was glad of it and said: 'Your bodyguard is waiting. You'd better go with her. You'd better get some sleep somewhere.'

'She's very sweet.'

'I love her,' he said.

The remark seemed to wake her, bringing her to life. 'Then you'd better stop loving her. She is one of those thwarted creatures who express it in other ways and –'

'You mustn't say such things,' he said. 'When we get out of this I must take you in hand. I will teach you etiquette.'

'When,' she said. 'When.'

'The Colonel may have news,' he said. 'We may be able to evacuate you.'

He kissed her again before he went along the corridor a few moments later, feeling unbearably severed and confused and lonely without her. He had the impression that the days since he had first seen her had swollen into years of incredibly slow substance that were incalculable, that would not drag themselves by.

Going into the central ward, for the first time since Mrs Maxted had died, he felt it large and empty by contrast with the little ward beyond the corridor, insufferably crowded with its women and children, the piano and the beds, the priests and the attendant nuns. Here, placed at the farther end, closer to the windows, for better light, he could see only four floor beds, occupied now by wounded Pathans. Then he saw a fifth, along under the opposite wall, with Dr Baretta and Colonel Mathieson standing beside it, talking; and a young nun, looking very much like Sister Courbet, waiting a few paces away. There was no sign of Father Simpson. Beyond the big windows it was so sunny, with the high fresh brilliance of mountain autumn, the sky blue and very lofty, that he felt an agony of longing to walk out there, down among the bare red peach-boughs, beyond the terraces, to smell snow and drive the sour horrors out of his nostrils and be free. Half-way down the room Colonel Mathieson came to meet him. They met by the beds of the four wounded Pathans, who lay staring under brown blankets drawn up to their chins as if to give support to savage and flattened moustaches.

'It's Sikander Shah,' the Colonel said. 'He bought it in both legs. Cannon-shell. He's pretty bad.'

'How bad?'

'About as bad as it can be. One leg will certainly go.'

'It will be a charming situation if he leaves us,' Crane said.

'Charming.'

'Where's Father Simpson?' Crane said. 'Did he parley?'

'I don't know. No one seems to have seen him,' the Colonel said. He turned, looking at the four wounded Pathans. 'There's another bad one here. The third along. They were all in a truck.'

Crane looked at the face of the third Pathan. Held rigid, drained of blood, it had something of the colour and texture of bleached brown paper. Under this it held for him a curious sort of familiarity and he said:

'He is one of our friends of last night. One of the woman hunters.'

The Colonel looked across at the Pathan indifferently. 'A diet of cannon-shell in the belly will make a nice change from raw meat and females.'

He put his hand in his trousers pocket, bringing out Crane's lighter. 'I am so sorry about it. I completely forgot. Is the hair-dressing done?'

'All but Kaushalya, who refuses.'

'Good for Kaushalya.'

'She has never spoken a word. She has never opened her lips. She just sits there.' Crane pulled out his cigarette case and held it to the Colonel, but the Colonel, who was looking at the four Pathans, shook his head.

But suddenly, rather savagely, he took one. He lit it clumsily and hurriedly, pulling at it once or twice; and then took it over to the third of the wounded Pathans, who accepted it between cruelly tired lips, from under a twist of fantastic moustaches.

The Colonel strode savagely up the ward. 'I just can't stand there,' he said, and Crane followed, scrutinized by wounded faces.

Calmly, with delicate dignity, Dr Baretta came a few paces down the ward. She smiled with an unembittered sadness made infinitely fragile by lack of sleep.

'What is the verdict?' the Colonel said.

'I should amputate the right leg,' she said. 'But there are no anaesthetics. We have nothing at all.'

'Must the leg come off?' the Colonel said. 'Is it absolutely imperative?'

'It is practically amputated now – there is practically nothing left –'

'It would be better to tell him,' the Colonel said. 'If you agree.'

He walked slowly up the ward. Dr Baretta did not protest. The Colonel stooped down by the Afridi officer, resting on one knee.

'How do you feel?' he said.

'I am just a little tired,' the officer said. He stared at the ceiling. 'I think I was knocked out.'

'I have something to tell you.'

'Please.'

'Would you care for a cigarette?' the Colonel said. 'Mr Crane has some if it would help you.'

'Who is Mr Crane?'

'He is the man from Bombay. From the newspaper.'

'Ah, yes!' Up to that moment the Afridi officer had spoken without the slightest deflection of his frozen stare at the ceiling.

Now he turned to the Colonel with a curiously sculptured formal smile. 'What was it you were going to tell me?'

'It is going to be necessary to amputate your right leg.' The Colonel felt himself begin to sweat unhappily, in distress.

'I see.'

'They asked me to tell you there is no anaesthetic – Dr Baretta cannot –'

'There is no need to tell me.'

The face of the Afridi re-averted itself, resuming more frigidly the straight upward stare at the ceiling. The Colonel, sweating and trembling a little, got up. Down the ward Sister Courbet, at Dr Baretta's request, walked away to find McAlister, her heels beating hard on the bare wooden floor. As their echoes passed away the Colonel moved a little away from the bed and the Afridi officer, his stare unchanged, spoke again.

'Is the young priest here?'

'No,' the Colonel said. 'He is not here.'

'When he comes, would it be possible to speak to him?'

'I think so.'

'Thank you. Will you find him –?'

'No more talking, I think,' Dr Baretta said. The Colonel moved finally away from the bed, trembling, wiping in a dazed way the sweat from the cup of his neck. 'We will try to get him ready.'

The Colonel and Crane walked down the ward. Through the door at the far end McAlister came in with Sister Courbet and another nun, and the Colonel said:

'Has Father Simpson reappeared?'

'Not to my knowledge,' McAlister said.

'He is not in the other ward,' said Sister Courbet. 'Shall I look for him?'

The Colonel walked on. 'It's rather odd,' he began, but Crane had stopped. McAlister had stopped too and it seemed to Crane that she looked upset.

'Mr Crane, I was rude to you and I am very sorry,' she said.

'You were not rude and it doesn't matter.'

'I was awful rude. I can't control myself.'

Crane smiled. 'We're all rude to each other and if we weren't we'd go off our nuts. Did you make her rest?' he said.

'I think she's asleep already.'

'It was very sweet of you,' Crane said. He grinned again. 'You have work to do. Did you remember to bring your carving knife?'

'Help me to be serious, please!' she said. There were pleading tears of affection and distress in her pale clear eyes. 'You don't help at all.'

'I'm sorry.'

She walked away up the ward and he turned and went through the door to where, in the corridor outside, the Colonel was coming back to meet him.

'I'm beginning not to like this,' the Colonel said. 'Nobody can find Father Simpson.'

15

Dr Baretta came back into the ward in the early afternoon. For a person so spare, so fleshless that she was like a peeled stick in her white hospital coat, she moved with strides of assurance, delicately and strongly. Three of the four wounded Pathans watched her as she passed; the fourth, too ill and now half-conscious, had turned away his face in some pre-comatose struggle and lay glassily gazing at the autumn afternoon beyond the windows. She went on to Sikander Shah. There had really been very little left of the leg and McAlister, who had seen these things in Burma and had no squeamishness about them, had been very wonderful and they had done what was necessary together.

She was surprised to find Sikander Shah awake and conscious. The traditional ferocious tribal toughness had been hardened through the fire of the experience and now it increased as he looked up and saw who she was. He had been put into a proper hospital bed moved from the smaller ward. It had had the effect not of raising him up but of transforming him from a merely crushed idol of flesh and bone to a figure with a curiously lethal and vicious stare that shocked her. She had in fact never really seen him until the moment she had been summoned to look at him that morning; she did not know of his tribal-convent conflicts; she was unaware that his ancestors had been kings; and he in turn had hardly been, in the first brutal hour or so of pain, aware of her.

Sister Courbet had followed her up the ward and now unhooked the chart from the end of the bed. Dr Baretta read its records and gave it back to her. She had not intended to do more than that and she was actually moving away from the bed when he called quite strongly after her:

'Where is the young priest?'

'He is not back.' She stood a little closer to the bed. 'It is no time to talk now.'

'I shall talk if I want to.' His lips were down-drawn in carved contempt.

'I am going to send you some sleeping tablets and you must not talk –'

'You are not Hindu,' he said.

She did not speak. The Pathan whose belly had been shot out by Tempest cannon-shell began coughing weakly, retching, and Sister Courbet moved away, leaving the doctor and the Afridi officer alone together.

'When I first saw you I thought you were English,' he said. 'I couldn't see very well. You are not anybody. I see that.'

She did not answer. She wanted to move away but for some reason she could not move; she felt transfixed by the furious magnetism of the Afridi's eyes, by naked dark contempt. She saw his tongue exploring with quivering thrusts the front of his mouth, as if he were gathering spittle. The accentuated jaw-bone, pale from loss of blood, sprang elastically to reveal white teeth.

'You are a tar-brush,' he said.

She did not answer. We could of course have killed you where you lay, she thought; and indeed there had been an odd moment, she now remembered, when McAlister had stood looking down at the bed with a sort of murderously bemused tension, a transitory moment of controlled antagonism held back like a catapult ready to fire.

'Get the young priest,' he said. 'I want to be taken out of here. I will not be mauled by parasites.'

Her eyes were simply fragments of glass in which there seemed to be no moisture at all. Her frail body, too tired to move or answer, seemed to have so little substance left that it could not fill its ducts with tears.

She made a great effort not to show these things and then saw, with amazement, that he was trying to support himself with his elbows and get up from the bed. All the incredibly indomitable tribal toughness leapt vividly into his face. She moved instinctively to hold him down. He spat out at her:

'Don't touch me! Keep your hands off me.'

She stood still, her strength gone. Her resources. dammed up, desperately holding back all her grief, her lonely bewilderment since her husband had gone out and never come back, broke suddenly down. She lifted her hands to her face, feeling tears flying up through her body in a broken flood. From the bed he spat something else at her, struggling once more to get up, and at that moment McAlister came up the ward.

'What goes on! What goes on!' she said. 'What goes on!'

She went past Dr Baretta and in a single movement of both hands, rather as if twisting a wet cloth, seized the shoulders of the Afridi officer and pinned him down.

He tried to say something, glaring at her with black eyes shot yellow now with streaks of sick exhaustion, and she snapped:

'Don't try any of your hanky-pankies with me or I'll whip your head off and show it to you.'

Unamused, faint and yellow now, he began: 'I want to –'

'Shut up!' she said.

'I –'

'Shut up I tell you! Shut up!'

A second later, almost as if driven to it by his own ferocity, he fainted clean away on the bed. There was a rush towards him from Dr Baretta and Sister Courbet, who had been standing apart by the other beds in frozen meek suspense, listening; but McAlister stood in front of Dr Baretta, holding her back.

'We can cope,' she said. 'What was it? What was wrong?'

'He wants to be taken out of here.'

'Wonderful,' McAlister said. 'Let's all go.'

'He has to be kept very quiet – it is quite impossible –'

'He's for the high jump anyway,' McAlister said.

Dr Baretta stood crying, tears floating with a curious bleaching effect down her face, giving it streaks of pallor.

'Don't cry,' McAlister said. Her incongruous gentleness flowed smoothly out, warming her voice. 'Don't cry, please.'

She put her arms about the doctor's waist. 'I love you. We all love you. There's no need to cry. We love you.'

'I am crying because I am tired.'

'If he wants to go so badly,' McAlister said, 'we might use it to get us all out.' She remembered the Colonel's suggestion of a bargain, a parley. 'Maybe we can bargain to get the women and children out. Don't cry. Have a wee lie-back somewhere.'

She pushed the doctor gently away down the ward. A Pathan made guttural noises like an appealing mute, pointing down at his bed. The doctor turned to attend, and McAlister went with swift steps after her.

'Away you go,' she said. 'Away. Out, out! He'll only be wanting a bottle or something and the blessed Virgin knows we can deal with that.'

Dr Baretta walked down the ward and through the corridor into the smaller ward beyond. After the big almost empty room isolated in the centre of the Mission it was very noisy there. Twice in the earlier afternoon a Tempest and two Spitfires had come up the valley, roaring fire into the lorry-park, empty except for the two trucks that had brought back the wounded up the hill. Cannon-shell had smashed the windows of the kitchen, hurting no one but setting every woman and child screaming with frenzy. It had taken some time again to calm the children down and finally Father Anstey had succeeded by giving lessons in English on a blackboard. There had been a few songs on the piano too and on the blackboard Father Anstey had written in chalk, largely, 'The cat ate the rat' and 'God is Good', so that now the air was full of the chanting recitation of small voices speaking primitive English in strange accents. The women too had been calmed by these things and sat about on floors, on beds, and on chairs with a strange shorn, stilted Anglo-Indian dowdiness, wearing Mrs Mathieson's dresses; all of them looking, Dr Baretta thought as she came in, half Indian, half European, their shortened hair stripped of adornments that would betray them.

Only Kaushalya was dressed as she had always dressed. Flamboyantly, sulkily, holding her head back against the wall, she squatted there smoking, dreamily watching Father Anstey. He had played several gay little tunes on the piano and was now beginning, in Hindu, with local variations, the story of the three bears. 'A very old story,' he said and Dr Baretta, looking on at it all, smiling, saw that Father Simpson had not come back.

16

In the confusion brought about by the wounded coming in at the main door of the Mission in the early morning the two guards had rushed out across the terrace, leaving the main door free for the first time since the raid had begun. Father Simpson in his blind anxiety to find Sikander Shah had blundered through the entire length of the ward before he saw the officer lying under the window just inside the door. He stopped to speak to him. He was thinking of nothing but the Colonel's excellent notion of getting the whole Mission evacuated by bargain; and then he saw that the Afridi officer, as if horrified at the descendant of kings being seen in the attitude of shattered mutilation, crushed by pain, had covered his face with both hands. The priest did in fact call his name but the hands, hideously clenched, did not fall away from the face and the priest did not repeat his call. Instead he saw that the main door was open and unguarded; and, in a moment, blundering and joyful and caring no longer for the Colonel's notion of bargaining or for Sikander Shah, he was through it and free.

He walked directly away towards the chapel, and in two or three seconds was beyond the cypress trees. That part of the garden had run very wild. Summer weeds and grass, under hot sun, had grown up to six or seven feet like thick bleached corn among dense masses of rhododendron. He disturbed a flock of minah-birds and they rose in a talkative black burst, scooping away down the terraces, here so disused that they were simply like the steps of a green waterfall rolling away into rocky scrub and woodland.

In the middle of it, blundering downhill, he slipped and fell. The smack of his body on rock and prickles brought him to his senses. He sat still. Since the moment of rushing out of the main doorway it had not once occurred to him why he was running. Now he remembered his impassioned, impatient anxieties in the wash-room.

He sat for some moments and said a prayer. He still had not found his crucifix. Even now it was difficult to restrain himself from fiddling for it across his bosom whenever he prayed. But now he did not mind very much. He was free; he need not go back; his purposes were superbly and simply manifest. Nothing need take him back until he had found Sister Teresalina and Dr Baretta's husband.

How he was to do these things was not quite clear. He sat looking at the mountains. A section of the snows of Nanga Parbat was quite clear. The sun on the eastern side had given the glacial face a vivid transparence; the great cols were flashing blue. He sat and said another prayer; this time with open eyes. I am in the wilderness, he thought, and I do not know which way to go; others have been in the wilderness before me and God has guided them. Indeed it is the substance and basis, he thought, of all we are: we are lost, each of us, severally and personally, in the wilderness of our time and it is by God and through God that we are found again.

It seemed suddenly very simple. He was still wearing only his vest and trousers and he sat fiddling with his braces. He looked down at the valley below. There was nearly always a little wind, even on the hottest days, from the direction of the snows, and now already it was stirring across the rice-fields, pushing back the smoke of the burning village on the other side of the gorge.

Through clearing smoke was revealed a peasant and his cow, dragging a plough across yellow rice stubble, the cow looking not much larger than a grey goat behind the primitive wooden share. Beyond them a fresh lifting of smoke disclosed the river, with road and bullock track, wrecked trucks under plane-trees, and the collection of moored house-boats that Father Anstey had seen. One of the boats was still smouldering like a large cigar.

He remembered then, with horror sharpened by three days of complete forgetfulness, Miss Jordan and Miss Shanks. In the distressing chaos at the Mission they had never been once in his mind.

He offered a prayer for Miss Jordan and Miss Shanks, again fiddling with his braces, now firmly shutting his eyes. When he opened them again the smoke in the valley had been driven still further back. A few white egrets had been disturbed by the plough. There was no shooting across the gorge; he could see wind shaking leaves from the boughs of the plane-trees; and now, all horror behind him, it was difficult not to believe that he was alone there in the tranquillity of an unblemished day.

Trapped by these deceptions and the beauty of the morning into a frame of mind that was almost exultant he went down the hill. His purpose had become suddenly clear; he was determined to search the Mission gardens from end to end, beginning with the farther lower boundaries, where nothing grew but wild pear and acacias and a few flimsy birches, and working up through the cultivated terraces of peach and vine to the arbours of cypress behind the chapel.

He crashed down the hill. Where he could not move the thick speared growth of weed and grass with his feet he turned and pushed through it backwards, sweating and blundering, ramming a way through with his great backside, making the crackling noise of running flame.

It took him until nearly eleven o'clock to beat his way along the entire length of wooded boundaries down the slope. By that time the sun was very hot and all the shining crust of Nanga Parbat was clear, its iciness no longer blue but paler, whiter, like a mountain of starch. He sat down on the lowest of the cultivated terraces and looked at it, sweating and hungry, feeling how splendidly and stereoscopically near it looked, and offered another prayer.

This combination of prayer and hunger brought a curious lightness to his brain, inducing an odd sense of cunning. Three days of banter under the tautness of hideous circumstances with Crane and Mathieson had sharpened his wits.

He thought of the Pathans.

'Like all Indians,' he thought, 'they will start eating before noon and if they get half a chance they'll sleep too.' In India,

150

he sometimes thought, there was more sleep by day than anywhere in the world. Always all over India incalculable millions of bodies were curled up on house-steps, under trees, by open shops, in fields, in the darkest recesses of shops: heat-stunned, hunger-drained carcasses rolled in dhotis that covered them like absorbing sweat cloths. He did not suppose the Pathans were very different. And if they are not different, he thought, it will be very quiet for an hour or so and I can explore the upper terraces and those behind the chapel.

He sat thinking of all this, glad that he had been able to collect thoughts that had always been so malleable and shapeless and wandering, and beat them into shape. It was rather what the Colonel would do, he thought. You had to be sharp. You had to think things out.

Thinking of the Colonel, he crawled on his belly up the slope to where, just below a potato-patch on which Father Anstey had surprised him on Saturday morning with what had then seemed so cruel a joke about the rabbits, he could see almost all the western side of the upper terrace, with the Pathan trucks parked beyond the orchard.

He did not stop there. His progress had the impulse of a hazy kind of divination. His head, from hunger, was very light and clear. He crawled to the extreme edge of the potato-patch and lay down. When the potatoes were up he was going to plant raspberry canes. It would be a splendid place for them: not only because the soil had been furrowed up but because he could have plenty of water. Beyond the edge of the potato-patch was the second of two wells that supplied the gardens. He had planted it round with cypresses only two years before. Now the trees were ten to twelve feet high, in a wide black-green square.

His recollection of the well, combined with the fact that he suddenly saw his garden fork standing where he had left it in his shameful haste on Saturday morning, made him very glad. The fork was a real English pattern, with four tines: he had got a Kashmiri smith to make it at the forge. Potatoes were lying about where he had left them, greened now by exposure to sun. There had been one of the big flat oval native baskets there too, but now it had gone. Perhaps Father Anstey had taken it up for him, he thought.

'I can drink now even if I can't eat,' he thought. 'I can rest and then I can go on searching.' He had crawled sloppily on his belly up the steps, like a grovelling and sniffing hound, and now his mouth was parched.

Over beyond the edge of the potato-patch was a screen of acacias and he was able to walk the last twenty or thirty paces to the square of cypresses about the well.

When he arrived there he wanted to shout with horror and joy and the shock of what he saw. He stood with huge mouth open, hands groping across his chest. All his curious blundering divinations, it seemed, had finally and incredibly flowered to revelation.

'Sister!' he said. 'Oh! Sister – Sister Teresalina! – Sister –'

She was sitting on one of the rocks that had been unearthed at the time of the digging of the well. By her side was the wicker basket brought from his potatoes. She had on her face a stunned watchfulness. It was so dead that for several moments he could not believe in the miraculous fact of her living.

And then she spoke to him.

'I knew it could only be you,' she said. 'You were so noisy. I could hear you coming all the way.'

She did not move for several minutes from the stone. He noticed that she looked straight past him, eyes apparently fixed on Nanga Parbat. Without tension, still neutral and stunned, she managed at the same time to convey an impression of being transfixed by something unforgettably awful. During these first few minutes before she got up he sat holding her hands.

All of a sudden she said, flatly, still staring: 'He is in the well. He was alive. They put him there. For quite a long time he was alive,' and he knew that she was talking of Dr Baretta's husband.

Stricken by a terrible sense of inadequacy, of being hopelessly equipped both as priest and man for revelation so fiendishly shocking, he was reduced once more to a trembling heap of flesh. He felt sweat streaming from him, in the hot noon sun; his whole body seemed to be in feverish dissolution.

'That's why I didn't come back,' she said. 'They dragged him along on his face. I could hear him screaming all the way. I was in the vines with the women when they went by –'

He felt he could no longer bear to hear these things. He plunged his head into his hands in groping, extinguishing thrusts of pain. 'I was frightened too,' she said.

When he looked up again she had got up from the stone. She walked away to the gap in the cypresses. He groped to his feet and walked after her. 'You must come back now. I will take you back,' he said.

She turned her face to him in a wooden smile. After the tension by sheer weariness the skin of her cheeks had fallen in loose collapse, sagging agedly from the bone. She seemed, he thought, more Spanish than ever: dark-eyed, racked by ageless and incomprehensible suffering, like a carved and tortured wooden saint.

She gazed at him as if not knowing what he said. He repeated: 'I will take you back. Are you strong enough? Can you walk?'

'I will stay here,' she said.

'Oh! No, no, no,' he said.

'You go.'

'Oh! My dear Sister – my God –' Shaken once again by his own inadequacy, he relapsed into incoherence, fumbling with his braces.

She said quite simply: 'I will wait here till you come back.' Her English, with its stiff, hard, almost masculine Spanish accent, had an effect of being recited, of being incontrovertibly pre-ordained. He made ineffective noises of denial and protest, spluttering; and she went on:

'I have waited here so long. It will not matter if I wait a little longer. I could not bear to go now. I will sit here to wait for you.'

'But after all this – you're exhausted – it's very terrible – you –'

'I can wait for you,' she said.

It had not occurred to him until that moment how exacting his task was. The distressing necessity of going back to the

153

Mission, of revealing the things he had found, was suddenly put for him by Sister Teresalina, who said:

'You must go to Greta.'

'Yes,' he said. 'Yes. Yes.'

He began to see it now: he was the bearer, by force of the bitterest ironies, of good tidings and bad tidings; he had come out into the wilderness asking for guidance and now he had guidance; he must go alone not simply because it was, in a sense, a sort of cross of responsibility that circumstances had pitched on him to bear, but because in a purely practical way it was safer. He remembered the Pathans.

'They will be eating. It's a good time to go. I will speak to the officer and I will be back in ten minutes.'

'He died yesterday,' she said. 'I heard all your prayers for the dead when you buried them up in the orchard. Are there many dead?'

Looking away, he did not answer.

'I think it must be,' she said.

Another attack of nerves made him tremble again in the very moment that she turned and sat down again on the stone. When he looked at her he saw that her look of stunned and dreamy neutrality had returned. She was staring down over the valley. Across the rice-fields smoke had cleared completely at last, revealing all the beauty of the earth flanked by forest, of dying plane-trees lining the brown fast river, of distant flashing snows.

'I will sit and look at Nanga Parbat until you come back,' she said. 'It has been very wonderful. I even saw it at night.'

Shattered by that final revelation he fled up the slope.

He was a little more than half-way up the terrace of peach-trees when he saw the two Afridi guards, rifles at the ready, coming down the path. He did not know that Sikander Shah had asked for him: first through the Colonel, then a few moments before the amputation of his leg through McAlister, who had been so impatient and fed up with such a request at such a moment that she had obeyed his order and called in one of the guards. The guard was the Afridi who had come in looking for women the previous night. He had been down in the village, burning houses, and had found women there; he was liverish and foul-tempered and truculent at being sent for by Sikander Shah, who was too stiff on discipline and small matters like tribal diversions and excursions into women-baiting that were as natural a part of fighting as killing Hindus. There were too many Hindus, as everyone knew. There were too many priests. Hindu males were meant to be butchered and Hindu females were meant to be raped; and he did not much care for officers, trained anyway by the British, who interfered with the natural elemental rules in these things.

When Father Simpson saw the two Afridis coming for him down the path he was torn between an extraordinary curiosity and a desire to run. His curiosity came from the fact that he felt he was really seeing the Afridis for the first time. Both of them were big men, turbaned and moustached, with long-skirted jackets belted by old-fashioned cartridge bandoliers in which they carried daggers. The younger had also a battle-worn duffle-coat stolen from an American officer who three years before had come up into the hills on leave. Their trousers fell baggily into folds above black and khaki puttees.

A moment later he turned aside from the path and began to run. For the Afridis the prospect of taking him calmly back to the hospital ward in an orderly fashion at the request of an officer changed in a moment to a ramp. As Father Simpson rushed through the avenues of peach-trees the Afridis were struck into delight by his blundering flabbiness. He was running and frightened; he had all the clumsy terror of a stricken animal who must be caught and baited.

They cut him off at the end of the plantation of peaches, below the orchard. He turned on them, roaring and stabbing at the air with both hands.

'Leave me alone! Leave me alone! I wish to see Sikander Shah! Leave me alone!'

The Afridis, laughing, seized him by both arms and began frog-marching him up the slope. He stumbled and fell on his knees, twisting himself free. He kicked out with both legs, cracking the elder Afridi on the shin, and the Afridi, not laughing, remembering the previous night, hit him across the spine with the rifle-butt. Father Simpson fell down. As his face crushed down on dry earth the Afridi hit him again with the rifle, beating him across the back somewhere about the point where his braces were buttoned. The force of the beating broke the buttons and the braces popped free. The Afridis howled with wild laughter and the younger took hold of the priest's trousers and wrenched them down. Father Simpson, turning, lashed out with both legs but the Afridis were too quick this time and simply hit the legs with rifle-butts as they flayed about the air. His kicking loosened his trousers still further and finally the Afridis seized his arms and dragged him to his feet so that the trousers fell down altogether. The priest stooped to pull them up and the younger Afridi, laughing, hit him in the buttocks with the rifle-butt so that he fell down again, pitching into the dust on his face. Again as he lay there the Afridis picked him up and again his trousers fell down. It was very funny, the elder Afridi thought, much funnier than when they had hit him in the face the previous night with the lamp, and he knocked him down again.

At the fourth or fifth fall Father Simpson made a savage lunge about him as he got up again. His trousers had now fallen completely over his boots, and he hit the elder Afridi full in the mouth with his fist. The blow the Afridi gave him in return was not only in answer to it. It was part of the Afridi's hatred of all priests, all British, all thwarters of soldiers' rights, all discipline; it came out of a boorish savagery left from his wild excursion of the previous night. It was delivered with a full-swing of the rifle-butt. It caught Father Simpson across the side of the head, below the left ear, knocking him down and out like a top-heavy ninepin, so completely and neatly that the Afridis roared with laughter at his scrambling futility to cover the fat white flesh of his legs and to get to his feet at the same time. Much better than being on guard at the Mission door, the elder thought, much better even than burning houses, almost as good as the first night at the Mission – and then suddenly Father Simpson got to his feet.

In the act of getting up his trousers fell down again. He did not care about that but with his free right hand he struck the elder Afridi across the ear. The blow did not hurt much and the Afridi, in contempt, put out his tongue and gave a belching sort of leer. It was something between an insult and a taunt and it goaded Father Simpson to final impulses of rage. He lashed across with his right foot and kicked the Afridi between crutch and thigh.

The Afridi, who had laughed so much that he felt like crying, now actually cried for a moment with sickening pain as he staggered down the bank and then recoiled. It was getting too much, he thought. With furious precision he hit the priest in the chest with the rifle-butt, just above the heart. The priest fell back on the bank, trouserless, stunned, holding his hands before his face. As he lay there, unable to get up, the Afridis hit him several times more, about the head, the chest, and on the lower naked parts of the body, jabbing the red imprint of rifle-butts on the white fat flesh like the marks of an enormous rubber stamp.

This systematic bludgeoning was halted by a voice yelling from the lorry-park. From the edge of the top terrace a small figure in khaki shorts, turbanless, brown and squeaking, came out from the trucks to shout that it was dinner-time. The elder Afridi, bored finally with the bloodiness and very hungry, hit the priest for the last time and turned away. The other had a new idea. He pulled out his dagger and slit the laces of Father Simpson's boots and then lugged the boots and threw them into his face. That made both the Afridis laugh again. And this final leer of laughter, with the blow of the boots on his face, was the last thing the priest remembered.

Half-way up the terrace the Afridis met the figure who had shouted at them. He was a tight-headed Pathan boy of twelve or thirteen who was carrying in his hand the ram-rod of a shot-gun. He came to meet them running, shouting that it was dinner-time. He had seen them bludgeoning the priest. It was his first war and he had had great fun following the Pathans about, riding on the backs of trucks, picking up bits of loot like ram-rods and cartridge cases and belt buckles; he had picked up besides the ram-rod a British army webbing belt and even a few cartridges.

As he ran down the terrace he began shouting loudly to the Afridis something about the officer Sikander Shah sending out an order to look for them. The elder Afridi, who hated officers and their interference and had wanted to take it out a little more on the priest, hit the boy with liverish fury across the face, telling him to keep his mouth shut. The other snatched the ram-rod out of his hand and swiped him with it, cutting his legs below the short khaki trousers.

As the Afridi strode up the slope with the ram-rod the boy ran after him, pleading for it. The Afridi took another cut at him and then threw the ram-rod thirty or forty yards down the slope behind him.

As the boy went back to fetch it he was crying not so much from the pain of the cuts across his bare legs as from the awful abruptness of his rejection. He couldn't for the life of him understand these things; he hadn't the vaguest idea what he had done to be beaten. He walked down the slope, crying, and picked up the ram-rod.

He stood with it on the path, looking down. He saw the priest, fifty or sixty yards farther on, lying on the bank, and he remembered watching the Afridis beating him. He walked down the path. When he saw the bruised and partly trouserless figure unconscious on the bank, with its boots lying against its face, he felt that the priest and himself were victims of the same thing. The Afridis had had a beating-up party and the priest was dead.

The boy crawled up the bank and lay down by Father Simpson.

'Sahib,' he said. The priest was so enormous and even in his beaten state so obviously an important person that he changed his mind and said 'Burra sahib. Sahib. Burra sahib.'

The priest was sick where he lay. For some moments he turned his head away from the boy, retching, letting bloody spittle and sickness ooze away down the bank of grass. When it was over he felt better.

'Where did you come from?' he said.

'Sahib?' the boy said. 'Burra sahib?'

'You speak English?'

'Little, little,' the boy said.

'Pathan boy?'

'Pathan,' the boy said. 'Pathan, yes, Pathan.'

'What do they call you?'

'Sahib?'

'Name?'

'Pir Dil Khan,' the boy said.

Father Simpson lay looking at the boy, too sick to get up. He saw that the boy had been crying; he could not guess why. The boy had the ram-rod in his hand and he could not guess about that either.

'What are you doing here?' he said. 'What is this?'

'Sahib?'

'This,' the priest said. He pointed to the ram-rod.

'Gun,' the boy said. 'Is for gun.' He held it to his shoulder like a rifle and the priest smiled.

He tried to pull up his trousers. He felt terribly sick and strengthless; but for some reason the trousers came up easily and he discovered the boy was helping him. He put his hand in his trousers pocket trying to find his handkerchief so that he could wipe away his sickness. Suddenly all the bruises of his ribs met in a single obliterating constriction across the heart, blackening him out again, and the handkerchief seemed simply to float away.

When he came round again the boy had wiped his face clean. He felt a little better. There was more blood in his mouth and he was very thirsty, weakly holding out his tongue.

'Water,' the boy said. 'Water. I fetch water, sahib.'

The priest, electrified by the simple mention of water, remembered Sister Teresalina; he remembered everything now that had happened. There crowded on him the accumulated hideous events of the well.

He sat up for the first time. For some moments he seemed to be centralized on a spit driven clean through his body. He was whirled about in sickening gyrations of darkening and lightening pain. He made a great effort to conquer these things. He managed slowly to stand up. The boy held him by one hand while he himself held up his trousers with the other.

At the edge of the terrace, below the orchard, he paused to conquer another wave of sickness and get his breath. He looked wildly and vaguely about him from bloody eyes. To the boy it seemed as if he were suddenly afraid and he said:

'Pathans gone. Pathans – no Pathans. Pathans gone. Afridi gone. No Afridi.'

It occurred to the priest then that the boy had seen the beating.

'You see Afridis?' he said. 'Down there? You see?'

'Sahib,' the boy said. He gave the curious oblique signal of the head, half-negative, half-positive, that meant yes. 'Sahib.' He waved the stick. 'Sahib. Sahib.'

Father Simpson turned and searched him with bloody eyes, speaking slowly from thickened lips.

'You must not speak,' he said.

'Yes, sahib!' the boy said. 'Yes, sahib!'

'No speak,' the priest said.

'No, sahib! No, sahib!' the boy said. He remembered the Afridis; he remembered what had come of that.

'You must not say what you saw,' the priest said. He moved forward up the slope, weakly, talking almost to himself, blundering slowly towards the final terrace, the boy holding him with both hands.

'No!' the boy said. 'No speak, sahib.' He was joyful and determined and not crying now. 'No speak!'

He knew now what happened after speaking. He had learnt the lesson of that.

17

Sikander Shah continued to ask for the priest for the rest of the day and occasionally through the night; but Father Simpson slept till seven o'clock the next morning, when Father Anstey found him awake in his own bed in the kitchen. Tortured by thoughts of Dr Baretta's husband, by the sudden appearance of the younger battered priest the previous afternoon and then by the spectral figure of Sister Teresalina, amazingly smiling, some time later, Father Anstey had not slept. He had spent most of the night in the central ward. At eleven o'clock another truck, bringing wounded, had driven in from the front, and soon after midnight a solitary Pathan had walked in, forearm shattered, to sit calmly on the ground of the ward until McAlister could dress his wounds. Most of the nuns were working with sweet and unhurried assurance among the beds; and all night the elder priest watched Dr. Baretta operating, under a small oil-lamp, with unshattered calm, on silent and complaintless Pathans.

Father Simpson, waking in the kitchen, could not for some moments remember where he was. When he saw Father Anstey standing over the bed he was at once reminded, as he had been before, of his awful moment of forgetfulness among the potatoes: how Father Anstey had teased him about the rabbits, how he had forgotten Crane.

He tried to struggle out of bed. He spoke vaguely and feverishly about his rabbits. Father Anstey said simply: 'They are all right. The boy has fed them. Twice yesterday and once to-day. They will probably get pot-bellied if he goes on like this.'

'The boy?'

'You remember – you asked him. It was the last thing you asked him before you came to lie down.'

'What boy?' He could not remember anything of these things. Distraught and sick, he simply looked about him, only to discover that the elder priest had gone. He tried once again to get out of bed and then saw, five seconds later, that the priest had come back.

'This boy,' Father Anstey said.

Father Simpson remembered. 'Pir Dil Khan,' he said.

The boy, still carrying the ram-rod, greeted this recognition with an enormous smile and a packet of cigarettes. 'No speak,' he said. 'No speak.' He held out the cigarettes.

'I think he stole them from Crane,' Father Anstey said.

'Steal?' Father Simpson said. 'Did you steal?'

'Yes, sahib. Steal,' the boy said. 'Steal. For you.'

'Everything is for you,' Father Anstey said.

'It is very wrong to steal,' Father Simpson said, but the boy smiled and the words did not seem to matter.

'He says he will go to the front and steal loot for you,' Father Anstey said. 'You are a very burra sahib. He was very upset because he thought you were dead.'

'I am going to get up,' Father Simpson said.

With puffy determination, he got out of bed. He wanted to send the boy away but a moment later Crane came in.

'Sikander Shah is asking for you again,' he said. 'Steady.'

Father Simpson staggered loosely about in his shirt. Crane and Father Anstey held him up.

'For me? Again?'

'He was asking for you all day yesterday.'

'Yes,' the priest said. 'Yes.' He was trying to remember more clearly now, in sequence, the events of yesterday. 'I was to see him. I wanted to speak to him.'

'Don't worry about it,' Crane said.

'It was about evacuation,' the priest said. 'Did they raid us again?'

'Three times,' Crane said. 'Twice yesterday afternoon. Once today. They're using Tempests and Spitfires in relay now. Six at a time.'

'Help me to get my trousers on,' the priest said.

When he staggered slowly into the central ward ten minutes later the boy following him with the ram-rod, like a puppy learning its first trick of carrying a cane. He had hardly reached the door of the ward when a flight of six Spitfires came over, punishing the entire hillside with wild and not very accurate bursts of cannon-shell that set the whole of the smaller ward screaming.

When it was all over he went into the ward. He was met at once by McAlister, who made sweeping motions with her hands at the boy. 'Out, out, out!' she said. 'Out!'

'No,' the priest said. 'Let him come.'

'He needs a bath,' she said. 'He stinks. And more than a wee bit too.'

'I can't remember when I had one either,' he said. 'I probably stink myself.' At the remark her sense of humour came back, making her smile as the boy, dog-like, followed the priest up the ward.

Half-way up the line of beds Dr Baretta came to meet him. Nothing of her cool graciousness had gone; there was no sign of all the revelations she had endured, he thought.

'I think Sikander Shah has asked for me,' he said.

'He is very sick,' she said. 'For your own sake you shouldn't stay.'

'Today I feel a man and a half,' he said, and went slowly up the ward to where Sikander Shah lay.

When Dr Baretta brought him a chair and made him sit by the bed he saw the Afridi officer give a glance of such carved and angular contempt that he was puzzled and aggrieved and said, sickly and sharply:

'I am very sorry I could not get away before. I was detained.' Dr Baretta walked away. 'I am very sorry.'

'Your face,' the Afridi said.

'I fell down,' the priest said. 'What is it you want?'

'I want to get out of here.'

The priest smiled with awful distortion; the bruised raw flesh of his face gave him astonishing and unnatural contempt.

'Shall we make it a reciprocal arrangement?' he said.

'I have no power to –'

163

'Yesterday we found the doctor's husband in a well,' the priest said. He spoke slowly, with tortured deliberation. 'For some time he had been alive. Of course he was a Hindu. Of course it has nothing to do with taking you out.'

'I have been terribly troubled,' the officer said.

'We have all the same common affliction,' the priest said.

The rapidity of his rush of bitterness had blinded him to the fact that the Afridi officer was weeping. He was overwhelmed by a blast of contrition: once again his tongue had run away with him; once again he had forgotten, blundered, contrived through his spasmodic stupidity to trap himself, to betray himself, to ignite evil and idiotic fires within himself, to make a mockery of his faith.

'You need not be troubled,' he said. 'There is no need to be troubled.'

The officer did not speak; his tears, woken and then held back by sheer weakness, had not fallen. They glistened on the lids of eyes no longer very barbaric; and the priest began to see, now, that he was tired.

'Tell me what we can do,' he said.

A guard peered in at the glass doors, shading his face with his hand. For a moment it distracted Father Simpson, so that he turned and looked out. The sun was shining, breaking through hanging smoke. It had been a colder night and the Pathans, down and across the valley, had lighted more fires.

He remembered all he was going to ask: freedom for everybody, evacuation, the bargain of which the Colonel had talked, and he said:

'The raids are getting too frequent. Surely you can give us two trucks and get us out?'

'I have already sent a message detailing the trucks.' He gazed past the priest vaguely and weakly. 'Who is that at the end of the bed?'

The priest, turning, saw the boy waiting there. With dog-like devotion he stood to attention, watching.

'He is a Pathan boy. He is with the men.'

'Tell him he must go away.'

164

'He is all right. We don't mind him –'

'Tell him to go,' the officer said. He spoke very slowly. 'It is against regulations to have boys about the camp.'

The priest turned to send the boy away, and Sikander Shah, at the same moment, said something sharply. The boy turned and hurried down the ward. 'You can clean out the rabbits –' the priest began, but the boy did not look back.

It seemed to him, when he turned again to look at Sikander Shah, that a great change had taken place. The face on the bed seemed to have moved farther away. It was defined in all ways less sharply; it was an object retreating out of focus. He said, 'I am very glad you have found it possible to evacuate us. Or at least the children and the women. The rest of us will stay. We shall do our best for you,' but the officer did not answer. His mouth had opened itself as if to say something and now simply remained darkly parted, like a quivering trap.

It was less from this than from a slight and terribly strengthless signalling of the officer's hands that the priest felt the truth emerge. In the act of turning to the boy he had let the hands go. Now as he grasped them again, clumsily, in what was intended to be a rush of comfort, they seemed to him already dead. The shock of it went through him like a purge, turning his body to water, making him tremble again.

Presently he heard the officer say something about 'A convent – I was at school –' but strength died on the lips, leaving them open, the dark mouth staring. With difficulty, his back a stiff cage of bruised flesh, the priest slipped from the chair and knelt by the bed.

'I will pray for you,' he said. He fumbled across his chest, as he had so often done, for his crucifix. It was not there. He was not disturbed by its absence, but prayed quietly, free of mechanisms and haste, his words no longer mere processions of recited thought.

McAlister, walking up the ward and seeing him kneeling there, slipped her crucifix off her neck and put it into his hands. By sheer strength of will he had already conjured up its reality so vividly – as if all the time it had really been there between

165

the officer's hands and his own – that for some moments he hardly noticed it.

It was only when the officer pulled it gently towards him that he became aware of it fully. Joy flashed through him: it appeared that the Afridi officer and himself were impinged, together, alone, under an immense arc-light. He could see everything with the candescence of revelation: the officer holding the crucifix, drawing it to his lips, an Afridi, a Moslem, an enemy folded at last, through himself, into the body of the church, the blessed, encompassing arms of The Holy Virgin and all the saints – but whether it really happened he never knew. In the clatter of six Spitfire engines – he knew they had got the range a little better this time because he heard the shattering of glass in the eastern wing where the chapel was – all the external impact of life about him came back. The obliterating roaring wings seemed not only to crush out all other sound but to extinguish, not in a single burst, but slowly, the extraordinary light holding himself and Sikander Shah together.

When the Spitfires had finally whined away down the valley he opened his eyes and saw that the Afridi officer had died. He prayed again for a few moments with unhurried calm. He could hear a good deal of screaming from the other ward and some yelling from the Pathans outside. He came out of his orgastic frenzy of death and joy and revelation slowly, crossing himself several times before and after struggling stiffly up from the bed. He walked at last in silence past McAlister, who had had rather less patience with the descendant of kings and the nonsense of his tribal pride and his insult of Dr Baretta, and slowly down the ward.

Outside, in the corridor, he met Crane and Colonel Mathieson and was back, abruptly, in a world whose remoteness he could not grasp for several seconds.

'They're getting the range,' Crane said. 'One more run and they'll be bang on. It's getting pretty.'

'Sikander Shah is dead,' he said. He could still see, in that final dazzling burst of light, the crucifix magnetically drawn to the Moslem lips.

166

'Blast,' the Colonel said.

'Almost the last thing he did before he died was to send orders for trucks to evacuate us,' the priest said.

'What trucks?' the Colonel said. 'Where?'

'I haven't the least idea.'

'The old, old story,' Crane said.

The priest did not answer. The light, with its centralized and dazzling emblem, had not faded. He could still see it where he stood.

'One bang from six Spits in the middle of us,' the Colonel said, 'and we won't need any trucks. They'd better get here soon.'

'I think they will,' the priest said. He smiled with patience, and now also with a certain triumph, under his bruised distortion. Still the light had not gone.

'If they don't get here by midday,' Crane said, 'we'd better think up something else – and quick too.'

'It's time we put out a cross,' the priest said. 'A real one. A big one. On the grass.' The light had become absorbed now into himself; he was shining and triumphant with its white internal glow. 'I should have thought of it before.'

18

By noon strips of surgical gauze and blanket, dyed by the women to varying shades of red, were drying under the windows of the smaller ward, where the sun came through. Since both Sikander Shah and Dr Baretta's husband had to be buried, the priest reasoned, the burial party, which would again consist of the Colonel, himself, and Crane, could also deal with the laying-out of the cross. But in his heart he did not believe these precautions would be necessary. He had great faith in the promise of the trucks. Moments of such rare spirituality as that with Sikander Shah were not transitory; death did not simply extinguish them. The trucks would come.

He had walked about all morning in a state of steely elation. The arrival of the trucks would mean not simply the end of all problems about him; it would crown the solution of his own. Rhetorical cadences of joy bounced through him as he blundered about the wards watching the women dyeing the cloth. He joked with Colonel Mathieson and the men, speaking with tenderness to Sister Teresalina, who had taken her place in the ward again like a doll of yellow marble, her face shining and embalmed.

During the morning he went several times to the windows of the two wards to look out, but the trucks did not come. He was not alarmed; these things, army orders and such things, he thought, take time. 'Even in Kashmir,' he told the Colonel, 'there are bound to be a few yards of red tape left over from Delhi,' and laughed with cruel distortion of his black-bruised face. The Colonel, who was getting more and more worried, could not bear it and walked away to ask Crane if there were not a possibility of finding a drink somewhere. The two of them had spent the morning raising the body of Dr Baretta's husband from the well. Like McAlister they were not fired with the glow of spiritual exuberances; they had no special use for the descendant of kings. The Colonel had the taste of death in his mouth and wanted a drink to get it out.

Crane knew nothing of drinks and was worried in turn by Julie Maxted, who had been drugged to sleep by day and then could not sleep at night. He felt her nerves had become like the over-delicate filaments of a lamp that had burned too long; they would snap if something did not happen soon.

The Colonel, tortured inside himself, his mouth full of the dry evil of blackened and rotting flesh, wandered away and presently met Father Simpson in the corridor again, rushing along with bouncing and blundering joy.

'Have you seen Pir Dil Khan?' he said. The Colonel blinked tired, sardonic eyes; not understanding this.

'The boy.'

'Ah, the boy,' the Colonel said. 'The soldier with the ram-rod.'

'I can't find him anywhere. He would be so useful for helping us to pack.'

'He went,' the Colonel said. He was stricken suddenly by the impossible idiocy of the significant word. 'Pack? What in hell for?'

'We shall be going,' the priest said. 'The trucks will be here.'

The Colonel, thinking it better not to argue about these things, said simply: 'He went off in a truck. I saw him. He was a bit miserable – said you and Sikander Shah had ordered him away.'

'Yes, certainly we did – certainly – but not like that – not in that way –'

'I want a drink,' the Colonel said. He had not bothered to shave. What was left of the youth in his face had grown a queer blond crust. Little bloodied tendrils crawled about the yellowed pupils of his eyes. 'Surely we've got something somewhere?'

'Nurse McAlister has emergency rations of tea if you feel –'

He stopped; he thought the Colonel looked not only tired now but sick. He began to say something but the Colonel let out a savage interruption that was not really a word but simply a bark of angry weariness.

'Of course there's wine – we grow that – we have the vines and we have always made it.'

'Where?' the Colonel said. 'Can I get some?'

'I imagine so – it's in the back cellar –'

'Cellar!' The Colonel made fresh and weary barks of despair. 'We have a cellar? Then why in hell didn't somebody say so?'

'It isn't very large –'

'Nor is the ward,' the Colonel said. 'At least the children could have gone down there. At least they could have sheltered.'

'Well, that may have been so,' the priest said. Indulgently he gazed at the Colonel's tired face. He was distraught and exhausted. A glass of wine would help him. 'None of them have been hurt and now it doesn't matter.'

'Have been,' the Colonel said. 'Have been,' and the priest knew what that meant. But the bitter obliqueness about his tenses did not distract or shake him now. He smiled with great patience.

'The trucks will come,' he said. 'They will be here.' He prepared to walk away.

'Where are the keys?' the Colonel said.

'Of what? – Oh yes, the cellar.' He put his right hand in his pocket, hauling out his chain of keys. 'It really isn't very big.'

'You'd be surprised,' the Colonel said.

The priest gave the Colonel the key of the cellar. He walked three or four steps away and then came back.

'I know you don't believe it about the trucks. But I do believe it. I can't explain why I believe it but I do believe it. I know it. I am sure.' Again he recalled the cross extended to the Moslem lips. He went on:

'We have been through a lot but there must be an end. You said that yourself. And I tell you I believe the trucks will come. They will come as certainly – as surely –'

'As surely as the Spits,' the Colonel said. He looked grimly up at the sound of planes whining up from the valley, and

170

then swiftly down at the watch on his wrist. It was almost twelve. 'They are getting to be so nice and regular,' he said.

'I am going to look for the trucks,' the priest said and abruptly walked, almost marched, away.

'And I am going to make a reconnaissance in the cellar,' the Colonel said.

The raid lasted fifteen minutes. Spitfires, coming in from the west, made the same mistake as before, turning too sharply, spraying only the eastern side of the hill. The Pathans had been digging themselves in below the south-western bank of cypresses; they consisted in that moment of nothing but four cooks and half a dozen sleepers from the night guard. Apart from a shattering of glass in the sacristy there was no nearer casualty than a stray shell through a petrol field-cooker. The explosion put the cook on his back and set fire to summer-dried grass in a clearing of thorned acacia trees.

It was while watching the smoke from the fire, after the planes had whistled away over the river, that Father Simpson saw two trucks coming slowly up the hill.

All the concentration of his joy broke in a single word. His bruised cheeks blew up with the tightness of an enormous paper-bag. 'Glory!' he shouted and the sound came out of him in an explosive burst.

Rushing to find witnesses to this miracle he found Crane in the corridor by the wash-room, with Julie Maxted. Her hands were stained with scarlet dye. There was no sign of the Colonel. Joyfully the priest shouted his news about the trucks and the three of them went running through the central ward.

By the time they reached the windows the two trucks had turned under the archway and were halting at the terrace end. The priest in the glory of this manifestation wanted to pray. He succeeded only in saying instead, over and over again: 'On time too. On time. On time,' as if it were all part of the final fulfilment of a divine time-table.

Drivers got out of the trucks. There was a sound of backboards slapping down. The priest jigged up and down with excitement and three nuns, followed by McAlister, came to watch from the windows too.

A sudden appearance from the first truck of nearly a dozen officers, with much kit, one or two in khaki drill and with peaked caps, hit Crane like a blow. He did not answer the priest's squeak of thankful triumph:

'Officers! They have come to take over! Glory – thanks be – Glory –!'

Several more officers got out and walked about the gravel.

'One can deal with officers – one can talk,' the priest said. He felt his faith in Sikander Shah extend to all officers everywhere. 'Now we can negotiate. The trucks are bound to –'

'The trucks are going back,' Crane said.

Caught between overwhelming joy and fear the priest could not speak. He saw a Pathan bearer, stacking rolls of kit, leap out of the path of a truck turning fast across the gravel as it drove away. He saw the scarlet hands of Julie Maxted rested on the window. The light in his soul still burned but now, suddenly, he felt it terribly and shatteringly dimmed. The second of the trucks drove away. Officers stood about the terrace in fantastic tribal accoutrements made real, here and there, by the touch of peaks and khaki. The priest heard Crane speaking as if from very far away.

'This, unless I am much mistaken,' Crane said, 'is the new H.Q.' He saw Julie Maxted's scarlet hands shudder on the window. 'Oh! don't look at them,' she said. They were outspread against the glass: skeletons of scarlet that shocked Crane suddenly more than anything that was happening on the terrace outside. 'I'll never get them clean again. Never.'

'Now they'll really have something to shoot at,' Crane said. 'Including us.'

19

The Colonel came out of the cellar at half past three: not drunk but uplifted, as Father Simpson had been uplifted, by a warm and private elation. Tired out, drowsy with three mugs of convent wine, he had gone to sleep for an hour, to be soothed by a series of dreams in which his wife had never died.

He had hardly got up from the cellar, into the corridor of the back kitchen, when the third air-raid of the day began. It came up the valley with a whistling roar, the planes so low that he thought for a moment the leading Spitfire had hit the roof of the smaller ward. He fell instinctively on his face, lying on the corridor floor until sometime after the last crack of cannon-shell. When he stood up again he felt angry with himself. He began to reproach himself bitterly for sleeping and boozing in the cellar instead of finding Father Simpson and organizing with him, as he had intended to do, a correct and orderly raid-drill for the children. The cellar would hold all of the children and even some of the women too. He had bawled at Father Simpson for not having remembered the cellar; now he had himself been guilty of an entirely different sort of forgetfulness.

As he stumbled along the corridor he was plunged into a hangover of self-reproach. He could hear a high wailing of Indian women from the little ward. Gradually his bitterness began to come back. But it was not until the door of the ward opened and McAlister, rushing out, the entire starched bust of her uniform spattered dark scarlet, said, 'Oh! there you are, Colonel,' almost as if reproaching him too, 'the ward's been hit!' that it possessed him completely again. It came over him in a sickening rush of misery. He managed to call after

McAlister, 'Anyone hurt?' and she called back sharply, almost off-hand, in the second before disappearing towards the larger ward:

'Two children and a woman. One of the Sikhs.'

He stood still, alone in the corridor, slowly striking his forehead with the palms of both hands. After some moments he went into the ward. All its life was clotted at the far end. Huddled women were wailing wretchedly on the floor; the glass of the far window had been smashed. Three nuns were busy with bowls and towels in the far corner, over one of the beds.

He stared at it all vaguely and helplessly. After some moments McAlister came back with Dr Baretta, and he said stupidly and helplessly as they went past, 'Anything I can do?' and McAlister snapped back, in her tart, thin Scots:

'Everything under control – thank you.'

He stayed long enough to hear the ward rent with the first scalding scream of a child as Dr Baretta bent and touched it on the bed. Then he went out. He did not know what to do. After some moments he blundered into the washroom. He dashed a little water in his face. The basin was splashed and stained scarlet with dye where the women had come to wash their hands and he was hit by the ghastly notion that once more he was staring at blood. He was sick with an entirely new wave of revulsion, hating himself so much that he stood swearing at the wet reflection of his face in the scrap of glass on the wall.

Outside in the corridor again he was torn between going back to the cellar, to get completely and obliviously drunk, and getting out of the building completely. He staggered away in the direction of the back kitchen at the very moment Crane and Father Simpson, who had been burying Dr Baretta's husband and Sikander Shah with the help of two Pathans, came into the corridor from the larger ward. Spitfires had sprayed with much improved accuracy all the garden terraces and the orchard, and for a few moments priest and Pathans and Crane had lain half in, half out of the grass under the apple-trees while tracer-shells scythed the hillside of many leaves. Crane was angry; the red cross laid out by himself and Father Simpson on the bare terrace had made no difference at all. He was angry too because at that unfortunate moment the Colonel, when most needed, had chosen to disappear.

It had been a hideous, exhausting, maddening afternoon, and now as he saw the Colonel staggering away down the corridor he shouted after him:

'Colonel, where the hell have you been?'

Crane's new reproach, coming so soon after McAlister's to join his own, had the effect on the Colonel of a lash. He made a bounding, startling turn, revealing for ten seconds or so a face he had not troubled to dry. For these few moments it was held there at the doorway, wet and anguished, without a word of answer, and then he disappeared.

'The Colonel must be going off his head,' Crane said. He walked a few paces down the corridor. 'Colonel! Colonel!' he called. 'Colonel –'

'Leave him,' the priest said; and Crane let him go.

Some moments later the Colonel was outside the building, feeling the first rush of relief at being alone. Fresh air, cool on his wet face, made him realize suddenly that he had not dried himself and he walked along, past the room where he and Crane had first slept, wiping his face on his sleeve.

When he stopped this and looked up it was to see the Pathan boy, Pir Dil Khan, coming down from the cabbages where Father Simpson kept his rabbits. The boy now carried not only the ram-rod but a full-sized cartridge belt of ·303 ammunition slung across his shoulders and in his hand two packets of looted cigarettes.

'For Father,' he said. He held out the cigarettes, beaming a yellow-toothed smile. 'For priest.'

The Colonel, waving him away, going past him without a word, was reminded by the cartridge belt of the rifle he had picked up on the first night of the Pathan raids. He had charged about with it for quite some time in the frenzy of looking for his wife before realizing it was as useless as a walking-stick. It was not loaded and there was nothing he could load it with; and finally he had pitched it into a pile of

175

pine-faggots that Father Simpson used for shading young crops in the heat of spring.

Now, remembering the rifle, he stopped. He called and the boy came back, running.

'Yes, sahib? Yes, sahib?' He beamed again his dirty yellow-toothed smile.

'The belt,' the Colonel said.

He lifted it over the boy's head; the boy did not smile.

'All right,' the Colonel said. 'Run away.'

Some time later he found the rifle in the pile of pine-faggots, where he had left it. It was a little dirty and he spent some time cleaning it, pulling the oil-rag through the barrel with steady thoroughness, putting his eye to the barrel in the sun. Gradually the weapon gave him confidence. He began to feel less badly about himself. It was pleasant simply to sit in the sun, watching the shining veined balls of Father Simpson's cabbages, smelling air and earth and rabbits and rifle-oil. It was a great change after the fusty, human, astringent hospital smells of indoors. He felt rather pleased too about the gun: he might even knock one of the bastards over with it, he thought, if they started beefing round again.

He was still sitting there, about twenty feet away from the rabbit hutches, the gun across his knees, rather in the attitude of a man waiting for one of the rabbits to bolt, when Crane came up from the Mission.

'There you are,' Crane said. 'The boy said – what the hell's the idea of the rifle?'

'Found it,' the Colonel said.

'Then lose the bloody thing quick.'

'I don't want to lose it,' the Colonel said.

'What's been happening to you? Where have you been?' Crane said. 'We had this ghastly burial business and you weren't there. Didn't you know Father Simpson's trucks turned up? Full of tribal brass-hats –'

'What trucks?'

'You don't seem to understand,' Crane said, 'that there has developed a charming situation –'

'What situation?' The Colonel held the rifle-barrel to his

eye and squinted. 'Where?' The situation seemed to him much as before. He felt awkward and miserable at heart and everybody was stuck.

'We've all been promoted,' Crane said. 'We are the new tribal G.H.Q. The big ward is full of red tape and grand opera.'

'When did this happen?' the Colonel said.

'Oh, never mind when the bloody thing happened!' Crane said. 'It happened. The place is top priority number one and you sit here playing with a rifle –'

'I've nothing else to play with,' the Colonel said. 'Of course I used to have –'

'For God's sake,' Crane said.

'We are getting on each other's nerves.' The Colonel put the rifle to his shoulder and took careful aim at distant snows. 'The tone of the place is going down. I'm thinking of clearing. Walking to Srinagar or something.'

'You're off your head,' Crane said.

'That,' the Colonel said, 'would not be at all surprising.'

Crane walked over to the rabbit hutches, not answering. He ran his finger-nails over the wire-netting mesh, remembering the evening he had watched the rabbits with Julie Maxted. The rabbits jumped about behind the wire and stared at him like fluffy, pink-eyed toys. They smelt badly and looked, with their twitching noses, stupid and ridiculous; he couldn't think why Father Simpson ever kept them. The Colonel was right: everybody was getting on everybody's nerves. He gave mad harp-like twangs of his fingers along the hutch-wires; the rabbits bounded about inside, more stupidly than ever, and the Colonel said:

'You can't see Nanga Parbat today.'

Crane walked back to him. He ought perhaps to be a little more understanding, a little more conciliatory, he thought.

'Funny how elusive she is,' the Colonel said. 'I've known chaps rush off on expeditions when she came into view –'

'We'd better get back inside,' Crane said. 'Come on.'

'I got the cartridge belt from the boy. Bit of luck. Awfully useful loot he has.' The Colonel put the bolt back into the rifle and slid it smartly backwards and forwards several times;

sunlight shone with dull reflection on polished metal. 'I'm not coming in. I like it here.'

'For God's sake what's come over you?'

'You go.'

'Throw the rifle into the bushes and be sensible. Come in before they beat you up like Father Simpson.'

'Not coming,' the Colonel said. 'I'm clearing out.' He grinned. 'I'll stay here until the next raid. Then I'll have a pot at the Spits.'

'It's a pity you didn't think of that one before,' Crane said. 'A little protective assistance wouldn't have been out of place this afternoon.'

The Colonel did not answer; there was no way of answering. He watched Crane walk down the garden path between the cabbages. Bright mountain sun slanting through late afternoon gave netted skeins to rows of fat green leaves; he could smell evening, with the smoke of fires, coming up the valley. He sat there for a long time with the rifle across his knees. He waited until the sun faded pink and orange and at last tender brown on the hills and there was no more chance of another raid. Once he heard machine-gun fire and cocked the rifle hopefully; but it was simply a sudden skirmish breaking out across the valley. When it was too dark to see much more he hid the rifle and the bandolier among the pine-boughs and went back into the Mission, thinking of the child who had died.

20

For the next two days he sat with the rifle in the cabbage-patch, taking pot shots at aircraft in the raids. Raids were now more frequent, as many as five or six a day, but the speed of them at low level was so great that he never succeeded in getting more than a single shot at the leading plane. He did not hit anything and once or twice he did not think it mattered very much. The life of the Mission receded; he felt he had no part in it. There was a great coming and going of lorries loaded with troops, of wounded coming in, of tribal officers swaggering operatically and sometimes, in khaki, with a sort of fierce correctness, through the central ward. There were many conferences, two or three times a day, into which Father Simpson blundered with fiery and unshaken faith, stubbornly demanding evacuation. The red cross of blankets and gauze grew dusty and dishevelled on the terrace and some of it blew down the hill.

None of these things mattered to him either. He sat in the cabbages. With glassy-eyed concentration he watched for aircraft, and Crane let him go.

On the third morning the Colonel was sitting in the cabbages waiting for the first raid of the day to come over when a jeep, driven by a Pathan officer in khaki, came up the hill. The officer parked the car at the end of the terrace and went into the Mission. The Colonel had not slept very much. Beyond the place where the jeep was parked he could see, under the apple-trees, sprays of crimson and yellow flowers on the graves of the dead: a contribution of Pir Dil Khan, who had raided abandoned gardens by the river. A little wind was blowing in from the mountains, spreading blue smoke from cooking fires down the terraces. Otherwise there was no movement on that side of the building at all.

He sat staring down the gardens, trying to remember whether this was the seventh or eighth day since the attack had begun; but he had lost count in some way and was no longer sure. For a time he had also kept a count of the raids, but now he had begun to lose count of that too and could not be sure if it were now twenty-one or twenty-three.

He sat looking at the jeep, counting back through the days. The officer did not come out of the Mission again; there was still no movement about the hill.

The Colonel waited for some moments longer for the officer to come out of the Mission. Nothing happened and presently he stood up. The entire procedure of escape now seemed incredibly simple. You simply got into the jeep, he thought, and drove it away. God knew where you drove it but the air-field operating Spitfires could not be far away. It seemed a credible and possible thing that he could talk some sense into somebody there.

He waited for some moments longer and then walked down the garden to where, on the terrace, the jeep was parked. He was so absorbed and excited that he had forgotten the rifle. He swung it boldly in front of him with both hands. The bastards would probably shoot him down as soon as he got out of the gate, he thought: but the notion of death came with neither fear nor shock. It would be awful fun: rather like the time when the Japs had captured him beyond Imphal. He had walked out quite simply then and had been free for nearly two days. There hadn't been a hope in hell of making it completely, but it had been tremendous fun and had given him a bit of devilish moral uplift, rather like cocking his fingers at his nose. Then, as now, it was the sauce and the fun of the thing that counted. They had been pushed around long enough by these cut-throats, anyway, he thought.

He got to within twenty yards of the jeep, his whole body so tense with excitement that he could feel the blood beating at the very edges of his vision, when the officer came out of the Mission. The Colonel, half-blinded by tension, went on for some moments longer before he realized exactly what had happened. He stopped himself only as the officer got into the jeep and drove away.

Half-way down the hill it suddenly occurred to the young peak-capped Pathan that the most extraordinary thing he had seen in several days of fighting was a civilian Englishman advancing with a rifle out of a cabbage-patch. He turned the jeep round and went back up the hill.

Two older officers, one disfigured with a deep-scarred lip that even long black moustaches had failed to hide, were at breakfast in the larger ward, now an odd mixture of hospital, tribal mess, and offices separated into compartments by rugs hung crossways on lines. The young officer had hardly begun to tell of the Colonel wandering about the Mission gardens with a rifle when Father Simpson blundered into the ward with the first of his daily protests. He came floundering through the ward with his face burning puffily, like one huge single purple and yellow bruise.

The elder Pathan officer spoke English brutally and stiffly, like a machine. His eyes, pitched deep into the skull, had a glittering and impersonal blackness, lacking entirely the confusion of loyalties that had swayed and shaken Sikander Shah.

The priest had not time to open his mouth.

'One of your peoples is going about the garden with rifle,' the Pathan said. The scarred lip made its machine-like statement naturally but stiffly, nakedly hostile. 'That is against orders.'

'It is the Colonel,' the priest said. He stood with belly thrust forward, facing the three officers. His aggressive bruised jowls had discoloured repulsively in the process of healing. His lips had difficulty in opening. 'It is just the Colonel – he is –'

'Colonel? An officer?'

'He was.'

'With rifle?' the Pathan said. 'How is that?'

'I don't know. I couldn't say. He does not mean anything –'

'It is against orders. He must be ordered in.'

'He is a simple man and he does not mean anything,' the priest said. 'His wife was killed.'

'You will get him in.'

'I will try – I am not responsible –'

'You will get him in.'

'I protest,' the priest said. His bruised lips quivered, 'I must protest – all this has gone on – it has gone on too long – I will not tolerate it – I must tell you now, I protest –'

'You will get him in,' the Pathan said.

The scarred lips were like a machine. The priest knew suddently that there was no forcing himself past the barrier of hostility: that this was not Sikander Shah, with his conflict of loyalties, that there was now no argument.

He turned abruptly, blundering out. His bruised jaws, dropsically shiny, seemed to be dumbly stuttering; his hands, quivering across his stomach, echoed them in pantomimic wrestlings with imaginary beads.

In the corridor he blundered into Crane. His words came rushing out:

'The Colonel has been seen in the garden with the rifle. It has made them still more hostile. I must talk to him. I must get him in.'

He strode crudely past Crane, talking as he went. He blurted out:

'This business – this awful business – this awful ghastly impersonal attitude – they have taken no notice of the cross. They have taken no notice of anything – it's getting beyond all reasonable bearing. I can't have it, I can't have it. I can't and won't have it, I tell you –!'

'I'll come with you,' Crane said.

'No, no, no.' The habitual protest stuttered out. 'I can do it. I can deal with it.'

'I'll come with you,' Crane said. 'It had to stop anyway. He'll end by getting us all shot.'

They went out together by the back entrance, behind the kitchen, the priest puffing slightly ahead, in a trembling combustion of anxieties.

The Colonel was sitting on the pile of pine-faggots, beyond the rabbit hutches, in the sun. He had placed the rifle between

182

his knees, the barrel perpendicular, its point beneath the chin. The effect was startlingly suicidal.

'You must come in,' the priest said. 'Colonel, you must come in. This new set of officers is quite different – they insist.'

'Hullo,' the Colonel said. He lowered the point of the rifle a little, holding it beyond his nose. Its gleaming circular hole gave him the effect of having a third, more watchful eye.

'Come on,' Crane said. 'They mean it.'

'They really do,' the priest said.

'I thought I'd get a squint at Nanga Parbat,' the Colonel said. 'Perhaps it's early. I'll wait.'

'Never mind waiting,' Crane said. 'Come in.'

'I'm not coming. I like it here.'

'Please, Colonel,' the priest said. 'Our only hope of evacuation is doing as we're told. This sort of defiance will get us nowhere. It will simply end in their doing something more ghastly –'

'All be buried in one grave,' the Colonel said. 'Cheers.'

The Colonel lowered the point of the rifle towards his chin again, grating the sight with his teeth. Crane felt his blood run cold at this scratch of tooth on metal, his mind frozen by a sudden thought that the Colonel was really sitting there waiting for a solitary and opportune moment to blow his brains out.

'Come on,' he said. 'Be reasonable.'

The Colonel raised the point of the rifle, creating once again the effect, almost as alarming as that of suicide, of the third and still more watchful eye.

'I'm waiting for Nanga Parbat,' the Colonel said.

'There has been trouble enough,' the priest said. 'Please.'

The Colonel gazed stubbornly, with three-eyed watchfulness, across the distant hills.

'Look,' Crane said. He had not even the remotest idea of what, in that moment, he was going to say. But suddenly, out of past confusions, he was jolted into an unexpected and sensible thought.

'We never got round to that game of chess,' he said. 'We

were always going to get round to it and somebody blundered in.'

'Awful lot of that sort of carelessness been going on,' the Colonel said. 'Bad show.'

'Well, call it carelessness. Call it what you like. But –'

'Call it etiquette,' the Colonel said.

He lifted the rifle, grating his teeth on the sight, once more freezing Crane's blood so that he wanted to yell at him. 'Don't be a bloody, pig-head clot, man! Get some sense into your damn skull and come in.' He was really getting a little tired, he thought, of the Colonel's studied attitude of a three-eyed mule.

He said quietly instead:

'If you don't come in voluntarily they'll fetch you in. That's all. It's one way or the other.'

'I'm happy here.'

'Play chess with Crane,' the priest said. 'He has wanted to play ever since –'

'I'm happy here,' the Colonel said. 'Quite happy.'

The priest, torn between a desire to let himself go in raging argument and a shaking anxiety not to let his tongue run away into a show of pointless stupidity, could not bear it any longer. He walked away to where the rabbits, squatting on dirty yellow cabbage leaves, sat crimping their noses, blinking pink eyes behind the wire in the sun.

Crane stood between the priest and Mathieson. The Colonel put the rifle-sight between his teeth, almost biting it. There was a queer sightless sort of lunacy about the eyes for a moment as Crane's shadow fell.

'For God's sake,' Crane said. He spoke quietly, with great effort, holding himself in check. 'The tension inside is bad enough without your making it worse outside. What about the poor devils inside? It's been tough enough for them. I'm going off my own head. What about Father Simpson?'

The Colonel did not answer. He was occupied, as always, with rifle-sight and invisible snows.

'Come on,' Crane said.

'No.'

184

'I shan't ask you again. It's too bloody silly.'

'If they want me they can fetch me,' the Colonel said.

'Don't yell neutral when they do.'

'Fair enough,' the Colonel said.

Crane walked away. His last sight of the Colonel was once again dominated by the queer sensation of the third, more watchful eye glinting between the curdled lunacy of the other two. The sun was quite hot among the cabbages; the dew of a coldish night had dried. As he walked down the garden he resisted a series of violent impulses to turn and look at the Colonel; and the priest, evidently haunted by something equally strong, kept his bruised jaw thrust outward, helpless and dismayed.

Out of hearing distance of the Colonel, Crane could no longer restrain himself and said:

'He'll probably blow his head off – it's more than likely.'

'Oh! no, no, no. Don't speak like that.'

'He's stubborn enough for anything.'

'He's had a very great deal to put up with,' the priest said.

'Yes, yes: we know.'

'I wouldn't judge him too harshly,' the priest said. 'Left to himself I think he'll come.'

At the back door of the Mission his certainty in that thought seemed to be shaken a little. 'Queer how there's been no raid,' he said, 'so far.' He looked up with squinting troubled eyes at the blue autumn empty sky.

'Probably thinking a Saturday special,' Crane said.

'Saturday? Saturday?' It seemed only yesterday, and yet at the same time a thousand years back, since Father Anstey had chided him in the potato-patch for his forgetfulness of the day, the rabbits and the coming of Crane. 'Saturday? Is it Saturday?' His surprise at these things gave a sudden urgency to his mind. Time was slipping away; he really had to do something about the Colonel, the women, the children, the raids, about everything.

'I will speak to Father Anstey,' he said. 'He'll go up. He will talk to him. There may be something about an older man –'

Together, in the passage between the kitchen and the cellar, they met Julie Maxted.

'You were supposed to do raid-drill,' she said to Crane. 'You were the man with the watch.'

'Oh! Lord.'

'Well, we managed.' She smiled; he felt all his anxieties become trivialities. 'We can get all the children and the women down in thirty seconds.'

'Splendid,' the priest said. 'Where is Father Anstey?'

'He is spotting,' she said. 'He sits at the window and gives us warning and then I march them down.'

'I'll go and find him,' the priest said.

Alone with Crane, in the narrow corridor above the cellar, she pressed her head back for a brief moment against the wall. He saw the soft dark throat gulp with emotion and then she was kissing him, pressing her body hard against him; holding his head so closely that he could feel the nails cutting through the hairs of his neck.

'I haven't kissed you. I haven't seen you,' she said. 'Not for so long. There's nowhere I can be with you.'

'God,' he said.

As she kissed him again she could feel the distraction in his own responses. She stopped kissing him at last and held her throat against his face. 'Don't be worried. There's no need – it's all right now.'

'It's not that any more,' he said.

'Then don't be –'

'It's the Colonel,' he said. 'The Pathans have ordered everyone inside the building. He won't come.'

'I understand him,' she said. 'I understand how he feels.'

'Everybody does. The more you understand the less he listens.'

'Don't worry – there's no need to worry.'

'He sits up there with a gun ready to blow his brains out,' he said.

As if she had really never heard what he said she kissed him again: his own hunger, frustrated for so long, drew on the

186

warmth of her mouth. She cried out quietly as he held her breasts.

'You can't let him stay there – that's an awful thing –'

'He just sits there. He just won't come.'

'You can't have tried,' she said.

'He's just stubborn.'

'I'll try,' she said. 'I know how he feels.'

She gave a little gasp of dry pain; she moved away from him and he felt he could not stop her.

He let her go and she called out at the end of the passage by the door: 'You act as warden if there's a raid. Nurse McAlister will help. You can have fun with her in the cellar,' and gave him a mocking, tenderly bright smile.

She walked out of the Mission and up the path by the cypresses to where, by the rabbit hutches, the Colonel was still sitting with the gun between his knees. She remembered the first evening there after the death of her mother: how they had taken a rabbit from behind its cage, how it had lopped among the darkening cabbages. She remembered the delicious sensation of warm rabbit fur on her neck; a feeling as if she had been wrapped in cotton-wool, all her agony soothed. The Colonel had not been so lucky; there had been no one to wrap the Colonel in cotton-wool. There had been no other way for him but to sit with the gun on his knees.

She broke off a cabbage leaf as she came up the path. The snap of its leaving the stem woke the Colonel from his bemused and not very vigilant watch for Nanga Parbat and Julie said:

'Oh! Colonel Mathieson, you're here. I hadn't the faintest. I came to feed the rabbits.'

'Thought they didn't let anyone out,' he said.

'They just let me run up.'

She broke off several more cabbage leaves, and then went to the hutches, opening the little cage doors, and putting in the leaves. The Colonel and she had played a lot of tennis together on the Maxteds' bungalow court across the river; she had known him longer than the priest or Crane. He played with great gaiety and energy; he smashed rather well; he never let you get him on the defensive; and in the evenings, after the games were over, she and her mother and he and Mrs Mathieson would sit in the garden and watch the stars glittering with leaping emerald flashes above the great majestic deodars. He always talked with gaiety and bantering wit, pulling her mother's leg because her father was so often away in Bombay. Her mother in her fluttering excitable way always fell for it and the Colonel made pretentious and public love to her. It amused everyone very much.

She took one of the rabbits out of the hutch, holding it in her arms, stroking its flattened ears.

'They go to sleep if you stroke them enough,' she said.

The Colonel began to grate his teeth against the gun-sight.

'I'm sure they don't get fed enough.' She broke off another cabbage leaf and the rabbit chewed on it, crimpingly.

'Over-fed,' the Colonel said. 'Fed too much.'

She sat down on the pile of faggots, holding the rabbit against her face.

'No raid today yet,' she said. 'Always the way. You get the raid-drill organized and then nothing happens.'

The Colonel stopped grating his teeth against the gun. He let the muzzle rest, instead, on the upper curve of his neck. It had the effect of lifting his eyes to the sun, revealing them queerly lightless and dilated.

'I'll bet they sent you to fetch me,' the Colonel said.

'Oh! no they didn't. Fetch you – why?'

'There was a young Pathan squirt with a jeep,' he said. 'I was going to pinch it and make a dash for it. Then he saw me with the rifle.'

'That would have been awful fun.'

The Colonel, who was starting to grate his teeth on the rifle-sight again, stopped and for the first time smiled.

'It would rather.'

'Where were you making for? Srinagar?'

'Hadn't the faintest.'

The rabbit struggled in her arms. She put it in her lap, stroking it. 'I thought we should have to eat them. You know, iron rations and that sort of thing. I'm awfully glad for Father Simpson's sake.'

She looked down the garden. Sun was pleasantly hot on the cabbages, making them glitter; the hills were shining and wonderful beyond. The Colonel waved the gun about, putting his finger into the barrel and letting the whole thing rock, by the weight of the butt, from side to side.

'We could still try it,' she said.

'What?'

'There's a jeep down there now,' she said. She stood up. 'No it isn't – it's a little truck.'

The Colonel said, 'Good God!' and stood up too.

'Sit down,' she said. 'Hold the rabbit a moment.' She was looking straight ahead.

She gave him the rabbit in a casual sideways movement and in the act of taking it he sat down. He experienced some difficulty in holding both rabbit and gun at the same time; the rabbit, struggling to escape, needed both hands; and finally he moved the gun from between his knees, for the first time, and laid it against the pine-faggots at his side.

'Where are you going?' he said.

'I'm going to have a look-see,' she said. She was already walking down the path.

'I'll come with you,' he said.

He began to stand up again but she turned swiftly. 'No: for goodness' sake. They've seen you once and if they see you again – stay here and nurse the rabbit.' She walked on and the Colonel called:

'The truth is they probably take out the rotor-arm. They've probably learned that trick.'

'We'll have to risk it,' she said.

She did not turn again. Walking on casually she thought only of the rifle. She had succeeded anyway in getting him to put that down. The notion of the truck was absurd; it was facing the wrong way; by the time they had turned it round the guards would be out, shooting them. There was a guard on the gate too. She would walk a little farther down the path, as far as the end of the cabbages, and then go back. She would let the

Colonel nurse the rabbit a little longer and then they could go in.

It was her last thought before she heard the first raid roaring at low level up the valley. She remembered thinking that there were more planes than usual. Already the greater roar, with the fierce high whistling, was beating everything to extinction.

She turned to run back, thinking of the children, anxious, a little frightened, her thoughts not clear. All she could think of was to shout at the Colonel:

'Put the rabbit down. Don't worry about the rabbit. Let it go. Let it go and come in. I must go in.'

'It sounds like two squadrons of the bastards!' the Colonel shouted. He had already let the rabbit go and was running down the path.

She turned towards the Mission and began running too. She could hear yelling among Pathans down at the camp, where the slit-trenches were. She heard the Colonel shouting. 'Get down, Julie! For Christ Jesus' sake get down! Get down! Get down!' and then the obliterating blackening roar of engines destroyed all other sound.

Bullets ricocheted off the walls of the Mission. She threw both hands over her head and fell down. She had the odd experience of smelling fire. A flame of curiously penetrative exactness flicked through the flesh of her right thigh. It seemed to knock her completely over the hillside, far away from the Colonel, who had now stopped running, far from the rabbits and the sustained scream of following planes.

Five minutes later, when Crane came rushing up the garden, it was to find the Colonel shattered to the unrecognizable shape, like the pile of women he had seen behind the chapel, of a twisted and bloody heap of discarded laundry. He could not see the girl. There seemed to be nothing living or moving in the garden except two white rabbits. A second had jumped free, seizing its chance to escape, when Julie had left open the door of the hutch. It frightened him far more than the sight of the Colonel as it scuttled in a scrambling white flash from under the cabbage leaves.

21

Night crept past McAlister, sitting by Julie Maxted's bed, on small waves of sound. The discreet coughing of the elderly German nun was like the dry half-sneeze of a little dog as it came over restless lines of sleepers from the other end of the ward; she could hear the Meran woman feeding her baby, talking to it somewhere on the darkened floor. Now and then a truck went down the hill.

Julie Maxted had been put into a bed in the corner of the ward by the corridor door: the bed was shut away from the rest of the ward by a small cane screen. Lying propped up, for easier breathing, in a half coma, the girl fought to breathe with dry irregular gasps that were like echoes of the coughings of the German nun. Through the previous day, after Dr Baretta had extracted splinters of cannon-shell from her groin, her temperature had floated up to a hundred and five and then down a little and then up again, and McAlister had tried to comfort Crane with a kind of cheerful dirge: 'She'll be all right once we get the damn thing down. We've got to get the damn thing down.'

McAlister had spent most of the night thinking of Crane. She had never felt the same since the moment of disturbing intimacy about the cigarette. For two years she had been try-ing to fit herself to take vows, to put the world of Glasgow and the world of Burma and its jungles and jungle fever and dust and heat behind her; she was trying hard to calm and straighten life after her breakdown.

She had been a very long time in Burma; five years, too long. They used to say women couldn't stand the climate. Up to the hills every six months, home every two years. Queer what you finally could stand. You stuck it out. Somehow you worked in places and temperatures, soaked under hot rain, blinded by white sun and dust, where they said white women had never worked. You got a little comfort from ghastly little transit camps where half the men boycotted nurses' dances and the other half wanted to make a meal off you under the nearest pipal-tree. Then a spell on transport, slinging wounded up on the roofs of Daks, watching mountain and river and forest and sea folding and unfolding below in a glittering stream, meaning nothing whatever. In the end nothing meant everything: transit camps, transport, hospitals, malaria, jungle sickness, dysentery, prickly heat, amputations, pain, hysteria, homesickness, death. Men came into your life, recovered, died, were time-expired; you crossed yourself and they were gone. Nothing meant anything except far off, ahead of you, a queer notion that you too would be time-expired, and you never were.

For these reasons she had been able to bear the ten days of Pathan terror much better than anyone in the Mission. She felt she had seen it all before; it was part of a nightmare mislaid. Life had taken another quick circle back and had picked it up. She had helped to amputate a million limbs like Sikander Shah's; she had seen him die over and over again, in deserts, by rivers, in jungles, in aircraft, in beds, on roadsides; officers, men, Cockneys, Americans, Africans, Indians, pilots, foot-sloggers, descendants of kings: she felt she had seen them all. She was terribly sorry about Colonel Mathieson; she had even cried a little when she had first heard of it; he was a gay, friendly, likeable man; she understood him and had even shocked Father Anstey a little by saying, 'He asked for it. He had it coming to him. I believe he even wanted it.' To her that was a fact so painfully obvious that the end of it all was natural: death was a kindly thing. She would have been able to bear it all in the same way if it hadn't been for Crane. For her there had been no moment in all the bloody hysteria of Pathan butchery to compare, in pain, with her moments of private, blinding distress, when she had held her own breasts with her own hands and tricked herself, with unbearable brightness, into believing it was Crane who touched her.

She had half fallen asleep and now she roused herself instinctively, looking at her watch. It was half past four. She looked at Julie Maxted. The yellow sweat-brightened face was quivering, convulsed by the difficult struggle to breathe. She watched it for a moment and then went into the corridor outside.

Crane was standing at the front end of the corridor, smoking. The wall light burned by the wash-room door and Father Simpson, rolled up in his habit and a blanket, was asleep beyond it.

'Hullo,' she said. She spoke in a whisper and Crane pulled desperately at the cigarette before saying:

'What news? I didn't dare come in.'

'All well,' she said. 'About the same.'

'What about the temperature?'

'Still up.'

'Can't we do something?'

'She's having a wee sleep. It's an awful shame to wake her. As soon as it's light Dr Baretta –'

'God,' Crane said, 'God blast them.'

He threw the cigarette on the floor and stamped on it; in two seconds he was lighting another.

'God blast myself,' he said. 'God blast me.'

His fingers trembled on the petrol-lighter. She heard his teeth chatter together as he withdrew the cigarette after the first painful hungry pull.

'Don't fret yourself so,' McAlister said. 'It's early yet – she'll be all right –'

'God blast me,' he said.

'Please,' she said. 'That's a terrible thing to say. Don't say it, please.'

For some moments he did not answer; he pulled savagely at the cigarette. She heard another lorry start, the engine roaring before it went down the hill. She looked at him with hungry despair; she was miserable because she could not help him and was glad when he spoke at last.

'What time is it?' he said.

'Going uphill for five.' She did not need to look at her watch. She stood hungrily transfixed, staring at him.

'Daylight soon. The trucks are moving.'

'Daylight – I'm not sure it's not worse.' He became aware of her hungry transfixation, misunderstanding it: 'Have a cigarette.'

'No,' she said. 'No thank you.'

'It'll do you good – no harm – keep me company.'

'No,' she said. 'It isn't that. It's just –'

'Oh! I forgot. You're on trial,' he said.

'What a trial too.' She smiled. He seemed to shiver. She realized suddenly that he was only half-dressed; he simply had on a thin shirt hastily thrust into the tops of his trousers. 'You should put your coat on. It's cold – the nights are cold –'

'No,' he said. 'It's all right.'

'Let me get you a drink.'

Outside, on the terrace, a lorry started up and moved away.

'No. I don't need anything.' He smoked savagely.

She grasped slowly the fact that he was almost unaware of her; she might have been Sister Courbet or Carlotta or simply one of the cropped Europeanized Indian women standing there; she was simply something neutral and anonymous in a white dress. All contact between them had been cut. What she said to him now seemed simply to travel on dark dead wires, evoking no responses. She wanted terribly to ask him, outright: 'What will you do when it's over? Where will you go?' anxious to shock him into some sort of answer, but the words seemed to become skeined on the edge of her lips.

'I think I will have a cigarette – please – may I?' she said.

With shocking directness he answered about something quite different:

'Go and look at her again – I've an awful feeling. Go and look at her.'

She was glad to go. She found relief, for the next few moments, in trained automatic behaviour about Julie Maxted's bed. Daylight was beginning to colour, with faint blue-grey, the cracks along the edges of the black-out curtains at the windows. A few Indian women were sitting up; the ward was beginning to stir.

She put the thermometer under Julie Maxted's arm and waited, looking at her watch. Calmer now, she took the pulse at the same time and then efficiently, not trembling, with her fountain pen made the morning record on the chart. The pulse had deteriorated a little; the temperature had not come down.

Going out into the corridor, pulling herself together by a great effort so that now, momentarily at least, she felt more calm and free, she saw to her astonishment Crane was no longer there. Father Simpson stood by the small wall-light, turning up the wick, revealing the air thick with cigarette smoke, the floor piled with ant-like ends where Crane had spent the night.

'Mr Crane – where is he?'

'He went out. He fell over me,' the priest said, 'he woke me up.'

'He shouldn't go. He hasn't slept.'

'Let him go.' The priest rubbed his hands vaguely and sleepily over his still bruised face. 'It will do him good – the air. I'm glad he woke me. It will give me a chance to see the officers before they go.'

'Trucks have been moving off for the last hour,' she said.

'I shall catch them.' He had slept in his shirt and trousers and now looked more than ever floppily truculent and unpriestlike as he went into the wash-room to wash his hands. She turned to go away but he did not shut the door, saying instead:

'You look tired.'

'Night nurses are never tired,' she said. 'If they were they wouldn't be night nurses.'

'Check,' he said.

'What did you say, Father?'

'It was nothing.' He came out of the wash-room, drying his hands. 'I'm just some way round the bend. Is it the right expression? I begin to talk to myself – and not only that. What day is it?'

'I don't know.'

'It may be Tuesday.' Light was beginning to show rose-grey on the small square of window. He finished with tender touches the drying of his face. 'I can't remember – I just can't remember. I am going to say Mass. Will you tell Father Anstey that?'

'Yes, Father.'

'Tell him we will have it at six. Tell him I will be ready as soon as I have finished the swearing match.'

'Oh! Father.' She smiled gently, her faith in herself renewed by the chance to mock him. 'Sometimes I think the reason we don't get out of here is because there are words you don't know.'

'Oh! no, no, no,' he said. He smiled too, his bruised face twisted with the queerest irony. 'Mr Crane and the Colonel have seen to that.'

She had not time to answer before in a movement of abrupt and ox-like blundering, almost a charge, he thrust his belly forward and went past her. She heard him mutter something that sounded to her like 'Forgive us our tenses' as he grasped and wrenched open the corridor door.

Less than a minute later he was back in the smaller ward. He blundered through with such enraged clumsiness, loudly repeating a grievance, something about 'All the officers have gone – there are no officers there – only two half-witted cooks and a wounded man,' that she had to whisper after him:

'Father! – please. This is a sick ward – there are people ill!'

He went straight on without a word to a storming invasion of the privacy of the kitchen. Father Anstey was getting up.

'Father,' he said, 'there are no officers left. I missed them. I was awake very early and it was my intention – and now they've already gone. It's monstrous that we should have to face another day –'

'Gently,' Father Anstey said.

'There is no gentleness left in me.'

'You sent a message about Mass –'

'There is so much absolute fury in my heart that I feel I cannot do even that.'

'You'd better have some cocoa,' Father Anstey said. 'You can't have these raging furies on an empty stomach. You'll have chronic indigestion. Sit down.'

'No, Father, no. I can't sit down.' He stood over-wrought, trembling.

'We will have a little service for everyone after breakfast instead,' Father Anstey said.

Father Simpson held his face in his hands, speaking convulsively, shuddering. 'I can't bear this suffering – I can't bear it. Mr Crane raging with himself like a madman. Miss Maxted so ill. The nuns getting no sleep at all – Colonel Mathieson –'

'We will have a little service,' the elder priest said. His Yorkshire staunchness, unvaried, never weakening, had kept him singularly free from excitement and self-reproaches. 'A little service and a little cocoa. Have we a candle? We could burn a candle for St Joseph. A cup of cocoa, a candle, and thou, St Joseph, beside me in the wilderness –'

'Father, you simply cannot joke about these things –'

'We will have the cocoa,' the priest said.

The cocoa was ready, in an enamel saucepan, on the stove, where the nuns had made it overnight. Father Anstey poured some of it out into two mugs, giving one to Father Simpson, folding the other in his two hands, blowing on it slowly. The blue eyes were brightly dilated: weary but calm.

'It will be nice to have a service for everyone,' he said. 'If there are no officers here couldn't we go into the chapel?'

'It was dive-bombed yesterday. It was hit again. Somehow I think not –' He was still agitated. Daybreak had filled the sky with small pink clouds. He blew steam from his cocoa. There was firing down the hill. 'Perhaps it would be better in the big ward. Away from the patients.'

'We will have the kitchen table in,' the elder priest said. 'I will say Mass tomorrow. Drink your cocoa.'

Father Simpson sipped his cocoa; it was sharply hot on his lips and Father Anstey saw them twist with pain.

'How did you bruise your face, Father? I didn't ask. You never told me –'

'There was nothing to tell.' He floundered, looking to left and right, taking refuge in gulps of cocoa that stung his tongue, bringing tears to his eyes. 'Nothing. It was in the dark –'

He stopped. Down the hillside the firing had increased. Bursts from machine-guns drummed across the gorge.

'More fighting, another battle,' he began. 'Why do they fight

197

here? What possible advantage do they gain from fighting for this place? I don't get it. I don't understand it. Can it be of strategic importance? I simply don't get it.'

'We are in no danger,' Father Anstey said.

Danger? That was absurd. He had not thought of danger. He did not mean danger. He was not troubled by danger. It was simply the stupendous pointlessness, the monstrous idiocy of it all.

Noisily the elder priest sucked in his cocoa. 'You must have patience. It may go on for days. It really isn't long. After all there were people in the wilderness for forty days and forty nights. All evil is simply an illustration of good – you know that. The wilderness is simply the frame for God –'

'You put things very well, Father. I have really been awfully blind to these things.'

The elder priest sucked down to the bottom of the mug. 'I like sugar at the bottom,' he said. He sucked again, noisily, crunching grains of undissolved sugar. 'We will have the service in the big ward. Shall we?'

Machine-gun fire broke out with fresh violence down the hillside. In spite of it Father Simpson felt calmer. The talk had done him good; the cocoa was like a bromide. He took another drink of it and was about to remark, catching sight of shoals of pink cloud sailing gently past the window, that the day was very beautiful, when suddenly there was shouting from the smaller ward, followed by stifled screams.

'Something is wrong.' He put the mug on the stove, all his agitation renewed.

'I've had the most terribly uneasy feeling all the time –' He blundered out through the door.

Father Anstey put his own mug on the stove. He had hardly moved, turning to the door, before Father Simpson was back again, in stuttering outrage.

'The two Pathan cooks have been in, looking for women. They have taken Kaushalya – the girl, the dancer –' He swung out his arms like a man struggling to steady himself in the act of overbalancing, and then turned to rush out.

'Where are you going?' Father Anstey said.

'Begin the service, begin the service,' the priest said, 'I'll be back. I am going after them. Begin the service.'

'Father – it's very stupid –'

'Begin the service. It will calm the others. It will help everyone.'

He strode out through the smaller ward and down the corridor and into the central ward. He walked blindly, borne on waves of resurgent courage which took him as far as the end of the empty ward. There, without the slightest warning, they gave out, leaving him stranded abruptly by the window. He stood helplessly looking out; the terrace was empty; he could hear bursts of firing down the hill. He thought of Crane. Where was Crane? He longed for the reassuring guidance and sense of persons like the Colonel and Crane. He was helpless; this was the end. Presently he found himself on the terrace, blundering about like a trapped rabbit, first this way and then the other. It could not be the end: Jesus our Father, God our Father, he thought, it couldn't be the end.

He walked along the terrace. The red cross of dyed blanket was a distorted mess, dusty, half blown away. Where was Crane? If God would not help them then Crane – no, he did not mean that. That was simply an accidental confusion of thought. He needed both. He forced himself to walk more slowly, to think with something like constructive processes. Where would they take her? and what could he do if he discovered where they had taken her? He was thrown into fresh confusion by the remarkable notion that she might even have gone willingly.

It took him five or ten minutes to search the second and third of the lower terraces. Under the exertion he came back up the steps in a sweat. He decided to find Crane. Firing had gone on almost continuously, in determined bursts, at the foot of the hill. Above him the sky had slowly emptied of cloud and was clear now, the great collar of mountain and snow intensifying the blue.

And then suddenly he saw Kaushalya coming in through the archway of the outer gate. He had never thought of that. He was struck too by the fact that she looked extraordinarily small, like a brown and scarlet doll. She had lost, he saw at once, that look of drowsy and contemptible calm; she had stopped looking like a sleepy brown chrysalis, bored or only half awake. She was walking very slowly, her head held so low down that the face was unrevealed; she seemed to be watching the scarlet toes of her feet pricking the dust below the sari.

He went towards her and when he came to her there was nothing he could say. She did not stop walking. He fumbled for a few words of Hindu but in the next moment gave it up, resigning himself simply to walking with her, not even looking at her lowered face for any sort of sign of what had happened.

He was glad when they reached the windows of the central ward to hear the first bars of a chant inside. He opened the door and they went in together. He shut the door and stood beside her, with his back against it.

The service had begun and he closed his eyes, crossing himself. He emerged out of momentary darkness to look at Father Anstey, clothed in vestments of crimson that were simply surgical bandages dyed, presiding over the kitchen table on which the altar cloth was a blanket. He saw the elder priest smile. All the nuns, with McAlister and some of the Indian women – he was never happy if they were converts through fear or force – were kneeling down. He heard more firing down the hill, but it seemed farther away now, and he did not notice it much. He felt dazed and happy. If there had not been a revelation there had been something very like it. It was all over and they were together with God; it was wonderfully quiet except for the chant of Father Anstey's voice and the responses and, far away, the noise of a truck coming up the hill.

He turned after some moments and saw Kaushalya's tears falling down on her hands. He was distressed and did not know what to do. It had always touched him terribly to see Indians weeping. He had once seen a Bengali weeping over the body of his son, run down by a bus; he had never recovered from the slow deep tears. It was not simply the universality of tears – it even seemed strange to him that a person of dark skin could weep at all – that affected him. There seemed something different in the weeping of those Asiatic beaten eyes, in tears that seemed to rise from sources deeper than Western tears, carrying with them inscrutable, unbearable poignancy.

'Don't cry, my child.' He knew that she did not understand; he knew that it did not matter. He reached down and held her fingers in his own. She did not look up. He felt her tears in a sense to be his own experience, cleansing him. He remembered how many misjudgements there had been on that first day of Crane's arrival; and now his own, out of them all, seemed more stupid and wicked than the rest.

The service went on and all the time he simply stood by the door, holding the Indian girl's hands, letting her weep. The tears continued to cleanse him; her flesh, by which he had been so sensitively repelled, was as beautiful as a new leaf in its smoothness, giving him comfort. This was enough, he thought; this – as always, in the way most unexpected of all – this was the promise of his revelation.

He had lapsed into a sort of half-dream, soothed by the chant of responses, and the contact of the girl's hands and by his own extending happiness, and he did not notice that the truck had now reached and was turning into the terrace-end.

It was a raising of voices outside on the terrace, immediately in front of the Mission, that finally disturbed him. At once his dream was broken; the extension of his happiness came bluntly to a stop. Deep inside himself he felt a spurt of fresh anger at the invasion of a precious territory, gained with such difficulty and at such cost. All the infuriating unreal condition of life was starting again, to provoke and madden him into being the person he did not want to be.

At the sound of voices Kaushalya had begun to cry more deeply, with small scared sobs. He opened his mouth to comfort her. At the same moment someone began banging on the door. In the second before rage made him turn to open it he saw a wave of half-turned faces among the Indian women kneeling on the floor.

Outside the door an officer in khaki drill, with a small black moustache and the crown of a major on his shoulder, began saying: 'Are you the priest –'

'Go away,' he said. 'Leave us alone! Why don't you leave us alone? Will you go, please –'

'I am of the Indian army,' the officer said.

'What army? What army? What difference does it make? We only want to be left alone –'

'I have come to fetch you, sir,' the officer said.

The priest stood swaying on the edge of the terrace. He could not speak. The word 'sir' brightened all his vision to such acuteness that he felt himself to be the victim of a curious illusory trick. The red cross that had lain and blown into a shapeless and meaningless mass on the terrace seemed suddenly to have sprung into air. It had stiffened and straightened, impinging itself on the side of a truck.

'It's all over,' he said. He spoke woodenly; his thick lips could hardly form the words. He turned to see McAlister coming out of the ward. 'It's all over,' he said to her. 'It's all over.' He stood stupidly, bruised mouth open.

'I am a major of the Indian army,' the officer said. He saluted McAlister.

'Oh! for God and glory,' she said. 'What have you got in the trucks?'

'Medicines,' the major said. 'Medicines. Many kinds.' He spoke with clipped and formal triumph. 'Even penicillin if you wish –'

'Oh! for Jesus' sake,' she said.

She began running across the terrace, the priest calling after her: 'Where are you going? It's all over – it's finished –'

'Mr Crane!' she said.

She ran up the side of the Mission and into the garden, across the path between the cabbages. Crane was not there. She found him half a minute later standing by the back door of the Mission, smoking, his feet surrounded by a circle of smashed white ends.

'There's a major,' she said, 'a truck – an Indian army truck. Oh! God, I can't tell you – they have things with them, supplies, penicillin –'

'No,' he said. 'No.' He stared at her in dazed helplessness. 'No. How did this –'

202

'Don't ask me.' She began crying bitterly. 'Don't ask me.'

'I could kiss you,' he said.

'Whatever you do, don't,' she said.

Words and tears began to choke her. She could not hold up her head. When she raised it some time later he had vanished completely.

Two mornings later Miss Jordan and Miss Shanks came struggling up the hill: past burnt-out hovels and ruined trucks, past
areas of scorched woodland where late leaves, shrivelled black,
gave no covering for stark and abandoned bodies stiffened as
tree-boughs on dusty roadsides. In a voice rather like the croak
of an aged and cultured parrot Miss Jordan called from some
distance behind Miss Shanks: 'Did you bring the strawberry?'
and Miss Shanks, without turning, waved above her head a
triumphant crimson jar of jam.

'And the shrimp?'

'And the shrimp.'

'Father Simpson absolutely adores it. He spreads it like
butter. I hope it kept. Did you remember –'

'Absolutely everything has been thought of,' Miss Shanks
said. 'Don't worry. Stop flapping.'

'I do worry. I can't help worrying. It's been so awful and
I'm sure they're starving.'

'They're not going to starve any longer.'

'Wait,' Miss Jordan said, like a child. 'Wait. You get so far
ahead.'

Miss Jordan, who never seemed to be able to catch up with
Miss Shanks because Miss Shanks at the last moment always
got bored with waiting and went on, seemed to be constructed
of bent and scraggy poles of bamboo. Like Miss Shanks she
carried a basket of food. Her body was so tall and thin and
fragile that it seemed not to be able to bear either the weight
of the basket or the weight of her head, on which she wore a
large turn-down straw hat like a yellow frying-pan. Both head
and basket bowed her down, the curvature of the spine giving
her the appearance of a hoop being slowly bowled up the hill

by invisible forces: up a little way and then poised on dead-centre for breath, up a little farther and then poised for breath again.

'It reminds me of that time we went on trek to Nanga Parbat,' she said. The basket of food was quite heavy and now and then she changed it from hand to hand, the flexible hoop of her body springily twisting.

'That was forty years ago.'

'It was worth it though.'

'This will be worth it when you see their faces.'

They passed a clump of bamboo and on the edge of it a dead Kashmiri who had lain for a week in the sun. Miss Shanks, who wore gold pince-nez, looked past it with the wry indifference of a skinny monkey. She was very small and quite used to these things. Violence in all conceivable and hideous forms, combined with a fatalism and callousness as blatant as the sun, was something that in India had long since ceased to shock her. Perhaps the week as a whole had been a bit much, she thought – she had made a hurried visit that morning to that part of the village lying beyond the house-boats and had seen where the heads of Hindu babies had been smashed like so many little brown oranges against burnt walls – but she was not surprised. Forty years in India, first as a mission teacher and then on retirement in Kashmir as companion-help to Miss Jordan, had left her with a sweet dry ugliness of face and a mind that in its reaction to poverty, to squalor, to pestilence, to fire, and to the altogether inextricable mess of India was almost mummified. She had become immunized to every kind of infection it had to offer; but she also loved it. She had resisted, with tart and charming stubbornness, staunchly supported by Miss Jordan, every kind of ruse to send her home. 'Partition?' she said. 'Partition? They may partition India but they won't partition us.'

What had been happening at the Mission she didn't know. Confined to the house-boat, locked in behind pulled shutters, ignored through sheer luck, the two ladies had never had a syllable of news except what had been given by planes and cannon-shell and the noise of fire and fighting. For once the infallible grape-vine of Kashmiri rumour had been cut.

She paused again to wait for Miss Jordan. The notion of relieving the stricken garrison up at the Mission had been invented by Miss Jordan rather as a child, bored with life, invents a game of escape. There was a kind of aristocratic childishness about her mind and bearing that was as faded and out-moded as her yellow hat, her crumpled stockings, and her suit of washed-out shantung. She seemed like a creature survived from days of viceregal grandeur, stubborn and embalmed and preserved by sun.

The business of relieving the garrison was quite unreal but it gave her, as she conquered a series of creaking dead-centres up the hill, a rising sense of triumph. She and Miss Shanks had kept their heads high; disaster had not beaten them down. 'Quit India' – that curt and brutal slogan scrawled on crumbling walls – had no more meaning for her than partition. They did not concern her; she had given neither a moment's serious thought. Now the field was cleared; everyone, except the few people at the Mission, had gone home; everyone had quit. For this lamentable and loathsome attitude of surrender she had nothing but contempt; and the journey up the hill, with the baskets, with the jam, the fish paste, the chocolate, the jellies, and the half-bottle of brandy for Father Anstey, was her demonstration against the spineless ineptitude of all who had retreated. 'They' – meaning Indians – 'may ask us to go,' she would say, 'but they will ask us back.' The presence of the British in India was as fixed and indestructible a moment of history as Adam in the garden of Eden; if sin had arisen from it, she felt, it was no possible fault of hers. The serpent came from elsewhere.

'Can you manage, dear?' Miss Shanks called, not turning round at all.

'Quite. Quite. Don't wait for me.'

'I can wait.'

Again Miss Shanks waited for some moments until Miss Jordan was ten or twelve paces away from her and then, bored again, did not wait any longer.

The hoop of Miss Jordan's curved and dried-out body resisted the pressure of the incline with springy pauses. She held her heart with her free hand, giving little hisses between long gold-stopped teeth. Again Miss Shanks called:

'Can you manage, dear? Shall I wait?'

'No: I can manage. I prefer to take it in my own time.'

At this moment two Indian army trucks, furiously driven, trailing comet-clouds of dust, came down the hill. Loaded with shrieking Indian women and children, evacuated and freed at last, they bore down on Miss Shanks and Miss Jordan with fury, pressing the two English ladies back into the shelter of roadside scrub. At the incredible sight of two truck loads of shorn black heads, strangely Europeanized and yet still more intensely Asiatic, the black hair wind-beaten, the children scared or laughing, Miss Shanks and Miss Jordan had scarcely time to look before the trucks, blindly racing, horns blowing joyously, had disappeared in their cloud-race down the hill.

This crazy passage left them both quite speechless. For some moments they stood choking, spitting dust. Then Miss Jordan, grasping suddenly that the evacuation of the entire Mission might have begun, that the triumph and pleasure of their own arrival might now be swept away as ruthlessly as the trucks tearing down the hill, thrust out the curve of her long crane-like neck and sprang out into the road and was for the first time ahead of Miss Shanks by some yards.

'We shall miss them – we shall be too late – they are going away –'

'Don't flap, dear.'

Swiftly, wryly, with monkey-like agility, Miss Shanks skipped in front. Dust, settling everywhere on thickly powdered dying leaves, fogged the road ahead.

'Yes, but I've an awful feeling they are all being taken away –'

'Don't flap, dear. They were laughing.'

The great rule of India, Miss Shanks thought, was not to flap. It was the mistake of which most Europeans were guilty when they first came. She supposed it was very natural; and there were people, Miss Jordan among them, who never really learned the trick of keeping calm. When Europeans first came out what they noticed most and what appalled them most was the riot of fecundity, the barbaric beat of light, the filth and fatalism of every day. But after a year or two, even after a month or two, you got used to that; after ten years you were brutalized into callous numbness – your refuge the bottle, the mail, the social round, the hills, perhaps the adulteries of yourself or those about you, the rumour, the bed, or the punkah; and after a few more years you began to say, with dusty cheerfulness, to those new arrivals gazing on India for the first time with the fresh and awful eyes of disbelief: 'When you've been here for twenty-five years – even twenty years – you'll begin to know as much about the country as I do – nothing at all.'

Presently, but quite slowly in the still morning air, the dust ahead of them cleared, and twenty minutes later, after many pauses, Miss Shanks more than ever like a wizened and in-exhaustible spectacled monkey, Miss Jordan springing with hoop-like jerks and pauses behind, they came to within sight of the gates of the Mission.

Miss Shanks yapped out a cracked exclamation of joy. 'They are all right! Isn't that Father Simpson there already?'

She stopped in the road, for a moment disconcerted, squinting through dusted spectacles.

'Isn't he with someone – I can't quite see –'

Miss Jordan had the better sight; her eyes had the beady brilliance of pigeon's eyes set deep into her angular head below the shadow of the hat.

'It's that awful girl,' she said. 'You remember we saw her hanging about – the dancer – the –'

'Say it, say it,' Miss Shanks said. 'I make no bones about it. Prostitute.'

'Ought we to wait?' Something like strategic decorum seemed to be necessary. The triumph of relieving the garrison seemed abruptly threatened.

'I wait for no prostitute.'

Miss Shanks, thin nose in the air, lenses flashing, began to go nippily up the hill.

'They are having the most enormous laugh together,' Miss Jordan said.

'I can't help that. I wait for no prostitute. I wait for nobody.'

'At least wait for me. We can face them together.'

Impatient, Miss Shanks waited; it was an extraordinary thing, this laughing; she seemed about to bound off like a monkey refusing to be captured; but finally, for the first time, Miss Jordan caught up; and now they locked arms and went up the hill together.

'He is saying good-bye,' Miss Jordan said. 'That's what all the laughing must be about.'

'I see her now,' Miss Shanks said. 'She is coming down.'

Kaushalya, carrying her cheap fibre attaché case, began to come down the hill more than ever like a doll of brown and scarlet, turquoise and orange: flamboyant and garish against the shantung and straw of the English ladies joined together in stiff advance against the sun. Thirty yards from Father Simpson she turned and waved her hand and Father Simpson waved in reply.

Miss Jordan and Miss Shanks continued to come stiffly up the hill, locked together, squinting at the sun. Almost level with them Kaushalya turned once again and waved her hand. In a single moment of flashing teeth, of dipping scarlet nails, of shaken turquoise, much of Miss Jordan's triumph seemed to slip back down the hill. From the girl there was a last gay burst of laughter and an incredible single singing word of English:

'Good-bye!'

Some moments later Father Simpson became aware of the two ladies advancing. He appeared for a single second to be coming down the hill. And then Miss Jordan, the triumph slipping still further away, said:

'Now there is someone else. Sister Carlotta, I think, the Italian one. And a man.'

But only a few moments later, at the gates, the priest came forward to meet them. In a moment of great shock Miss Jordan wanted to run back from a face she did not know: hideously bruised, ghoulishly discoloured, almost unrecognizable and yet full of joy. It did not seem at all the moment to shout. 'We have brought you the shrimp! – some strawberry –'

'How wonderful!' he said. 'How marvellous to see you!'

They felt there was nothing to say. Beyond the priest Crane and Carlotta were talking together. In her high reedy voice the little Italian nun was saying: 'I have been so happy. My throat is sore from so much singing – but otherwise I was so happy.'

It was impossible for the English ladies to understand these things. From the Mission, across the terrace, they saw two other women, Sister Courbet and McAlister, coming towards the gates; and Miss Jordan, grasping the basket that now seemed so stupid, said:

'You're so busy, Father – so many people. We brought you a few things –'

'How kind – how wonderful!' he said. 'It's so wonderful to see you. Will you go in? Sister Carlotta will take you in – Father Anstey will be absolutely delighted.'

'Yes, thank you,' they said.

Going across the terrace, following Sister Carlotta, Miss Jordan said:

'There are graves. Look – under the apple-trees,' and the triumph, killed by a new burst of laughter from Sister Courbet, slipped finally away.

At the gates Father Simpson was saying to Crane: 'After you've said your good-byes I will walk down with you. They would have given you a truck from here, you know –'

'They've got a jeep across the river. Nice to walk for a change too.'

'You will be in Bombay tomorrow.'

'Ought to be,' Crane said. 'You never can tell.' He was going to Bombay to find Maxted and bring him back to Julie. 'Any luck and I'll be back by Saturday.'

'Sister Courbet and Nurse McAlister are coming to say good-bye,' the priest said.

Sister Courbet was very shy; she smiled quietly and simply said 'Good-bye' and after shaking hands with Crane, rather formally, in German fashion, she walked away.

'Good-bye,' he said.

McAlister stood alone, looking past him.

'All well?' he said.

'All well,' she said. 'She's having a sleep now.'

'She does nothing else but sleep,' Crane said. 'I came in to say good-bye and she was asleep.'

'She will get over that.'

'She'd better,' Crane said. 'Look after her.'

'We shall be here.'

'I said look after her.'

'We shall be here,' she said. She smiled flatly, straight past him, down the hill.

With cherubic bruised face upraised Father Simpson breathed with gasps of pleasure at snow-touched air and sun. Far beyond the river and the rice-fields all the mountains seemed to be uplifted. The priest half-shut his eyes in a curious attitude of sensuous exultant prayer and Crane, feeling the wonder of a moment that could not be expressed otherwise than in the sort of foolery that had kept himself, the Colonel, and Father Simpson from going insane about the graves under the apple-trees, said:

'Is it in order to kiss Miss McAlister good-bye, Father?'

'Perfectly –'

'Oh! no,' she said. 'No.'

'I have no authority to forbid it,' the priest said.

'Please,' she said. 'Not here.'

'That makes it worse – Father Simpson will grant a special dispensation –'

'Oh! no,' she said. 'No. I told you – I asked you –'

While her mouth was still open he bent down and kissed her with a sort of affectionate jocularity, lightly, on the lips.

He felt her shoulders quiver as he held them for a moment longer. He did not sustain the kiss and it seemed, from the vibration of her arms and the tautness of her mouth, as if she did not want it sustained.

'Good-bye,' he said.

'Good-bye.'

'Thank you for everything,' he said. 'And that goes for you too, Father. For everything. For the hospitality.'

'It was nothing,' the priest said. McAlister did not speak. 'Perhaps hospitality is hardly the word —'

'For the etiquette, then.'

'For the etiquette — for the hospitality — for the love — whatever you like to call it.' The priest smiled, gently, ironically, but in some way beatified, the bruised globe of his face smoothed. 'Perhaps love?'

'The exercise has done us all a power of good,' Crane said. He knew that the priest was thinking of the Colonel, that his joy was touched by a bleaker glint of pain. As he gazed at the mountains it seemed too that he might, in a dream, have been looking backwards, with tender astonishment, at the man he had been; and Crane felt that it was time to go.

'Good-bye,' he said again. He turned to McAlister; she was looking past him.

'Good-bye,' she said. 'We shall see you soon.' She spoke impersonally, not simply for herself but as if for everyone. 'We shall think of you.'

When, some moments later, the priest and Crane walked down the hill she still stood motionless, watching them.

'She has become very calm,' the priest said. 'She used to be terribly tempestuous.'

'Yes.'

'Perhaps I should not have said that.' A little of his hesitation, his lack of faith in himself, clouded his face momentarily; he seemed about to be trapped once again by a hideous misjudgement, a moment of his former nervous vanity; but for once it did not trouble him. He seemed to ride over it, serenely, striding forward with undiminished happiness and calm.

'None of us are quite the same,' he said.

He turned, now some distance down the hill, and waved his hand to McAlister, laughing. Crane turned and waved his hand and laughed too.

For the last time she waved her own in reply. Beyond her all the mountains, just as the priest had seen them, clear and uplifted, glowed with such brilliance of morning light that far off, pure blue and crisp above snow, the sky seemed to quiver. The spur of rock that had so often troubled Father Anstey hung in brown suspense above the river, and across the rice-fields all the leaves had fallen from the planes.

More about Penguins and Pelicans

Penguinews, which appears every month, contains details of all the new books issued by Penguins as they are published. From time to time it is supplemented by our stocklist, which is our complete list of almost 5,000 titles.

A specimen copy of *Penguinews* will be sent to you free on request. Please write to Dept EP, Penguin Books Ltd, Harmondsworth, Middlesex, for your copy.

In the U.S.A.: For a complete list of books available from Penguins in the United States write to Dept CS, Penguin Books, 625 Madison Avenue, New York, New York 10022.

In Canada: For a complete list of books available from Penguins in Canada write to Penguin Books Canada Ltd, 2801 John Street, Markham, Ontario L3R 1B4

H. E. Bates in Penguins

Fair Stood the Wind for France

'*Fair Stood the Wind for France* is perhaps the finest novel of the war ... The scenes are exquisitely done and the characters – tenderly and beautifully drawn – are an epitome of all that is best in the youth of the two countries. This is a fine, lovely book which makes the heart beat with pride' – *Daily Telegraph*

Also published

The Darling Buds of May
A Breath of French Air
When the Green Woods Laugh
Oh! To Be In England
Dulcima
The Four Beauties
A Little of What You Fancy
Love for Lydia
The Purple Plain
Seven by Five
The Song of the Wren
The Triple Echo
The Wild Cherry Tree
The Jacaranda Tree
The Grapes of Paradise